Bad Boys
and Black Sheep
■ ■ ■

Western Literature Series

Bad Boys
and Black Sheep

■ ■ ■

Fateful Tales from the West

ROBERT FRANKLIN GISH

University of Nevada Press
Reno   Las Vegas   London

Western Literature Series

A list of books in the series appears at the end of this volume.

University of Nevada Press, Reno, Nevada 89557 USA
Copyright © 1996 by Robert Franklin Gish
Jacket design by Erin Kirk New
Manufactured in the United States of America

The paper used in this book meets the requirements of
American National Standard for Information Sciences—
Permanence of Paper for Printed Library Materials, ANSI Z39.48-1984.
Binding materials were selected for strength and durability.

Library of Congress Cataloging-in-Publication Data

Gish, Robert Franklin, 1940–
Bad boys and black sheep : fateful tales from the West / Robert Franklin Gish.
p.   cm.   — (Western literature series)
ISBN 0-87417-280-2 (paper : alk. paper)
I. Title.   II. Series.
PS3557.I79B3   1996
813'.54—dc20   95-47238
CIP

First Printing

05 04 03 02 01 00 99 98 97 96   5 4 3 2 1

For my son, Timothy
For my grandsons Matthew,
Joseph, and Daniel

"No pleasure but meanness."

—Flannery O'Connor,
"A Good Man Is Hard to Find"

Contents

Acknowledgments

I owe some considerable gratitude to the persons who aided and abetted me in the composing and committing to paper of these stories of mischief and misadventure. Although these good and benevolent souls assisted me in my many queries and observations, they share no sin, blame, or guilt for any apparent waywardness, villainy, or misanthropy found herein.

For that matter, some of the prototypical, indeed, "mythic" personages who form the bases for some of the characters in these stories are similarly absolved from any complicity in the distortions and violations of my authorial imaginings. If some of the characters at times appear to resemble seemingly recognizable, "real" persons to too great a degree, the reader should be reminded again of what the author comprehends most acutely—the "lies" of fiction play havoc with historical and biographical "truths" in the name of story and tall tale.

With that kind of *apologia* in mind I wish to offer my most truthful and good gratitude for the encouragements and assistance of certain knowing and naïve supporters and collaborators. In large part these individuals aided me in hiding out at the appropriate times and in garnering the various kinds of support—emotional as well as temporal—to sustain the stamina that writing stories such as these requires. In another kind of mischievous collusion, others of these individuals helped me in confirming certain facts and feelings from "life," which manifest themselves here in the far-fetched vagaries of the imagination.

Benny Padilla continues to prepare and supervise the recurrent and *muy sabroso* New Mexican soul food that keeps me going. Terri Yokley's over-the-table courtesy goes much beyond condiment.

Ron Nelson and Deborah Marie Simmons gave me great insight into the California located "over the grade" of Cuesta Ridge and back some forty-odd years into the past. Kimi and Clyde Ikeda showed me hospitality much beyond a weekend spin in their 1972 Porsche 911. And John Corsaut and Merl Townsend clued me in at just the right time about Henry Elfrink's manual and some of the technical aspects of the Porsche 550 Spyder.

Gerald W. Haslam, Gerald Locklin, and Raphael Zepeda continue to welcome me into the fold of California writers, and for this I am thankful. David Congalton's dedication to writers and writing continues to inspire me.

Margaret F. Dalrymple, my editor, pointed me in the right direction with the most graceful and charming of shoves. She must surely represent every author's ideal editor. Thomas R. Radko, my publisher, has my most fervent appreciation and gratitude for repeatedly reinforcing my need to write and, as David Thomson says, to suspect the capacity for story in everything. The entire staff at the University of Nevada Press combine friendship, cordiality, and professionalism in the warmest of *relleno* ways. Sara Vélez Mallea and C. Shannon Sandifer merit my special appreciation.

Bishop's Peak, sentinel of the Central Coast and the city of San Luis Obispo, inspires me daily. Warren Baker, Robert Koob, Paul Zingg, and Glenn Irvin have my gratitude for affirming my work.

Judy, I say, yet again, thank you for keeping me good and true, and for your matter-of-fact faith in the finishing of what, when started, was two futures now long shared as one. Robin, you remain an abiding inspiration in your laughter and determination, most dramatically demonstrated one special Santa Fe night. Tim, thanks for telling me your bad boy stories after the fact and saving a father all that extra worry. Annabeth, thank you for those Indianapolis and California apples and for the resonating road melodies of "all night long." Stuart, thank you for your continuing counsel. As for the Butzier boys, may you someday read this book and confirm its composing in the hope that your days will be blessed with the strength of goodness and love in a benevolent and passionate manhood.

Namesakes

I remember the night they came. That's when all of this first started for me, and for Frank. Living up to the legends and all, living out the legacy of our father's dreams. What Father must have wanted all along—damnation!

It was late night, before the set of morning chill, sometime between summer and fall, and the night was full of sounds: familiar sounds, strange sounds. The sounds of changes, transitions, of beginnings and endings.

Frank and I used to listen to the sounds and try to name what we thought we heard and where we thought we heard it. We played that game a lot, almost always at night or in the evenings. Except it wasn't really a game. It was a combination of what we had done that day—what we'd seen and all—and what we imagined, future or present or past. And where we'd been together, or alone—around the house or far down the creek or over by the road. Maybe atop the big hill up by the freshwater springs and the caves where I hurt my leg and had to spend the night all that long time ago.

That's when I really told the tales, that night by myself in the cave and afterward, when Frank finally pulled me out. That's where I first heard it, and thought I saw it, the devil cat that stalked me then and haunts me even now.

It wasn't easy combining truths and tales, what happened and what almost happened or could have happened, mixing up facts and fancy, blending history and story. We tried to make it all seem real and believable, me and Frank. But then Frank would start to stretch something, and I knew he was out there in his far fancy. I let him go, too. Frank would always start me to thinking.

I kind of enjoyed hearing him take those sounds and locate them and then just distort the hell out of it all. He had a morbid turn of mind, and his sounds and stories always tended toward the scary. It was part of being my older brother, thinking he could scare me all the time. But he wasn't that good at telling lies. I could beat him at it. Stretching the truth, I mean. I could always see right through him. I know Mother did, too.

"I depend on you boys. You're my eyes and ears while I'm here in this bed," Father would say. And then he would ask Frank some pertinent questions about the place, or about me or Mother, or if we'd seen any strangers, or any lost cattle or hogs and such. Frank would answer. If he ever did stretch things, it was to make it easier on Father or because Mother had told us to say what we said.

Father would ask Frank a couple of questions related to the main subject at hand; then just to be sure, he'd turn to me. "That so, Jesse? That what happened?"

And Frank would give me that look of his. The one where he cocked whichever eyebrow Father couldn't see and stared the holy bejesus through me. And I would say, "Sure, Father. It's like Frank says." Except now and again I'd have some fun with Frank and pipe up, "But he forgot to tell you that . . ." And then Frank would die a hundred and one deaths, and I'd make him squirm for a bit before I came back from some elaboration and made Frank's account twice as believable, even with the things I'd invented.

I guess it came from knowing Frank like I did and from lying awake at night trying to identify all the sounds and our asking each other questions about each other's versions of the truth, each other's lies and legends and stories and all. Frank usually asked me more questions than I asked him. It was part of our legacy, I guess—talking. Always cussin' and discussin'.

Mother talked the least of all. You almost felt she'd talked herself out. She seemed sad and forlorn, even then. Father would ask Frank questions, Frank would ask me questions, but it was Mother who had the answers—without the questions, without all the talk. She was the one who kept the place running. She would ask Father just the right question, by way of telling him and us what to do. And then he would turn those questions into advice and counsel, into instructions for us boys, and even back again for Mother. She kept us going, Mother did. But the funny thing is, she was living Father's legend, his "truth" turned lie. Just like me. Just like Frank. Fulfilling Father's fate.

The one story we all knew for true was that Father couldn't get out of bed. Mother said his spine was being eaten away by TB. Frank and I both knew he was in awful pain. Knew the sound of that pain. I thought I knew it too from when I was left in the caves and my leg was broke and it hurt awful bad. When the cat shrieked and cried and came for me—and then at the last minute backed away into the fade of fever.

So I knew Father's pain, recognized the cries and how he had to be suffering. I suffer still, carrying this limp and not being able to run flat out, or even to walk right. Carrying this craving to reshape the truth.

We all knew the sound of Father's pain. We could hear it during the day when we'd be gathering eggs or popping off chicken necks or working with the cow trying to get the milk coming or feeding the couple of steers we were trying more to keep alive than fatten up. We could hear it when we'd be helping Mother dig potatoes or when we were digging fence posts or stringing what wire we could gather. We could even hear it out in the woods when we were trying to build a snare for a wild hog, or whatever critter, large or small, came along and was dumb enough to step in the wrong place. Meat for the table. Sustenance.

Sure, I believe Father was in plenty of pain, and we all knew the sound of it. So much so that the times in between his cries were all the more special. But those silences were amplified by us waiting to hear Father's shrieks come tearing again through the night, or the morning, or the afternoon. Waiting through the hot, humid air of summer or as the chilled air of autumn became winter. His pain came at all times, anytime. And the question, much beyond words, would come, near or far, "Why?" or "Where?" Usually it would be a mix of "Why me, why this pain?" and "Where are you, Louise? Where are you, boys?"

And we would come as fast as we could. Or if we didn't or couldn't come, we had some good reasons ready. Father wanted answers, even if there were none. Wanted truths, even if they were lies.

He had his answers, too, in his more comfortable moments. He had his stories, his truths. How he knew some famous people—good people, regardless of what others said about them, or about him. How he rode with them in Missouri, and how he came to head for Indian Territory and met Ada Louise Walters, mixed-blood Cherokee and Irish, and how Sam and Ada Louise Meeker came to settle here in the Cookson Hills. How he named us boys after two of his friends. They'd be coming to see him one day. They had something for him, something long overdue. He was waiting for that day, he said. Gave him something to live for, it seemed. Gave all of us hope, he said.

"You'll see. You'll see. Just wait. . . . I'm gonna tell 'em about you boys, about the namesakes and all."

And as we waited for the shrieks and beyond that for the special coming, that hoped-for-beyond-hope visit and what it would mean, we all began to wonder and silently ask ourselves whether Father and his dream were what we were living for, maybe all we were living for, and was it worth it. Truths and tales and all those lies in between.

That kind of questioning and wondering was behind all the other questions, all the other talk. The questions Father and Mother had for each other, the ones they had for us. The ones Frank and I had for them—and for each other. The questions and answers about the sounds, even as we would lie there in our small room at night listening and waiting for the night sounds, with a piece of oilcloth hanging over the door separating us from the kitchen, and beyond that from our parents' sparse, smelly room.

All the sounds seemed the same, at least at first. There was one large sound of song and then there were smaller sounds of many songs. Not all songs were happy, you know, and even the happy songs were sometimes tinged with pain and ache and sorrow, beats and rhythms, loud and soft, held long and cut short. There were the sounds inside my head and inside our shack of a house. The sounds and truths of then—and of now.

There was Father's song:

I'm an old bachelor, all ragged and lame.
From North to South Carolina I came.
I married a damsel, and the very next day,
Trouble began.

And there was Mother's song:

See those tiny tracks in the snow.
Wonder what they are and where they go.
I'll bet a tiny little rabbit hopped across the
snow . . . last night.

And there were the songs and sounds outside—all the chirping and croaking and buzzing and humming, the music of the earth seemingly never ceasing. I could hear the crickets in our room and in the kitchen, where the old flat-topped cast-iron stove burned low, and their millions of relatives just outside, and the cicadas in the hickory and oak and sycamore trees, and the mosquitoes coming through the open windows, the gnats and flies and beetles and bugs, and the frogs croaking and singing by the pond and all along Drowning Creek. And a fish, maybe a giant bass, jumping and slapping the surface of the pond. And somebody's hound, maybe Old Trouble hisself, treeing a coon. And the owls and nighthawks and bats. And the night. And the hills.

And the shriek. Except it wasn't Father. It was another kind of shriek—savage and full of wildness. The sound of pain and pleasure, of hope and despair combined, the sound of sheer screaming without any mind or motive other than the cry, the sound itself.

"What in the Sam Hill blazes was that?" Frank whispered.

I could tell he was as surprised and scared as I was. But I rallied, even to the dying fall of the fearful wildness, and said with a quickness of memory and old knowing, an inspiration that in its familiarity was as much reflex as imagination, "It's the panther come forever and new again to the hills. I've seen him. I told you before. He's come from up by the caves. He's come to kill us all—Father and Mother and you and me—and take us out of this miserable, godforsaken life. He's come to answer the questions, to give purpose and meaning to the talk, to give truth to the lies, to fulfill our lives, being born unto death and the Devil's keeping. It's Old Scratch hisself, Frank. And he's in these hills. Old Scratch, hisself."

"Wha . . .what, Jesse? Old Scratch, his . . . hisself?"

That pretty much scared the shit out of old Frank. Him and his mealymouthed morbid stories seemed pretty small now. He didn't say a thing after that, not for a while. Then he rose up on his cot and looked over at me and whispered, "Shut up with that Revelations, end-of-the-world, Bible-thumpin' preacher talk, Jesse. Listen. Something's happening in the hills, and some of it's comin' our way."

And I waited for the shriek again. Maybe it was Father, after all, crying out in the final pain and anguish of the death throes—his spine finally snapped, crumbled and shattered in two, into particles of bloody bone dust. Maybe it was the Devil's own feverish black cat come to kill us good and final. But then I heard it. Heard what Frank was hearing and telling me to listen for. Heard it syncopated against the insect chorus of the last songs before the deaths of winter.

It was horses, all right. Horses' hooves pounding ever so faintly but getting louder far up the creek road and coming our way. They were running hard. It was dark up there, darker than the Devil's dark heart, and they were running hard in and against the darkness. Then the running stopped, and we heard a shot. And another shot. And then a cry, another shriek of wildness, but muffled.

"Listen, Jesse. Those were shots. Rapid shots. Pistol shots."

"Sure enough, Frank. Shots from the Four Horsemen, Frank. Shots that killed the Devil's own cat, Frank. Shots that will ricochet back and kill the killers, Frank. Shots that will come to kill the

Antichrist and . . . us, Frank." I spun my own truths, elucidations of hallucinations from the delirium and body twistings of my cave times—me feverish, lying there in the dark, hearing the underground spring trickle and drip and seeing all those things. And now they returned to haunt me and my memory and my talk.

Then we both listened, and before long we heard the horses running again—our way. And there was no mistake; they were coming to our place.

"They're comin' here, Jesse. They're comin' here. Why would riders be comin' here? Why would riders be comin' here, and in the dead of night?"

"I told you, it's the Devil's own riders, Frank. And they're coming for Father. They're coming to make him pay for all he asks of us. Coming to make him pay for all his sins. Coming for us, since we done his bidding, blood of his own blood. Sins of the father. Coming to take us with him, Frank. Not even Mother in her goodness can protect us boys now, Frank."

And then we heard the snorting and blowing of the horses stopped outside our thin walls, and we could hear voices mingling like bugs come into the gift of tongues. Voices outside talking, asking questions. And inside, the voices of Father and Mother stirring against their own fears, awakened out of who knows what dreams or nightmares, to hear riders, maybe Marshal Parker with his boys, finally come into the Territory, finally come in the middle of the night.

"What ho, the house!" came from a throaty voice just beyond the darkened porch.

"Is this the place of Sam Meeker? Show-Me Meeker from over Kearney way, over Missouri way?"

"The slim-skinny son-of-a-bitch Sam Meeker who used to ride rowdy through the streets of Joplin? It's us come to pay up old scores, Sam. Come to parcel out your just deserves."

"Boys, is that you? Is that really you? Frank? Jesse? Finally come to visit?" But Father wasn't talking to us. He was yelling from his bed to the night riders.

"Louise, it's the boys," he yelled. "Don't shoot a thing."

And I looked past the oilcloth to see Mother standing by the window, holding Father's double-barreled shotgun, shaking in the cross fire of voices come to resurrect the hopes and dreams of her husband and to shatter whatever illusions had kept him and us living alone, dependents to a dream, in these remote and hidden hills.

Then a lamp glow came into the kitchen, and Mother in her ragged robe went to the door to let in two riders in long duster coats, heavily spurred, clinking and clanking out of the noises of the night. And they took their hats off, big-brimmed hats coated with the red hill dust of Drowning Creek Road, and they nodded to Mother and shook her hand and apologized for their unholy, foul language. The one with the mustache leaned over and kissed her hand and said softly, "Nice to meet you, ma'am. We heard about you and Sam and you taking care of him."

Father's voice sang out with a happiness we'd never any of us heard before. "In here, boys, in here." And both men walked past the oilcloth curtain into where Father lay. Then we heard Father cry out, "Tend the horses, sons. Tend these fine friends' horses."

When we got back from unsaddling and wiping down their sweaty, lathered-all-to-hell horses—a big chestnut bay and a stocking-footed sorrel—and giving them a little of our alfalfa hay, the two riders were already taking off their boots, and their pocket watches and vests, and their gun belts. They'd brought the lamp into our room.

Mother was back in the bedroom with Father. Then Father yelled out, "These gentlemen are dead tired, and they're going to sleep in your cots tonight, sons. You sleep in the kitchen by the stove and be ready to help Mother with a big breakfast feed."

So we took an old patch quilt, Frank and me, and started to turn in next to the stove.

"Which one of you is Jesse?" the man with the mustache and thinning hair asked.

"Me," I said. "I'm Jesse, and this is my brother, Frank. We took good care of your horses."

Then both men laughed hard and deep, and they shook our hands and tousled our hair and turned in—the one that did all the talking taking my cot and the taller man taking Frank's. "We'll talk in the morning," the man in my cot said. "We need sleep. So you boys sleep with one eye open, now. But wake us early. We got to ride on."

One-eye-open sleep comes hard, what with all the new noises in the house. Every cough, every breath, every creak of the floor. Sometime after midnight I heard one of the men get out of bed and go outside and spit, and then take a piss off the porch. Then he came back in and more or less stepped over me and Frank, and then he leaned down like he was going either to cut our throats or to cover us up. But all he did was grab the silver-coiled handle and lift open the stove and spit again, this time into the fire.

The sizzle of his spittle lingered the longest time and kindled thoughts of hellfire and the hiss of the cat from up by the caves. I vowed to remember to ask them in the morning if they had heard that shriek tonight and if they really did shoot and if they hit anything in the darkness of the creek road.

Mother got us up with the sun, and we stoked the fire and helped her fix a big breakfast of biscuits and eggs and side-pork. We all pretty much tiptoed around, whispering. Then Father called us bedside and told us to go saddle the horses and have them ready.

Oh, they were beautiful horses, fine-blooded horses for sure, the likes of which we never saw in the hills, except maybe when we headed into Grove for supplies or something. When we got back and reported to Father, he told us to be sure and wash up and comb our hair.

"You dry on one end, and I'll dry on tuther," Frank told me as usual.

Father asked us to slide his bed into the kitchen, and then we all arranged ourselves around the table waiting for the two visitors to come to breakfast. They came out from behind the oilcloth pretty much ready to ride. They had their guns on and their shiny, singing spurs, and they had their hats and long dusters at the ready. We all sat down for a big feed after Father said a prayer, like I remember him doing before he took to his bed. He even held his Bible, the one he used to read from and tell us about before he took the final bad turn to the bed.

"We sure are thankful for these fine friends, Lord. These two fine boys here who share their good fortune with the likes of us. And we sure do thank you for this loyal wife, Ada Lou, and these two fine, obedient sons here and how now their lives will be considerable easier, thanks to these two old friends come here to do your bidding, Lord, so that a sinner like me, Sam Meeker, and his family can hold out here in these hills for the coming of Your Kingdom, Lord. Watch over these two boys as they ride on today to further their work. Blessed are the poor, Lord, as you know. And blessed are those who taketh and giveth away and share with the poor, for theirs shall be the kingdom of heaven. Bless this food, Lord, to the good of our craven and cracked, our wrecked and wretched bodies. In His good and holy name. Blessed be the Meekers. Forever and ever. Amen."

Then we all ate up hardy. The two men took up the napkins Mother had laid out and used them nice and politely. They poured their coffee, hot and black, into their saucers and cooled it with their hot breaths, and they talked about the time they kept a little clerk bastard counting and ducking his head under the counter.

"Either that or eat lead! Right, Sam?" they said. And Father laughed a croupy laugh from his propped-up pillow.

When we had finished they asked me and Frank to come outside, said that they had something for us, too. Mother and Father said it was okay, so we stepped outside, and they asked where the horses were and if they were tied up. And we said, "Sure, they're still in the barn, ready to go but all bridled and tied safe."

Then they walked us over by the big walnut tree in the yard. The one with the mustache pulled out a gun from his waist belt, a big Colt .45 Peacemaker with a long six-inch barrel, and asked me and Frank, "Do you two youngsters think you could hit that big hardwood tree over there if you took real good aim?"

We took our turns with the gun, and we both hit the tree and saw the bark splinter about the same time we heard the shots. We were only about twenty yards back from the tree, and the shots were loud and powerful. The tree took the bullets, which lodged there next to each other.

"Just remember, boys," the older-looking one, the stocky one, said, "A woman, a dog, and a walnut tree, the more you hit 'em, the better they be."

And then the two of them looked at us and at each other and laughed again and proceeded to take turns shooting at the tree with the one pistol. The booms and pops sang out fast, and the bark splintered and cracked like they were taking a double-sided ax to it. They reloaded once and kept on shooting. Then they stopped and reloaded the gun one final time. And then without shooting they handed us the gun. Frank started to take it, but the barrel was so hot it burned him and he flinched back. And I reached out and took the gun by the handle.

I said, "Would this kill a panther? The one you shot at last night in the dark?"

They laughed some more and said this is for that bastard Parker or any other goddamn lawman who comes here after you or your pa. Said this is to protect your father and your mother and yourselves.

"You're brothers, you know. Like us. If you're gonna have our names, you got to learn to hold to them." Said that's what namesakes means. "Panthers comes in many forms, boys. Like good and bad. Panthers comes in many forms."

Then they went and got their horses and rode 'em out of the barn fast and didn't even wave at us when they went by. Me and Frank walked over to the tree, the gun barrel still warm, and we looked at what they had done with the bullets. We saw they had shot their initials into the tree. You could see the bullets spelling out a big *J* and over it was an *F*, so that it looked like *F̶*.

This was the same gun, this big, long-barreled .45 Peacemaker, that went off when Frank and I were trying to get to the caves one day, looking for the panther. The gun that killed Frank dead to the Devil's own liking. And this is the tale I would give anything to lie my way out of. I try to imagine it taking on different endings. Try to create a happier ending—for Frank especially, but for me and for Mother and for Father.

They allowed how Frank and Jesse would be heartsick about it. They kept asking me about it, all the details, asking me to describe just what happened. And I told 'em, too, first one way, then tuther.

And I shot 'em both to smithereens. Father with his pain and his prayers. Mother with her silent, knowing, sad eyes. I told them like I'm telling you, Frank, and you, Jesse. We heard it. Remember? The Devil hisself came into these hills that night, and that's the sorrowful truth. The truth of damnation. The truth of a legacy that will sing out in a final night shriek any moment now when the panther comes round again calling our names.

Horned Moon

The night drive through the canyon and hitting the owl made me think of my life and destiny more acutely one final time. Of course, it has always been out there, crying, circling, searching, waiting to swoop down and slam into me—memory colliding with the moment. Then it hits, just like the flutter and thud of an owl hitting car chrome and glass. Whether I seek it or it seeks me is confused beyond answer.

We had invited my colleague Eldon Cross and his new wife, Darlene, to dinner to celebrate their recent marriage. We were late leaving because of my lingering on the phone. The restaurant reservation was for 6:30 P.M., and we were just going out the door when Sidney called. And I had to talk with Sidney. I always talk with Sidney. He calls, I answer. He's had considerable control over my destiny, presenting me with choices as to where I want to be, where I should be. He offers, I accept. I don't underestimate Sidney; I owe him a lot. But the chance he gave me to get away from what my deadwood boss had called a "no-exit" job at a treadmill college hasn't really changed anything. Seems like there really is no escape from some things.

Anyhow, I talked until a quarter after six or so, my wife and our guests making polite chatter while they glanced anxiously at our Pier One furnishings and their watches, and then we grabbed our coats and raced to the car, and I headed down the hill toward the main road that would take us to the coastal highway and on into Cambria for the damn dinner with the newlyweds—a dinner I didn't especially want to attend, but I guess obligations are obligations. Destiny is destiny.

We were all festive and friendly enough on the surface, but there was a bit of an edge to the conversation in the car because I had spent too much time talking to Sidney. Maybe he planned the call, the timing and all. I don't know. Maybe I wanted to stall. You know the theory: you're late because you didn't want to go in the first place.

Like I said, I talk with Sid every chance I get, and we have so much to catch up on when we talk that I lose track of time—especially in an instance like tonight when I didn't particularly want to go to Ian's or Robin's or any other upscale restaurant. I wasn't in the mood for California New Age cuisine—you know, roasted garlic and goat cheese with an overpriced bottle of Tobin James or Wild Horse chardonnay in a frosty glass and vacuous talk about the weather and sports and travel arrangements to New Zealand. I was more in the mood for barbecue and mesquite than incense and coastal vino. Actually, I would have preferred raiding the refrigerator and watching videos. But I owed it to the prior agreement to go, made (of course) in a different mood, and I owed it to Margaret, though she was no doubt going more to please me than herself.

Anyway, Margaret saw everything of what happened, and she knew as instantaneously as it happened just how significant it was to us. We loved together. We cried together. We were frightened together, and then in that moment, we shared the history of it, the mystery, magic, and superstition, and how it came first to me, and then indirectly to her as my wife.

I'm convinced Sidney knew too, was involved in all the events from long before I first spoke to him and accepted his offer to move to the West Coast, to the very edge of the continent, to the rim of the world as I then perceived it. Sidney's a benevolent man, I know. Made a benevolent offer. But he knew, too. He must have. He's a real smooth talker. You like him instantly, but then you start to wonder why you like him so much. Why you wind up doing his bidding. On first impression, Sidney's not the best-looking guy, not in any Denzel Washington sense, but he's very charismatic. When he enters a room, you notice him. He's really much younger than he looks, but his life shows hard on his face and gives it character and inscrutability. Put him in a white linen jacket, an Armani polo shirt, and a pair of Italian loafers, and the guy is pure class. And so disarming.

I didn't know the right or wrong of the move—just that I had to leave Rock River, had to escape all the whining, all the excuses, all the talk about burnout and deadwood, or try to. The move to Rock River was supposed to be a move toward the future and proving up as a professor, a solid job in a solid-sounding place. But names can be deceiving. And so can plans and great expectations. I had read about it before, studied it: the mutability and mortality themes of great literature. But academic claptrap about Sophocles and eternal sadness, about Dickensian darkness and Hardyesque irony were more on the page than on the darkening plain of my soul. Or so I thought. But what a change the convergence of one night and a family curse can bring.

I knew deep down as soon as I got in the car that things weren't right tonight, or, from a different perspective, that the time was right for what started to unfold and what brought me here, lying awake in bed thinking of Celso, waiting for him and what must now unfold under the high, horned moon suspended outside my window like a waiting, omnipresent owl. Celso. Sidney. Celso and Sidney. Now there's a pair. And you have to wonder about this business of the strong surviving and the weak withering away.

I shouldn't have been driving in the first place. The Crosses were supposed to take us in their car but begged off due to lack of seating space. I mean, there's quite a bit of room in a Buick Riviera, even if you do have bags and miscellaneous boxes from afternoon shopping piled up in the backseat. But they had their reasons for wanting us to drive. "More room for the beautiful people," they said and laughed, and we pretended to agree. I'm pretty much re-signed to the notion that whatever is going to happen will happen. "*Que será, será.*" Not much I can do about it now, if there ever was.

So that was one thing, along with lingering too long on the phone with Sidney. Wrong car, wrong driver. Or right, depending on how you approach things like destiny or fate, or whether you're super-stitious about choices and chances—making them and taking them. Anyway, as we bounced down the hill road, the Pacific, as usual, overwhelmed me, spread out there in front of us flat and dark and silently pounding, wave after wave, into the rock jetty, so that all you could see were the high geysers of white water and spray danc-ing up into the darkness to meet the peculiar slivered light of the horned moon.

When I got to the intersection I almost forgot to stop because of the moon's pull on me. It was pulling me up beyond the waves so I could sit between its horns, or maybe fall on them, impaled. The pull of that moon was hypnotic. It was a dark moon, just a line of light showing, with the two horns curving up. A moon right out of my childhood, when all of this started.

Back then we used to sit out on the back porch and watch the moon come up over the Sandia Mountains, and sometimes, when I was delirious from some fretful childhood fever, my mother would recite nursery rhymes like "Hey, diddle, diddle!" and I would actu-ally see the cow jump over the moon, lift my drooping head and raise my tired little arm and point to the moon. And then she would start to tell stories about hard times in the Oklahoma hill country, butchering wild hogs and skewering squirrels, and about Celso, or Ruth Muskrat and the Bushyhead boys, and how one time Chero-kee Charlie Parsons gutted a guy over a bottle of bootleg whiskey and a miscued smile. She was always talking about changelings and how the shadow people would sometimes take a healthy child with them into the hills and place an unhealthy or deformed child in its stead. The shadow people liked to do such things out of mis-chief and, worse, malice. Or I would sit quivering in my mother's lap listening to the chants of "Burn, witch, burn" emanate from the yellow-lit dial of the moon-domed Philco radio.

Before we hit the owl—or it hit us—everybody commented on

the moon, Margaret in particular, since she was beside me there in the frayed front seat of our old Volvo 240, and since she knew me well, all my hopes and all my dreams of escape—and all my fears that I couldn't put it behind us. She's almost as superstitious as I am about the things in nature, about the ocean, and the moon, about all the nocturnal creatures, owls and the other birds and beasts, all the bumping night things I told her about. How they seem to be trying to tell me something. How I seem to be trying to tell them something, to communicate with them. And I do. Maybe Margaret does, too. I shouldn't underestimate her. I told Sidney about the animals too. I'm pretty sure I did. Maybe not in so many words, but he's an expert in communication. An expert much beyond the communication allowed through human speech.

I'm pretty close to Sidney, close enough to tell him such things. He's shared some of his fears with me, too. Like the time he went back home to Memphis and had to sleep all night with a shotgun beside his bed. Something, as an educated man, he hadn't done in years, not since his own childhood when anything could come out of the night for him and his parents—a cross of fire or a noose thrown over a tree limb in the moonlight. Yes, Sidney's told me some things about his fears and how he gained the power to retaliate and put the fear of God in those who trespassed against him and his. I believe him. Sidney knows about hatred and evil and misadventure, sure enough.

Naturally, once the Volvo hit Highway 1 the drive was beautiful. That drive is so spectacular, so sublime, that even after a year out here it's impossible for me to take it for granted. The ocean stretching out forever into shifting lines of darkness and invisibility; the mounting swells and cresting waves ever and always breaking white and washing onto the long stretches of beach, creating sand spits and dunes that run for miles; the estuary that attracts the slim, white, elegant egrets and the hunkering blue herons, and almost infinite numbers of other species of birds that make their rookeries high in the old eucalyptus groves in the hills above the beach.

The whole place is charged with the spirits and shadows of the Chumash Indians who first lived here and developed their canoes and their fishing and their sacred culture long before cars and the oil derricks and petroleum tankers anchored off the coast like rusting specters of death, sucking and pumping the ancient juices of the earth. But the ocean perseveres and still prevails, no matter the pollution of one violation after another.

East, across the highway, are the rolling hills, the *cerros* and *morros*, named by the Spanish sailors who thought they discovered them and in their naming claimed this place, these soft, rounded mounds of earth modulating softly to the east into the mountains of the guardian coastal range. I've seen wildfires come over the tops of the morros so fast that nothing could get out of the way and you'd think they would drive you into the ocean. Even so, these round hills serve as buffers between the nearly distant mountains and the line of extinct volcanoes that claim the coast with their ancient craggy prominence and try to claim the ocean itself with the jutting, jagged Morro Rock offshore. It's a curious monolith, like a giant shark's tooth or spear tip, thrust up through the water from below, ambivalently asserting its sharp, towering presence, yet cowering too before the ocean's vastness.

The Central California coast is a sublime and savage place much suited for dusky romance, for the wailing of women and their demon lovers, for the shadowy pursuits of Celso and his kin. Sidney said I might find it exhilarating, inspiring, provocative—though it wasn't depicted in the slick Chamber of Commerce brochures in quite that same way. Neither Sidney nor the brochures ever said outright, "It's a place for facing up to who you are—and were."

Take a dark, horned moon and hang it over a vista like that, and the awe of it all quells you into the intuitions and silent knowing of mortality, of the grave and what lies beyond. You start thinking about creation and destruction, about geological forces and where things come from and where they go and whether the profound, stalwart perseverance of Morro Rock and the not-so-placid Pacific and the wild, picturesque mountains are what they really are in their essence and ideal. See for yourself sometime if you don't believe me. Take a drive up the coast from Morro Bay to Cambria and, amid mundane and mediocre talk, you see that change is what prevails there, like the phases of the moon and the ceaseless motions of the sea, and how you can't run from who you are—not even at the edge of the world, most especially at this particular glorious and ghastly edge of the world. Sidney set me up for all this. It's his fault. He's to blame—or to be thanked for the finality of it, for the eventual resolution.

But leave it to Eldon and his self-conscious "Hey, I'm funny" interruptions. "Did you hear about the fellow who went to see his doctor about groin pains?" he queried from the backseat, looking over at Darlene, his shopping mate and partner in crime, and winking, both of them framed in the rearview mirror like two sophomoric kids in a photo booth at a fair. "'Growing pains?' said the doctor. 'No, groin pains,' said the patient."

"Oh, Eldon, don't tell them that one. Don't listen to him, you two. He's just intolerable. But it is kind of funny. Oh, go ahead. You're just terrible, Eldon, just terrible. Isn't he terrible, Margaret? He knows more dirty jokes than he could ever possibly tell. He has a new one every week." Darlene's ways with cosmetics gave her an almost clownlike visage, and in the darkness of the backseat, with the passing car lights illuminating her caked-over wrinkles, she was mawkishly grotesque. I mean we were like some warped version of Lucy and Desi, Fred and Ethel.

Imagine having to listen to that kind of chatter at the start of the evening and in such a setting. Imagine having to endure the banter between two middle-aged newlyweds who, in their own minds at least, were out on some perpetual date, funded by the insurance money of Darlene's first and recently croaked hubby. So of course I stepped down hard on the accelerator. But four cylinders and an eggbeater Swedish sedan don't give you much quick release. Margaret reached over and patted me on my groin, and then we smiled at each other in commiseration of the froth and nonsense bubbling up from the backseat.

I keep the Volvo tuned up and in good driving condition, so once in high gear, it can sail, square and boxy as it is. Speeding up the Pacific Coast Highway is usually a beautiful thing, like I told you, but the moon this night was so very strange. It was influencing more than the physical world, more than the tides. At the spot just where the highway takes a turn between the rolling hills on the coastal side and the larger mountains outlining the encroaching inland darkness, I caught a brief flurry of feathers and an instantaneous glimpse of wings and a round, smooth-saucered face and two moon-yellow eyes reflecting the sliver of moon, and then the thump of feathered, hollow-boned softness hitting windshield glass and hard roof metal. And I knew.

"An owl!" Margaret spoke out in a voice at once subdued and shrieking. "No, no, Jason, we hit an owl. I saw it rise up from the side, then try to pull up. Oh, Jason, it was so beautiful. Did you see it? Did you?"

"Damn it all to hell," I remember saying, for I too had seen the owl's face. Saw its angry expression, the anguished contour of its futile effort to escape. Margaret and I looked at each other in immediate recognition. But I said something like, "It either saw us too late and couldn't escape, or maybe it flew into us, seeing only some moving, twilight morsel." But we knew. We silently said, "Celso! Celso!" and we prayed for our very souls.

"Just a bird, folks. Just a big bird. Why all the bother, unless it was one of those spotted owls come down from Oregon and then you've got bad trouble. Uncle Sam will fall on you faster than shit out of a sparrow's ass, faster than crap out of a condor."

"Oh, please, Eldon, please give us a break and don't trivialize it so," said Margaret. You could tell she had almost reached her limit, could carry the Crosses no longer, but was still trying to be tactful. I looked quickly into the side-view mirror, but all I saw behind us, streaming past Eldon's dumbfounded expression, was the white stripe receding down the highway into darkness, and to the side from where the owl flew, the dark, horned moon still new to the sky.

And I was back again in the storied hills, back where a certain wind, or a rustling of leaves, or omens and feelings of bad luck take on serious, life-changing meaning. Maybe it would be a chilling draft, goose bumps at some alien sound, but you would know things weren't right, were somehow out of kilter, and you would wonder and try to take precautions. Back in the faraway hills where Celso reigned. And I heard again my mother's anxious, palsied words about changelings.

"He came for you again last night, son, in the shadowed moonlight. But I slowly reached over and pushed you out of your bed, where I kept the stainless-steel, guardian scissors, and onto the floor and tossed a cover over you, and he couldn't find you, son. And he found only your father in his snoring, oblivious sleep. And me, rising up to curse the ugly damnable visage standing over the bed, and defy him, point the shaking gun at him, hold up the Bible your grandma gave me and order him to be off. 'Who are you, who are you?' I said as usual. And his usual reply, 'Father and mother have I none.' Then my ritualized reply, 'Get thee behind me, Satan. Get thee behind me, Devil and all your demons! I command you in the name of the Holy Father! Or face again the silver bullets of this gun, the stabbing of my scissors.' And then in the quickness of a flutter of wings he was gone. And I picked you up from the floor and put you again safely in your bed, and I placed that Bible next to you and waited, gun at the ready, for a time before I slept. And it wasn't a dream, son. It was real. But I've fixed it so you'll know when he comes. For he will. He will. It was my parents' promise, and I'm sorry. But it was the only way to have me and for me, in turn, to have you, son. The only way. But I'll give you the Bible and you'll take it wherever you travel. Damn his ugly black soul. Damn his relentless soul determined to see through the exchange—and mine."

So it all came back to haunt me again and frightened me even more, given the incongruity of the time, inane and profound, under the waxing and waning of a horned moon in the sky, hanging there still from childhood. Sometimes, when I would be walking in the late evening and see a hunchbacked night heron waiting for an unsuspecting fish, or a grotesque, perching pelican smiling at me, or a one-legged gull sleeping on a pier piling, I would think of my mother's words and I would shudder and say, "Satan and all your evil throng, get thee behind me." Night birds always brought it back, even the evening quail and doves from the hills here on land's edge. Celso always came at twilight or in the deepness of night when the moon was phased just so.

The drive to Cambria after we hit the owl was pretty much bordering on terror—at least it was for me, and I think for Margaret. She didn't say much after she put the stopper in Eldon. Neither did he. And Darlene just pouted and sulked through every curve in the road, every clicking turn of the odometer. I pulled up at the restaurant door about fifteen minutes late and let everyone out and on their silent way to check on our reservation; then I drove on to the parking lot. When I walked around to the other side of the Volvo and checked where I knew the owl had hit, there was nothing: no blood, no downy paste of feathers stuck to the car, no evidence of any splatter or dent. But what did I expect? Spirit owls don't die. Celso didn't die, for his life is legend and memory and prophecy. Willfulness.

Once at the table, the Crosses thought they knew what bothered me, and they did, I guess, on one level. Margaret knew more deeply, for I had told her everything, as a precaution and as a protection. I don't think she believed me at first, but she was worried about me, my state of mind, my emotions, and she was believing of what she witnessed in my behavior.

Darlene Cross knew nothing of the spirit world beyond her facile dismissal of superstition and indigenous rites and rituals, "primitive" values and beliefs. Eldon had once known, and believed, but Darlene was trying to drive that stigma out of him. What did they now know of predator and prey, hunter and hunted, of a predestined rendezvous with the past? After some wine and an appetizer Eldon soon rallied and took his tail out from between his legs. "Old Jason here is pretty pale, pretty pale. Order up, pard. It was just an owl. Now let us tell you about what we bought today in Santa Barbara. You've been to the shops in Old Santa Barbara, haven't you? Well, we spent the whole day there—and a few hundred dollars, wouldn't you say, sweetheart? Tell 'em about it, Darlene."

Tales about her shopping exploits were enough to brighten up Darlene. And so it began—through the appetizer, the entrée, the dessert. And two bottles of chardonnay, one of which I tried to finish off personally. I saw their faces, heard all their words; I let them talk and watched what soon became a strange pantomime of moving lips and meaningless gestures with me trying to get soused on a bottle of wine I absolutely loathed. Just about the time I was ready to order a double Drambuie, it was over and we were walking back out to the parking lot. I gave the keys to Margaret, and she took the wheel while I started complaining about a bad headache much in advance of our arrival home. No way were we about to invite them in for postprandial conversation. I'd had it. Margaret too. She drove sixty-five and seventy all the way back.

I tried to locate the exact point of collision on the highway, but there was no trace of anything—no wings flapping lifeless up from the asphalt, no bundle of feathers along the side of the road in the peripheral sweep of the headlights. But the moon, the horned moon, was still there, suspended over Morro Rock like the dark moon hanging over the Oklahoma hills where the outlaws ran, and where Celso plied his trade and bartered for the bodies and souls of humanity.

That image of all of those ancient and mysterious pasts, all those predictions of future moons, stayed with me as we sped along the endlessly turning coastal highway, our way lit by that ungodly beautiful horned moon: two souls in the front seat, and the car itself burdened by Crosses sitting side by sticky side in the back like heavy albatross weights around our vulnerable, frightened necks. So we hurried back down the coast, the small, winking moon strange and obscurely prominent in the sky and on the water, and no sooner had we pulled into the driveway than we watched the Riviera pull away into who knows what ignorant and naïve night dreams. Dreams of the uninitiated.

A few headache pills swallowed, a rush to bed with no thought of anything but sanctuary, and a promise to awaken Margaret if the hauntings, the dreams and nightmares, came again. She slept, so beautiful against the pillows and bedding she spent so much time choosing and color-coordinating to ward off our insomnia.

But they came, the dreams, the wakeful, worrisome dreams of the dying and dead. And my last quick but lingering sight of our collision with the owl began to merge with the visage of the man I knew as my grandfather, and the pieces of his part in my fate started to slither and slide together like the patterns in a kaleidoscope. There were the puzzle-cut pieces of the faces of the owl and of Celso—and of Sidney—and they were flip-flopping with the composite features of me and my grandfather and Margaret, and the stunned, insipid faces of Eldon and Darlene Cross. And there was Morro Rock, reaching skyward toward the horned moon while my grandfather jumped from the rock and floated across the sea of my dream. For he was the first one to know and resist the will, the negotiations and prophecies of Celso. And I was with my grandfather again, heading into Oklahoma Territory, sick and on the lam, a stolen horse under us, galloping hard, and my grandfather, ghost-like, once known as Howard Gates and now newly nameless, was lashing the horse's neck with the reins and slashing into its flanks with long, sharp-roweled Mexican spurs, tired, ever so tired, and sick, in need of sanctuary and nostrums, in need of tonics for health and healing, and wanting the hiding and the alibi and the alias essential to his desperado ways.

And he came to Celso and received that elixir, that *healing*. I knew the outlines of motive and result and can fill in the in-betweens, for I share in them just as I share in the vision and visage of the horned moon and the hooting now heard high and eerie in the tall coastal pine outside the bedroom window of our picturesque California bungalow.

The sound and the dream will awaken Margaret soon enough. What I must do, once and for all, is finish it—end it here on the edge of what Sidney has now set in final place. But there is time to wait with some greater patience now in the knowing that it will end. Wait for the falling together of the pieces in some final pattern. Turning the granular crystals and colors and features, back-lighted by the horned moon, and the owl flying out of the edges of my vision and colliding and fusing into the fragments of the kaleidoscope of my nights, of this night. High time to see once again, more clearly, what must have faced my grandfather, and through him my mother, and now faces me in a rhythm as recurrent and inevitable as the moon's horned and owl-faced phases.

"Here it is, my good man, Horace, the elixir, here in this small, dark bottle. Take it, good sir, and be welcome. Good for the ague and the agony that afflict you. Good to halt your croup and your shivering fears, good for the transforming powers of yet another new day, another new starting and facing of life. Take it, my good man, and just see if what I say isn't true. See if the transforming contents of this smoky-glassed melding of heated and blown sands of time will not regenerate you, will not change and eradicate what shows so painfully in the wrinkles of your haggard face and austere, bony body. Take. Drink. Revive and live."

And the small, stooping man reached out his scaly-fingered hand from the shadows of his encompassing dark shawl, embroidered delicately with semicircular patterns all stitched of golden, glistening thread, and he offered the bottled gift to the supplicant before him. And my grandfather said little to the smiling presence standing over him, and realized little in his exhaustion and illness. He accepted the offer and raised the smooth, warm bottle to his dry, weather-ravaged lips. And he partook of the strangely cold, sizzling liquid. And he shuddered in the swallowing and the sealing of his fate—and his progeny's.

My grandfather needed only rest, for himself and for the stolen horse that had brought him to these remote badlands. He had come into the Territory from the south, riding for days, eating little, knowing only that he had to put some fast distance between him and the others. For the spoils had been less than expected, and the quick, selfish sharing was done amid silent, accusing good-byes—each rider heading off into hoped-for obscurity, soon to become legend for some postponed, yet inevitable, greater oblivion.

And now the horse, turning its head to observe the transfer and the thirsty imbibing, pawed the ground and snorted as the man drank the effervescent liquid to the distant screams of animals caught up in the nightly clutches of quick death, predator savoring prey. The strange medicine burned in the man's throat and stomach and thought—and in his almost immediate delirium he dreamed of lightning and strange trees catching fire in instant destruction. Ravens soared through his knowing, and bats, and his fevered face was fanned by the slow-flapping wings of what resembled an owl, ascending into the limbs of the burning trees.

The horse, feeling the spasms of its rider against its own pained, exhausted body, found its way to a farmhouse hidden in the dankness of the darkening heavy-wooded hills. The isolated, silent woman who was to be my grandmother took the rider into that house and tended to his delirium with broths, and cool compresses cut with steel scissors from flour sacks, and Scripture readings from the Bible she carried alongside the scissors in her apron. She hung his gun belt and long-barreled pistol on the bedpost and ran her fingers over the carved dragon that curled on the now yellowed ivory grips. And she took his stained wallet and his ivory-handled straight razor, and a curious dark-glass bottle, and placed them beside his bed. And she wondered just who had come her way, and where he had been. And she sat beside him and comforted him and read aloud from her Bible. The words escaped from her mouth and circled around the kerosene lamp and comforted the sleeping man.

Then, as this man come to be known as Horace rallied over the next months, and as the woman joined him in that bed, he would not let her remove the bottle, even long after it was empty, as if it were some precious memento, some amulet or charm. And his gun, too, he insisted must always stay there. He checked it often and would even reach for it late at night or in the small hours of the morning, surfacing out of deep sleep in which he would babble about the strange hunched man who had helped him, a man my grandmother recognized, in her own shuddering, as once living in those hills, who had died old and crippled and much defamed long before she was born.

She recognized him as the full-blooded Cherokee named Samuel Celso, who was known to have had the powers of special medicine, magical powers of life and death. It was said that he could change himself into different animal forms, and that his ways were ephemeral and ghostly. He had an eye for young children, and he was finally shot as he hovered over a small baby. The baby's father had worked long to convince his wife of Celso's evil will, and he had of necessity crafted the special bullet, a bullet to be fired only late at night, as prescribed by lore, under a high and dark, horned moon.

But when the man ran to his crying child's room, my grandmother remembered, he found only an owl perching on the side of the child's crib. The man shot at the owl and cursed it with strange words as it flew through an open window and into the yellow iridescence of a full moon. The next day Celso was seen limping around a corner heading back into the hills with his arm bandaged and suspended in a gunnysack sling. And the man knew he had hit the owl. But others knew, though they did not all have the courage to say it, that the moon had not been right that night, so whether the old medicine man would live or die depended on the vying powers of the moon and the metals of the special bullet and other forces of the night. There had been a trail of blood leading to Celso's shack, which they burned to the recitation of the prayers of their beliefs.

My grandfather insisted that the man he had met, the man who gave him the bottle, was proof that Samuel Celso lived, and that he visited his patient again and again in hastening, rapidly recurring, suffocating dreams, asking for his payment in the form of my grandfather's mind and body and soul or in the relinquishment of his firstborn. And in one way or another such a debt would be paid.

I have the razor and that same gun my grandfather kept by his bed and brandished in large moonlike arcs whenever the anguish became too much and he began to rave that the debt had been called and he was in dire danger of being swept away on the wings of owls: the gun he finally turned on himself when my mother was small; the gun she found in his hand, her own insane father, him still bleeding but already dead; the gun she gave me just before she died, along with her mother's scissors and the Bible I clutch here in my hands. The gun, the scissors, and the Bible were no small solace for her, and I remember seeing them all those years, one under her pillow, one in a dresser drawer, one on top of the pine dresser where she would go to search out her protections, deal with the dreams of Celso and her father when the visions were too strong upon her and she vowed she owed her salvation, such as it was, to those paper and steel legacies. Each is a comfort in its way, for I brought them here to the edge of the world, a further final remove of the westering path and setting that my grandfather sought in his run to the Territory and his attempts at a new start.

Margaret despairs now of everything, even her complaints of sharing our bed with this dragon-handled pistol, these Nordic steel scissors, this cracked and worn black leather volume of the Word of God. And she is beyond despairing as she yearns in sorrow past sorrow for a child we cannot, dare not, allow. And soon her despair, though perhaps her liberation, will spread to this final episode, this final night when the gun I now clutch will shatter the night when I take aim at the spirit owl who comes to us out of the years and across the continent, finding us on a destined drive along the coast, under a horned moon in a world only the foolish can pretend to understand and enjoy.

Sidney knows this all so well, for I told him much more than I told Margaret. And now with his spectral voice lingering in my ear, emanating from the tree outside my window, I finally understand that he was Celso's own emissary and that in inviting me out here, luring me here to the beautiful, wicked edge, he always knew more than I ever imagined. Whether he will explain it to Margaret or whether she, or the Crosses, or even you will care after tonight can't concern me. I do what I must, for this small bottle is finally and forever empty. The moon and the sharpened razor shine, and Samuel Celso and his spirit owl await.

Silver Dollar Man

It's hard to say just when things started to get worse, but there were signs, a whole series of events that stacked up like a tower of silver dollars until it toppled. And all the events taken together built into what I'll call the Kohldhaas incident. That was the real turning point between then and now, or maybe shopping for the new pants just before that. Of course, the brightness of the dollars started to tarnish along the way, and the old pants wore thin and took on a sheen, but after the Kohldhaas incident things never were the same for Hipa, or for the family, and surely not the same for me.

The nagging. There had always been the nagging. Mema's will for a spic-and-span house, or in larger terms an orderly life, started long before I came on the scene, I guess. To tell the truth, it was hard for me not to choose sides. I loved them both but I had special empathy for Hipa. Him old, me young. Kind of like two sides of a coin. But after the Kohldhaas incident I watched Hipa get older fast and head into a sharp decline. It's hard to imagine . . .

29

but I think the nagging got worse in the aftermath of what happened there at Kohldhaas. For one thing, Hipa seemed to get on people's nerves much more than before. When she heard about it, Mema seemed to go over the brink and lose patience with just about everything. Thus the nagging. Always the nagging. Variations on an old motif, you might say, but always and ever the same old tune: "If you can't take your shoes off when you come into the house, at least try to wipe off that damnable automobile grease. You're getting it all over the carpets. Next thing you know, I'll need plastic runners for the whole house. And if you can't make your way around a warehouse, well, just how will you be able to navigate plastic runners, pray tell?" That was the basic tune, but the volume was amplified after Kohldhaas.

I would sometimes be coming in the door with Hipa and hear Mema scold him like that, about the grease on his shoes, about other things—but mostly when the nagging started to pick up it was about the grease. And then that would always slide, smooth as the grease itself, into old grievances, a barrage of scolding about old transgressions, old infidelities, old disappointments, lingering frustrations. Ancient inadequacies. There were a lot of years stacking up, you can imagine, ready to topple.

Long before Kohldhaas, Hipa had to get a leg brace for his weak right knee because all the cartilage was deteriorating, grinding down into nothing. The brace hooked into his shoe just under the heel, so he couldn't take his shoes off very easily because he had to take his pants off to get to the leg brace to take it off. One thing led to another, like the old song about one bone connected to another, and another, and so on. It became quite an ordeal for Hipa just to walk into the house, just to sit down and take off his leg brace.

Then, there was the problem of where to put it, and when to get a replacement or a realignment of all the mechanisms. It was a complicated contraption made of chrome-plated steel shafts that ran up each side of his leg, guided by a couple of padded leather harnesses around his calf and just above his knee. He had to sit down to remove the brace and usually didn't feel like he could go without the extra support until after dinner, when he went to his black vinyl recliner (chosen so it wouldn't show the grease smudges) to smoke a couple of pipefuls of his favorite Maple Leaf tobacco in his aluminum-stemmed Falcon pipe. He had to have both, one in the other. No substitutes. Maple Leaf tobacco in his Falcon pipe. He bought large tins of the tobacco and had backup bowls to screw into his pipe. He used to send me shopping for him. "Down at Payless . . . they stock it down at Payless. Second shelf."

I used to think he had a kind of high-tech style, a flair of sorts, with the metal brace and that metal pipe. If you've ever seen a metal-stemmed, removable-bowl Falcon pipe, you know what I mean. Sometimes you still see them in faded cardboard displays in out-of-date, out-of-the-way drugstores. There are still a few Falcon aficionados around today, and whenever I see the displays I tend to want to buy whatever pipes are left and take them all to Hipa. But it's too late for that.

I guess Mema didn't think so highly of Hipa's changing "style," his metamorphosis into what she saw as decrepit old age. She hated old age, even as she slid into it herself. There was the grease on the soles of his feet, the spilled tobacco, the burned holes in his chair. And there were his pants, his worn, shiny-seated pants.

"For heaven's sake, can't you keep that brace from wearing through your pants? Every pair of slacks you own is either frayed and frazzled and threadbare at the knee, or worn clear through, or riddled with little burn holes from that damn pipe. They're beyond mending—all of them. I'd be ashamed to go out in public if I were you. I'm ashamed for you!"

I would overhear that, too—maybe at the dinner table or maybe in the living room while I would be watching TV or reading, and Hipa would be sitting there in his reclining chair with his leg brace propped against the little walnut end table where he kept all his smoking paraphernalia: the tin of Maple Leaf tobacco, the leather pouch he always kept filled to the brim, a disposable lighter or two, some Diamond wood matches, his pipe cleaners and all-purpose pipe tool, and an extra pipe bowl—that extra high-tech advantage of the Falcon pipe, the epitome of 1970s pipe smoking, if you were progressive and an explorer like Hipa.

That was one of the neat things about my granddad: his style, and how, even as he got older and should have hung on to things like briar pipes, he was inclined to innovation, that is, he was inno-vative and a risk taker in regard to his pipe. As for his clothes, Mema was right. He held on to his clothes way too long. He wasn't a connoisseur or a collector or anything. He was about the most practical, functional man around. And when things didn't function anymore, well, that tended to break his spirit, cramp his style.

His pants would usually be draped over the end table by his chair, placed neatly under the brace, all of this serving as a kind of ornate curtain to the stage of his little walnut table. He had to reach behind the slacks, being careful not to disturb the balance of the brace and shoe, to get to his smoking equipment. All of this led to new problems. Mema didn't like him sitting in the living room rummaging through his table in his boxer shorts, and she would shake her head and almost stomp her foot and say so.

"What if someone comes to visit? Are you just going to sit there in your underwear? Can't you put your pants back on? I just don't understand it. Always fumbling with your pipe. I think sometimes after all these years you're finally hopeless. Don't you have any respect for yourself, or me as your long-suffering wife of all these years, or your grandson there? Don't think he doesn't notice these things about you. He's got eyes in the back of his head. All young folks do. His mother and father do, too. They see these things. How do you think we all feel, seeing you sitting around in your undershirt and shorts?"

And they would both look over at me, and I would pretend not to hear anything and scoot up closer to the television, or bury my nose a little deeper in whatever book or magazine I was reading. I tried not to take sides, except in a personal, private sort of way. Sure, Mema wanted to keep her house nice and all, but Hipa didn't have any extra energy after a long day working at the garage. Just putting his pants back on was a genuine effort. He had his routine, and when he settled into his chair and arranged himself he was pretty much in for the night. When I stayed with them I would try to turn in before they did, leaving them sitting in their chairs doing their end-of-the-day, end-of-the-trail battles over their domain. Mema's chair seemed the true throne of the house, elevated, barri-caded by countless self-help, how-to-do-it books. Her well-worn Bible rested atop it all.

Hipa got away with quite a bit, when you stop to think about it. Even the pipe smoking in the house. Even his greasy hands, fingernails, knuckles, wrists. Even his crusty elbows and his insistence on a bath every Thursday afternoon, his afternoon off, "Whether I need it or not, Stephen, whether I need it or not." He knew he was goading Mema and kidding me, because he would chuckle to himself and his gray-blue eyes would sparkle a bit.

He had the saddest eyes I have ever seen. His eyes were sad and forlorn even when he was a child, even in some of the earliest photographs of him and his brothers and sister. I always wondered why his eyes were so damn sad, even when he first started out in life and everything was fresh and new before him. How could a little kid know about old age and remorse? Not that life doesn't have its sadness for everybody, but how was he to know that, all dressed up in his little jacket and trousers, trying his best to smile over the flourish of the bandanna tied in a bow at his neck?

It was hard for Hipa to stand in the shower and to get in and out of the bathtub. Sometimes he would call for me, "Hey, Stephen, you want to give old Hipa a hand?" and I would open the door into the steamy bathroom and help him step out of the shower. I would try to respect his dignity and hand him a towel right away, but he had no qualms or inhibitions whatsoever and would stand there drying off, telling me jokes about the days he and his brothers used to go swimming in the ponds and creeks back in Oklahoma before it was a state, when he grew up Cherokee free. Or after he moved to New Mexico, when he would take my dad swimming up by Alameda at the flumes.

"*Ahyahketsga na usdi gasohiʔi*, Stephen. Just remember that when you want to embarrass somebody at the old 'municipal' pool. When the courage and Indian mischief come on you and some bully tries to act bigger than he really is. Just talk Indian to him. We got to keep our Indian blood, boy. And you got some too. Don't you forget it."

I won't bother translating all of the Cherokee words he taught me. They were cusswords, mostly, and insults. I tried to talk Indian like he suggested, but I never heard him mutter even a single profanity in front of Mema. She tried to play down her Indian heritage.

I still wonder why Mema didn't force Hipa to wear a bathrobe or a smoking jacket or something, but such refinements weren't for him. Not after a bath. Not in the evenings when he was in his chair. I don't think such civilities ever really registered on him, being born in Indian Territory and bathing only in the creek beside his house.

Now and then I tried to picture Hipa in a quilted smoking jacket—you know, some Walter Pidgeon–type attire tied with a silk sash, with a hundred little fringes dangling at the ends, and him there in a fine leather chair with his feet propped up in some elegant house slippers, smoking an expensive pipe and reading the *Wall Street Journal* or *Forbes* magazine and saying, "Anna, my dear, would you please bring me and Stephen some refreshment?" Naw, that wasn't Hipa.

That's probably why he was never big on buying clothes, either. I mean, when a man grows up without indoor plumbing, with maybe a new shirt and overalls and a pair of shoes once every year or two, you can see how habits form. Hipa was what you might call an essentialist, and his needs were few. I realized that from those stories he told about the time when he was a boy like me. That's why such a simple thing as buying new pants and new shoes for the big oyster-on-the-half-shell reception at Kohldhaas Distributors was such a big deal . . . and such a turning point for Hipa and for me.

In the old days, when I was maybe ten or twelve, he used to take me to town with him. We would jump into his old Ford pickup, which I loved almost as much as he did, and run errands—"gallivant around," Mema came to call it. First, we always stopped at the bank. Hipa kept his daily deposit of checks and cash in a hand-tooled leather wallet from Old Mexico. It had ornate flowers carved on both sides and was double-laced around the edges. He liked to carry it inside his shirt next to his stomach, and you could usually see it through the thin cotton material, especially in summer.

He used to hold up his wallet and tell me, "I picked up this little beauty in Juárez, Stephen. Got it for a song after some hard negotiation with the best small businessman in that whole Ciudad de Juárez. Don't let 'em tell you anything stamped *Hecho en Mexico* is cheap stuff. This piece of cowskin here is good, and it's pretty to boot." Of course, it had Hipa's grease smudges all over it, and the lacing was frayed from use, always going in and out of his shirt.

He carried a turquoise-colored canvas money sack for change and for the silver dollars he liked to hear clink and jingle. It had the words BANK OF NEW MEXICO stamped on it in bold black letters and the drawstrings were tipped with little red wooden beads. Sometimes he let me carry the sack of silver dollars, and I would marvel at the weight of it and try to guess how much money it held. I would swing it with some little bravado and Hipa would say, "Hey, Pretty Boy Floyd, hold on to them silver dollars, pal. We could head for the border and get lost forever with all the money you've got right there in your two little hands." He was always talking about Pretty Boy Floyd and Jesse James and Will Rogers and Jim Thorpe, and a whole bunch of other Okie folk heroes. And that was just fine with me, because I could imagine myself as every single one of them.

Hipa didn't wear a leg brace then, and he could step pretty lively into and out of the truck or walking downtown into the bank and along the sidewalk. We always went into the Model Shoe Shine Parlor, where Mr. Cheers would shine our shoes and our spirits. Hipa liked Mr. Cheers, and so did I. He was a porter on the Atchison, Topeka, and Santa Fe Railroad before he opened his shine parlor. He had old train calendars all over the walls, and I would sit there listening to him pop the shine rag, and those trains would come right off the wall to the rhythm of his shines. "All aboard, now, all aboard," he would say when customers climbed into the big elevated chairs and placed their feet on the metal foot stands. "Coming home," he would say to the accompaniment of the pop and beat of his shine rag and his brushes. "Coming into the station, now, people, into the station," he would say when he finished and touched your toe with his final blessing.

"What's this young businessman been up to these days, anyway, Mr. J? Is he your assistant again this summer? Ready for some good Griffin wax and a nice dye and polish around the heels and soles of those scruffy business brogues?" He would turn to me after finishing Hipa's shoes to a high, mirrorlike gloss and start with the old horsehair brush and saddle soap and his cut-handled toothbrush around the edges. His hair was as white as the lather of the saddle soap, and I was always struck by the similar patterns and textures I saw in his bent-over black skin and white hair and the lathered-up dark leather shoes he could transform into works of art before your very eyes. I wondered if he got in trouble at home for the polish stains on his hands.

Hipa liked to talk to Mr. Cheers, and they would complain together or laugh together, and then Hipa would give me a silver dollar to give to Mr. Cheers, who'd give me a kind of salute with his polish-stained fingers. Then Hipa would thank him and remind me to thank him, and the two of us would head back along the sidewalk with a spring in our steps and smiles on our faces, to where we had parked the truck. Usually Hipa would whistle and flip another silver dollar into the air with his thumb. He'd catch it a few times and then wind up giving it to me, with a wink.

"You always respect fellows like Mr. Cheers there. He's a good businessman. Knows how to greet the public. Likes people . . . and people like him. Don't ever put down a fellow like Mr. Cheers. Never. Always treat hardworking people with the respect they deserve. You just remember the value of hard work and a silver dollar, and you'll be okay."

Hipa liked to carry silver dollars, and he always saved them when they came over the counter at the garage. He was a regular silver dollar man, Hipa was. In the fall, when the state fair came, he always had fifty or sixty silver dollars for us to drop into the turnstiles at the rodeo or to bet on horses or ride the Ferris wheel and the Tilt-a-Whirl. A silver dollar here, a silver dollar there—they mounted up. But Hipa liked to spend them. He'd buy the family cotton candy and candied apples. He'd let me take about a zillion shots at the metal ducks in the shooting gallery, and every now and then I'd win a stuffed animal amid the clang of the hits and the smoke of the rifles.

"What a shot! What a dead-eye Dick!" the guy with the apron would say as he pointed to me and yelled out to the passing crowd. "This little Dick just won a big teddy bear, folks. Lookie, lookie here! Dead-eye Dick. Yes sir. Betta, betta . . . load 'em up again. Wowie! What a dead-eye Dick." And I'd take the little bear and look up at Hipa, and we'd smile.

Just about anything we wanted to spend money on was okay. Hipa saved silver dollars all year for those fair days. I mean, he loved the state fair, and we all loved going with him. When I was really little, I remember going to a couple of the rodeo dances with Hipa and Mema, and I watched them kick up their heels together. They were a good-looking couple, all spruced up and having the time of their lives. Any time the band played a fiddle tune or something like "Ida Red," or "Faded Love," or any Bill Monroe or Bob Wills tune, Hipa would holler, and he and Mema would twirl and two-step all around the dance floor.

I thought about those days and how Hipa used to spend silver dollars to buy things when, a few years later, he asked me to take him to the mall to buy a new pair of pants, a new shirt, and some shoes for the reception at Kohldhaas Distributors. He wanted to look his best because his son and grandson were going to the reception, too, as his guests. When we headed off on that special shopping trip, Hipa asked me to drive. He preferred to drive his truck himself, of course, but by this time he was getting older and the leg brace slowed down his reaction time some.

"Take him to Penney's and get slacks, a shirt, and some new shoes. He definitely needs pants and shoes," Mema scolded. "And be sure you don't let him make you drive all over town in the doing of it, either. He'll make you take him all the way to El Paso if you let him."

We weren't out of the driveway before Hipa pulled his small spiral-bound notebook and his Papermate ballpoint pen out of his pocket and went over the list: Donut Land, the Indian Hospital, the mall, the guy who made his brace, the new Juan Tabo road out by the mountains and the tram, then back to the valley to see where the new bridge would cross the river. I mean, it was the itinerary for quite an outing.

"Let's just go to the mall first and then see about fitting your brace to the new shoes if we find a good pair. Just the essentials for now. Okay, Hipa? We don't have enough gas to drive all over the city."

We compromised by adding the Indian Hospital, where I ran in for some more of Hipa's arthritis medicine. Then we went up to the new Winrock Mall. I parked the truck as close as I could to the main mall entrance, and we walked slowly into Penney's and the men's department. We found the shoe section, and Hipa picked out his same style of plain brown Nunn Bush oxfords. Then we found the shirt and slacks section. We rummaged through some sale shirts and a couple of racks of pants, and Hipa tried to explain to a dippy, overdressed salesclerk just what style and color and cut of shirt and trousers he liked. The clerk picked out a couple of shirts, but Hipa insisted that he didn't like the collars. Finally he found a shirt he liked, and we turned to looking for the right slacks.

"The pant for you is over here, sir, on the sale rack." As I followed Hipa to the sale rack, the patronizing clerk started to get on my nerves. There was Hipa hobbling around, and this smart-ass kept saying "pant." Not *pants* or *slacks*. Every time Hipa would say "trousers" this guy would say "pant," as if to correct him. What a shit-face, pissant of a salesman. I mean, I was angry.

I realized for the first time that I felt sorry for Hipa, and I was partly mad at that. All of a sudden, I thought Hipa needed some protection, some greater respect and loyalty than what I was seeing. And I realized that I was a bit ashamed too—at Hipa's age and his crippled leg. So what if Hipa was old? So he had a brace and limped along. So his clothes were pretty worn and not all that fancy to begin with. Who was this sissy clerk to assume even a small degree of arrogance with a guy like Hipa, a hardworking man all his life? I knew what Hipa meant about Mr. Cheers. But I tried to hold it all in, and aside from a grimace or two I let the smirks on the clerk's "pant" face pass. Besides, Hipa soon found a pair of trousers he wanted to try on, so I walked back to the dressing room with him and saw that he was situated okay behind the curtain. And then the most embarrassing thing happened.

Hipa had no more than got out of his old pants—with the trouble of the brace, you understand—and into the new trousers and stepped out from behind the dressing-room curtain when he said, "Stephen, I've got to take a leak real bad." I checked with the haughty little salesclerk for the location of the nearest rest room, which wasn't too far down the hall, and I went back for Hipa to take him there. But it was too late. He had already wet all down the front of his new trousers. I'll never forget his face all pained up, his sad eyes tearing in anger and in humiliation.

"Ah, shit, Stephen, I didn't make it, I just didn't make it. I'm sorry."

I helped Hipa down to the rest room anyway, and he took the pants off and finished up in the toilet and washed his hands. And I just took the tags off the pants and told the clerk to ring up the sale and give us a bag and we would take the pants and a new pair of underwear. He knew, though, judging by the sneer on his face. But I just took the new underwear and went back for Hipa and got him braced up and into his old pants again. The old pants were heavy in my hands with the weight of silver dollars bulging in all the pockets. Hipa told me to pay for the new shoes and shirt and trousers with the silver dollars, so I counted out about fifty silver dollars and put some in my pockets and carried some in my hands and went back to the counter to settle up.

That sissy clerk had never seen that many silver dollars before, except maybe in a movie. He raised an eyebrow when I plunked the silver down on the counter. Then—I couldn't help it, I swear—I put my face up close to his face and said, "If you say one word about this much silver to the manager or to the police until we're long gone, I swear I can't be responsible about what the old man will do. He's one mean son of a bitch." And that damn twerp almost had to head for the dressing room to change his own *pant!* I hope he thought I was some Okie bandit.

I carried the shopping bags out to the truck. Hipa didn't say much, just fumbled with the silver dollars still in his pocket. Then I drove straight to Oscar's Five Points Cleaners and dropped off Hipa's new pants. Hipa and Oscar were old friends, so Hipa felt better about leaving his new trousers there. From there we wheeled over to the shop, where this real technical-looking guy fitted Hipa's old brace to his new right shoe. He was all measurements and numbers and had about ten pencils in his shirt pocket and one over his ear. His workbench was filled with pieces of chrome and miscellaneous shoes and artificial legs. I was glad when we got out of there.

When I asked Hipa if he still wanted to go to Donut Land, he just asked me to take him home but not to tell Mema about what had happened. I tried to liven him up and insisted I was hungry for a coconut or maybe a sprinkle donut. I tried to joke about the sissy

salesclerk and speculate about what kind of a donut he would order and what he would do with it. Hipa said in a low voice with a
real straight face, "That midget would probably order donut holes."
I found that funny as hell, but Hipa didn't crack a smile. All the
expectation and sense of adventure charted out on the list in his
little spiral notebook were now just so many strokes of ink.

I had never ever heard him ask to go home. There wasn't much
else to say, so I just sat there in silence, going with the flow of the
traffic and listening to the muffled clink of the two or three silver
dollars left in his pocket.

Come the day of the big oyster-on-the-half-shell shindig at
Kohldhaas, it wasn't hard to pick up Hipa's dry cleaning. Oscar
himself waited on me. "Here you go, Stevie boy. Good to see old
Jake get some new pants. He needs 'em. Most of the others are
close to falling apart. What's the occasion?"

"The annual oyster feed at the equipment company where he
gets all his compressors and pumps and hoses for the garage. You
know, that place north of town on Second. He goes every year. This
time he's invited me and Dad to go with him."

"Well, good. It seems to me your grandfather is failing somewhat lately. Slowing down, you know. Is he doin' okay? Still after
those silver dollars? He's a regular silver dollar man, that Mr. Jake
is."

"He's tapering off a bit, I guess. Now and then he has some new
grief, like with these new pants . . . , you know. The body's getting
older. His leg is giving out, slowing him down. It's hard for him to
drive anymore."

"Well, you tell Jake hello. Tell him I still check his pockets for
those silver dollars. He used to tell me to keep whatever he forgot
and left in his trousers. And he always forgot one. Always."

From Five Points up to Granite to pick up Hipa's brace wasn't
that far, but dealing with the engineer wasn't as pleasant as talking
with Oscar. The bill was more than I expected, but the technician
agreed to send Hipa a statement. Some big credit risk—a guy who
always paid his way with cash, and silver dollars at that. That engineer was a cold fish, all measurements and numbers. He said he
had made the new brace a bit shorter and that he had decided to

narrow the straps and the leather harnesses. It wasn't exactly that way on the specifications, he said, and it wasn't that way on the old brace, but he knew what was good for his clients. He had also leveled out the heel on the left shoe and made the right heel so many fractions of an inch higher. It gave me some pause, but I assumed he knew what he was doing.

It was a pretty curious contraption, that brace and its attached shoe lying along the truck seat, next to the other lone shoe back in its box with the tissue paper protruding from under the lid. Made me feel like I was riding with a ghost. I got a kind of feel for what it might mean to have to walk around with that heavy, shiny thing with its hinges and harnesses trying to stabilize you and rubbing you raw in the process.

Anyway, I dropped it all off with Mema, who was still curious about the new pants being dry-cleaned before Hipa wore them. But I held to our story about them needing quick attention, some alterations and some pressing, and that only Oscar could handle it, knowing Hipa like he did. Mema bought that okay because Oscar took care of all Hipa's cleaning.

Just a little after eleven the next morning I drove Hipa and my dad to the reception. My dad had attended the event before, so much of our conversation focused on whether or not I was man enough to down raw oysters. That came before any beer drinking. "Raw oysters first. No brewski till a guy can down a raw oyster or two."

Hipa was on my side and reassured us. "He'll love 'em, just like his father and his grandfather. If he can swallow sardines, he can gulp down a raw oyster. Then on to mountain oysters or brains and eggs. Now, those are meals to separate the men from the boys. Raw oysters will just whet his appetite, Joe. Then there's . . ."

"Now, Hipa, don't get carried away," my dad interrupted. "Steve's just sixteen. He's got plenty of time."

But I knew what Hipa was going to say. He'd been getting a little raunchy with the passing years, as I got older and as we rode around together in the truck. He'd say, "Now this might sound gnarly, Steve, and you could sure get me into trouble, but did I ever tell you about the old gal out on Mushroom Road I used to deliver coal oil to?" I could tell lots of tales on Hipa, some of the things he told me here and there, but I'm a loyal traveling companion. He made me promise to keep a few secrets, and I kept them.

Hipa's spirits were back, I could tell, and he looked pretty spiffy in his new getup. Pants creased. Nice dark brown shoes and the silver shine of the brace showing over his right ankle when he walked. A new lime-green shirt, lightly starched and accented by his favorite turquoise bolo tie. He'd overdone it a bit with the Bay Rum aftershave. But he was happy and ready for the big event— really looking forward to it. To being with us. You could tell he was proud of us. And he liked oysters, too. He really had an appetite worked up.

When we entered the place, it was jam-packed with all ages and shapes and sizes of men, talking, laughing, shaking hands, patting each other on the back. Some of them were all doubled up and near collapse, gasping and wheezing for air because of their laughing. Some fellows had their heads thrown back with their mouths open wide with laughter, faces flushed, plastic cups sloshing over with beer.

You could tell all of the guests were guys like Hipa—middle-class, blue-collar guys, independent garage dealers with no pretenses at all about themselves or their businesses. Even the two guys who greeted us in the office area of what was really a big warehouse, and who turned out to be the owners of the company, were just ordinary-looking guys. A bit overweight but no sharp-dressed tycoons or anything.

After the introductions and handshakes, we joined into the press of bodies all heading for the food. What faced us were two big, high-sided tables of galvanized metal, filled with crushed ice and piled high with oysters. Four or five young guys of varying ethnicity stood behind the tables opening oysters and filling the plates. All the talk was loud, and there was quite a bit of jostling with people coming back for seconds or another beer.

Hipa was in front of Dad, and I tried to keep close to him. He was laughing and I could see he was having a good time. But he looked a little unsure, maybe a bit peeved or disoriented. Kind of mixed up. I got my plate of oysters and a Pepsi-Cola and followed

Dad's nod to move out of the crowd and across the room to where we could stand at a makeshift counter and eat. I was trying to balance my food and drink and keep the course set by Dad when it happened.

I heard it first. The yells, and then a clunking thud of metal and soft weight hitting cement. Then, amid the momentary hush and silence, I saw Hipa. He was flat on the floor, and his plate of oysters and his plastic cup of beer were scattered and spilled, on him and on the floor around him. As my dad and I rushed over to pick him up and check the damage, I watched some fat reveler mouth the words, which reverberated through the rafters of the warehouse, "Damn drunk son of a bitch. Can't even hold a beer or two." Then the laughter picked up like a chain reaction, surging out in ripples and waves of volume until the noise level was as high as before and the party resumed.

All Hipa said was, "Damn new brace. Damn new pants. Tripped me up." But he had that same forlorn, sad expression on his face and in his eyes that I had seen in the Penney's men's department on our ill-fated shopping trip, and in that old dress-up picture from when he was a kid.

We didn't stay, of course. We got Hipa back out to the truck after we picked him up, but I don't really recall the details. What I do know is that he was never the same again after that.

A few months later, maybe a year or so, I watched with my own sad-eyed sorrow as Hipa tried to eat a Styrofoam cup from the edges down to the base, oblivious to all the family standing around his hospital bed. And I remember hearing the doctor tell my dad something about Hipa being overmedicated with conflicting prescriptions, tranquilizers, sleeping pills, pain pills, cough syrup, nose drops, arthritis medicine, you name it—all from the Indian Hospital where, apparently, Hipa had obtained prescriptions for much more than arthritis medicine, each prescription with a different doctor's name on it.

To complicate the situation, there was a heart attack and a pacemaker implant and the overall diagnosis of "multisystem disability." Then it was time for the nursing home and counselors and therapists and a whole bunch of talk, mean and confused. Everybody hated to see Hipa come to such straits, and to tell the truth, we all hated the bother of it. All the errands and the demands and the confusing, contradictory litany of requests and needs.

I tried as much as I could to visit Hipa in his room at the Vista Grande Rest Home, taking him tobacco and maybe a malt now and then. "Maple Leaf" or "Chocolate," things like that were about all he would say. He was always glad to see me, I could tell. His old Falcon pipe was his one remaining possession, and he liked the Maple Leaf tins to keep things in, like his pocket notebook and his Papermate ballpoint pen. I'd bring him my sacks of whatever I was supposed to drop off, give him a pep talk, and maybe coax him out of his bed or out of the small corner chair where he would sit with a housecoat draped over his shoulders. He never put it on fully. He had to wear pajamas, and I had to buy a couple of pairs for him, but I got them at Kmart. I never went back to Penney's.

Hipa didn't have the freedom anymore to sit around in his recliner decked out in his boxer shorts. Maybe Mema found some satisfaction in that, but I don't think so. The room was small and smelly, like the whole place. You know how those nursing homes smell with the stench of urine and feces and vomit and blood and stewed cafeteria food. There were odd voices and noises, laughter mixed with cries of pain, old people coughing and muttering and babbling this and that. Hipa still kept his leg brace out and visible, leaning against a pair of pants and a shirt. He was ready to go. I would maybe wheel him around the lobby and over to the observation area, where he could look out at the sky and the trees and the changing seasons. He started calling me Joe sometimes, Dad's name.

"Joe," he would say and then point to something or gesture for me to do something for him. He got me confused with my dad quite a bit.

Dad visited Hipa, too, and often he brought Mema. She would start up her old habit of scolding Hipa about his pipe or his new housecoat, letting him have it for not putting his arms through the sleeves and not tying it around his waist like he was supposed to. Or maybe it was his toenails, which were too long or something. But she was paining all the time she was complaining, you could tell. Maybe she was remembering their old rodeo times two-stepping together, or maybe she saw shadows of herself in him, of what awaits us all. She tried to talk him into handing over his pipe a couple of times when I was there, even though it was only a pacifier to him now.

There was no smoking in the place, and Hipa just kept dry tobacco in the Falcon. He never lit up, or so we all supposed. I sometimes thought I smelled the residue of Maple Leaf pipe tobacco on him and wondered if he ever charmed an attendant or another patient to light it up for him. Over time the tobacco disappeared and I replaced a few tins for him. More than likely, it just dribbled out on the floor because you could see little pinches of it sprinkled around his bed and chair. Maybe the staff just kept flushing it down the toilet.

Hipa didn't stay in that place very long. He went downhill fast, falling in a steep drop after he tripped and fell to the floor in front of me and Dad and his friends at Kohldhaas Distributors, covered with food and fear and shame in the midst of celebration. The last time I went by to visit Hipa, I charged up the battery in his old Ford truck, washed off all the months of dust and bird shit, and opened it up to blow out all the engine coughs and sputters. "Open her up and blow out the cobwebs, Stephen. Open it up," he used to tell me on our errands into the city.

I picked up a Wendy's double cheeseburger, a small order of fries, and a chocolate malt made with fake ice cream and tooled over to see him. I found Hipa in his corner chair, got him to recognize me and rally to the enticements of Wendy the fast-food siren, and I asked him if he wanted me to wheel him around the place. He did, and looked up to tell me so with his eyes. Then a funny thing happened. He pointed to his leg brace beside him and over his shoulder to his pants draped over the back of his chair, all wrinkled from him sitting against them.

He wanted to put on his pants. So I helped him get them on. They were the same new pants from our Penney's shopping trip. We got one shoe on, but I didn't bother to tie it, and the other shoe and the brace were impossible to lace and position, given his weakened condition. His legs were so scrawny that they looked like little tree branches. But he wanted to take the brace with us anyway, so we just put it so he could hold it, laid out across the arms of the wheelchair.

We dodged a few patients along the way, like a truck with an extra-wide load. He was happy, you could tell. When we got to the Vista Grande observation window to see the Sandia Mountains and the high blue sky and the thick trees of the bosque and river valley, and the parking lot in the near distance, I pointed and told him to look.

"There's the truck, Hipa. Running like blazes. I blew out all the cobwebs just like you told me." He looked at the Ford and I know he recognized it. I could tell in his eyes as I bent close to him, and in his smile when he turned his head and looked at me. Then he said a funny thing.

"Oysters," he said, and tried to move his leg brace and shoe, which looked like an old useless shell. And I thought of all the trays of oysters at the Kohldhaas reception, and all the rows of braces back in that engineer's workshop, and all the legs of all the people they represented—each one, at one time, with someplace to go. Some song to dance to.

And then Hipa tried to reach into his pants pocket. "Cheers," he said, just as clear as could be, and a big shiny and solid Eisenhower silver dollar pinged and ricocheted off the spokes of the wheelchair and fell, wobbling for a time, flat and still to the floor beside his scuffed, unlaced shoe.

Man of the Cloth

Blackie was good with all kinds of fabrics—real and synthetic. He could stitch by hand, and he could make the big Singer Duro-stitcher live up to its name. It would sing soft in a whisper, and it would sing loud in a coughing sputter or in a high-velocity whine. And Blackie could turn the fabric at just the right time, and at all kinds of corners and curves and angles. He had double-stitching down to a high art, forward for a spell and then quickly back over and adjacent and across his original stitch. Ridging was, after all these years, a piece of cake. Ribbing, high or low, he almost could do in his sleep. And tucking was no big deal—not for George R. "Blackie" Blackburn, Man of the Cloth. That's what the sign over the door announced. He had thought of using the slogan "Brave Little Tailor" but decided that would confuse his customers, since he didn't sew clothes—not that he couldn't if he wanted to. But furniture and car upholstering are another line of work. "Man of the Cloth" said it best—denoted what he did in his work and suggested a certain integrity.

"Fuck and tuck, fuck and tuck," he would say under his breath to the accompaniment of his sewing machine. "Back and forth, push and pull," he would mouth with the to-and-fro motion of his hand-stitching or the pushes and pulls of his lacing. Tufts and pleats, they were his specialty. That, and quilting. He was an artist with thread and needles and tacks, nails and staples, and, now and then, tape and adhesives. Tape had its special uses, and Blackie Blackburn knew all the tricks of technique and was always dreaming up original designs of ornate concept and pattern.

All of his designs were originals of one sort or another, and whether it was a seat cover for a car or a completely rebuilt and upholstered couch, whatever left Blackburn's Man of the Cloth upholstery shop bore not just the mark of competence and quality, the imprint of a master craftsman and artisan, but the flair and the imagination of a true artist. To be sure, Blackie liked to preserve new car seats. He was obsessed with cars and seats and chairs of pristine condition, and he brought in a considerable proportion of his income by stretching and shaping and conforming both smooth and raised-design plastic seat covers. Part of his passion to preserve and protect also involved restoration and repair—nothing was too far gone for Blackie to try to mend or patch or rebuild or cover over.

He hadn't had a drink for nearly four years and he was himself much on the mend, but this was only the most recent time he had tried to patch up his life. There had been other times. The demons of drink weren't the prime cause, but they had always been there, in various ways, and for various periods of time even before David.

Blackie cut out almost all the drinking and the partying when he met and married Helena Ruiz. He agreed to a Catholic wedding almost without thinking. What did it matter? His parents had long ceased to care about church and religion and their own vague and insecure Protestant upbringing.

Once Blackie and Helena were married, their lives took off straight and fast toward the attainment of the still credible American Dream. The first job, at Redding's Tent and Awning Company, quickly turned into a spot as foreman of a team of eight workers. The FHA loan came through for the house, and the children came, first Bradley, then David. Things blossomed and bloomed and improved yet again. They started going to church once or twice a month, and soon they were attending mass each Sunday. Blackie took the necessary orientation classes, came to accept the teachings of the church and the papacy, and officially converted in a formal baptismal service attended by Helena and their two sons. But then, one sunny spring Sunday morning, right in the midst of the hustle and bustle of getting the boys ready for church, the family dream they were living turned into surreal horror and tragedy.

"Daddy! Daddy! No! Stop!" But it was too late to heed Bradley's fragile, terrorized words of warning. Blackie felt the right rear wheel pass over an extraneous bump, like a slow stitch over an extra fold of cloth, but the car had passed over something much more precious than a piece of cloth or a stray toy. The car had backed over his son David, who was crawling under it to locate a little toy lawn mower that clattered when he pushed it. "It can't be true!" But it was.

Blackie knew fully and at once and forever that there was no God or goodness, no faith or creed of whatever sort worth a second's thought or devotion, nothing of any meaning or significance that would allow a father to back over and kill his son . . . on a Sunday morning, on the way to church, or on any godforsaken day of any black, blasted week or year or aeon.

And just as he never forgave God or himself, Helena never forgave Blackie. Nor did his older and suddenly only son, Brad. Not then and not through the almost twenty long, sorrowful, guilty, intervening years. And every day, every minute Blackie worked, in every whine and whir of the machine and the patterns and colors of the thousands of spools and miles of thread, he tried to repair and remedy, patch and restore the horrible tears and wrenching of that morning when all he meant to do was move the station wagon out of the garage and park it in front of the house so they could all be safe and sound, comfortable and together on their way to hear the blessings of Father Willis Hayes, S.J., priest and servant of the Church of the Holy Family and the Blessed Mother.

Helena turned against Blackie totally as they worked to restore Brad to some psychological normalcy after the trauma of witnessing his brother's death. Father Hayes's counseling and his advocacy for faith were ineffective and unconvincing in the face of the reality of David, lying contorted and still on the driveway concrete, of David lying dead—all decked out in his blue corduroy suit, his starched and ironed white shirt, and his red snap-on bow tie. "Hail Mary, blessed mother" indeed. Indeed.

The divorce had come soon. Helena never forgave, never stopped blaming Blackie. And he had admitted that for one second, just one, he was admiring the fancy-stitched fleur-de-lis design on the new seat covers instead of paying full attention when he was moving the car. The iris was a onetime favorite family flower, and purple iris lined both sides of the driveway. All during the intervening years Blackie remembered seeing them, the long-stemmed, cascading flowers, when he bent down to David. But there were no iris at the funeral, only white roses, honeysuckle, and gardenias.

Helena remarried and moved to Nevada. Then came Blackie's fall into the abyss, his descent into the snake pit of drink that leveled him out, flattened his will and ego flatter than a thousand steamrollers would the hottest of asphalt paving. Then he pulled himself back out of the gutter of despair and self-pity and guilt through the opportunity to work again, first as a helper to a friend who had once worked under Blackie when he was in charge at Redding's, then eventually in his own Man of the Cloth shop. His own little upholstery shop gave him the real and symbolic means for attempted reparation. "Workaholic" came to replace alcoholic in his self-image and motivation.

Then slowly over the years, very slowly, Brad began to forgive. He forgave his father and the forces of fate enough to invite Blackie to his wedding. And Blackie went, reinforced by the resolve of the past years of sobriety and hard work building up his own shop—trying to stitch and sew and patch his life back together. Helena was there, down from Reno. She said her hellos and was civil, as was her well-heeled and officious husband, a Rocky Mountain Bell bureaucrat named Bill Carosco who, in conversation, revealed his abiding and unctuous loyalty to his wife and his job, to communication in marriage and to communications stock and his IRAs and his Keogh, and his company money purchase plan. "Helena and I are sittin' pretty, Blackburn, sittin' pretty with retirement just around the corner. Three cheers for the two women in my life—Helena and Ma Bell. No state taxes in Nevada, bud. It's the next California."

"Well, here's to you, Carosco," Blackie said as he raised his long-stemmed glass of sparkling apple juice. "I was never much good at communicating—with Helena or anybody else." And that was the sum of Blackie's speechmaking, except to congratulate his son and his new daughter-in-law with simple sincerity and eloquence. "I wish you two the best of luck." But he came away more committed than ever to bachelorhood and his life as an independent small businessman and "man of the cloth."

And now, just barely a year after the wedding, Brad called with the news. "It's a boy, Dad. Six pounds and eight ounces. Named him David George Blackburn. Yes, at University Hospital. Barbara's fine. But . . . the baby has some breathing problems that concern us and the doctors. Just wanted to tell you. Sure, I'll keep you posted. Yes, I'll tell her. Good-bye, Father."

Blackburn's curiosity about his grandson's possible or probable resemblance to him and his concern about the boy's breathing problem took him first to the mirror over the sink in the shop washroom and then to the timeworn and frayed photo of his two sons, which he had carried with him for as long as he could remember. It was taken in a photo booth at the state fair and it had lasted all these many years. Now was a time to look smart and get ready to see a new Blackburn boy! A new face to see a new face fitted with the old.

Brad's naming his son after his dead brother and his father was fine, maybe another step toward forgiveness and a family patching up of the old tear, the old tears. As he took the fragile photo carefully from his wallet, Blackie's eyes welled up with new tears as he tried to look beyond the tattered edges and broken lines of the sepia photograph, beyond the wrinkled, sallow visage in the mirror, beyond the past and present faces of family genes and family ghosts and into the imagined fresh face of a new grandson, another boy to carry on the loss of what might have been, and the hopes of what still might be.

Blackie looked again at the face staring back at him in the mirror as he took the photo and slid one edge under the rusty chrome lip that framed the mirror. Shaving was always a solace to him in times like these, and in the crisis times in between. He turned on the faucets and picked up a hand towel from under the sink and held it under the steaming hot water. He wrung it out, moving his tough, calloused hands along its square folds. Then he held the hot terry cloth up to his face and kept it there. Looking over it, through the steam, he imagined the likeness of the doctor who had delivered and was caring for his new grandson, David George Blackburn.

Blackie conjured up the visage of the new doctor, a spectral doctor who in a different person had also attended his dying young son, and himself and Brad. And in that physician's caring image, the family lineage fused and melded into one glowing face. There had been a time when he stood over a sink like this, even, in remembered moods, over this same sink, thinking of ending it, obliterating the face in the mirror. Still, shaving was always relaxing for him, and he revered the possibilities of it, the making new and clean and smooth of the old. For some strange, genetically encoded reason, he always shaved with one hand behind his back. He wondered if Brad did too, and if his grandson would someday.

Now Blackie imagined the incisions and the sutures endured in birth and birthing, and he thought he knew and felt the small similarities and the vast differences between fabric and skin—the living, marvelous tissue and organic complexity of humanity. And soon all the other larger meanings beyond clichés started to emerge. "The social fabric." "Cut from the same cloth." Such sayings were numerous, but now he suddenly understood them beyond the mundane slogans. And as he took the shaving mug and the brush and started the at once physical and spiritual ritual of a much-needed shave, he wondered if he would ever, ever restore his own face, repair the person staring back at him to any outline or shape or form whatsoever of any possible atonement and exoneration.

"Unless ye become like unto a little child . . ." Some of the Scriptures came back to him, remembrances from the church classes and the funeral all those years ago. And Father Hayes. "Only in a new life," Blackie mused as he fingered away the excess lather around his mouth and sideburns. "Only in a new life like Brad's and Barbara's new little boy. Only in my new, grand grandson."

Suddenly, a nick of the skin and some blood, and he reached for a styptic pencil to staunch it. Then, trying for more care and precision in the razor strokes, he thought, almost out of the steaming and misting air and the fogged-up mirror, about his friend Clyde and the stories he told about barbering at the University Hospital—where David was now. That's what made him think of Clyde, he guessed. He could see Clyde's face in his own barbershop mirror, and the barber license in which he took such pride blurred into Blackie's tattered photo of the boys.

Yes, he could see Clyde standing over him, razor in hand, and going around the ears with that hot, scraping sound and the smell of lilac vegetal and rose hair oil. Silk shirt and bow tie. Clyde was a dresser, something of a dandy. A man of expensive tastes and clothes, threads that bespoke a higher station in life. An authentic gentleman of the cloth, at least in externals.

"I tell you, Blackie, she thought I was a doctor. She actually thought I was a doctor right up to and even through the time we screwed right there in the hospital storeroom. Then, after she found out, it didn't really matter. We were lovers—and friends. But talk about doctor's privilege, Blackie, those guys are at the top of the walk. I mean, it started innocently enough. She jumped to the conclusion on her own just about the first time I walked down the hall on her ward.

"'Hello, doctor,' she said softly and smiled and then swished and twitched her nicely fitted, tight-little-uniformed self down the hall. Great mobile lesson in anatomy, she was. Great legs. Great everything, Blackie, if you know what I mean. Pretty little smile. Stays with me yet, I'll tell you, Blackie. White, hard rows of strong, healthy teeth. You know what they say about most nurses. Let's say not even the good lookers, just most nurses—never getting enough of men, Blackie. Well, who am I to resist such cordiality?

"'Why, hello, nurse,' I say and thank my lucky stars for my new leather barber bag when I realize that's what did it for her. Saw my little black bag, she did, and took me for a doctor. Pays to wear these nice silk shirts, too, Blackie, worth saving up for, sure enough.

"'Doctor Clyde P. Kelley, on call, at your service. That's me.' So I go on to the next ward to cut this old codger's hair and give him a shave, just like I'm giving you here around the ears and down your neck. Except this is a full-face shave—and wouldn't you guess it, the guy has Parkinson's disease or palsy or something and I about slit his throat for him right there in his hospital room!

"Anyway, I mean his hair is really long, but as for him, why, he's not long, not very long at all for this world, Blackie, if I can speak so, which works well with the nurses, by the way—talking poetical and all. So I'm thinking about Her Highness Miss Starchy Whiteness and laughing to myself about trying to spruce up this cadaverous-looking guy a bit before they plant him, and trying not to hasten him along with a slip slash to the jugular, and listening to him mumble about whatever-hell-war he was in with Teddy Roosevelt, for Christ's sake, and whatever martial, marital combat, whatever senile anecdote his feeble, jelly-brain mind could retrieve, whatever volume and control his shaky voice could muster, telling about all the loves he's had and this and that. And all the while he's being ever so thankful that he still has a full head of hair, and telling me about the special shampoos he's used over the years—all the way from tar soap to Grover's mange cure, and I start actually imagining I'm this doctor, see, in the midst of brain surgery or something, and I think, maybe, just maybe, I can get in the good little nurse's white panties one day soon and operate. . . .

"You know, the plans and positions start to materialize. I mean, I'm so caught up in imagining myself as Doctor Kelley, so deep in thought that I cut this guy good a couple of times. Then I take the razor and start stropping the hell out of it, thinking it's just too damn dull, and I get the damnedest hard-on just thinking about the good nurse and start to take little triangles of skin out of this old guy's cheek and chin when I resume shaving him, little pieces of skin as if surgically removed for a biopsy or something, but he doesn't know shit, this old coot, and just keeps shaking and talking, blood coursing down his face and turning the remaining lather pink as an undercooked T-bone.

"Even when I shift to cutting his precious preserved hair I cut so many gaps in it that it looks like a splotchy mesa-top driving range for special education classes. But I butter him up about his full, healthy head of hair, so he'll ask me back. And I'll be goddamned, Blackie, if it doesn't actually to hell happen and before long my little black barber bag of tricks opens up to some worldly delights, right there on that spiffy little nurse's floor—first one room, then another, all the time with faint little cries coming to my ears, if you get my drift.

"The codger keeps asking me back to shave him. I put in my strokes. And all the time I'm playing doctor with Miss Nurse. Yvonne Penhurst turns out to be her name. Perfect anatomical specimen, Blackie, like I say, perfect. And she says she's got a sister studying to be a nurse, too, or a pediatric nurse, or something. Wanda Penhurst. Just imagine, Blackie. The two of 'em and us two—me a doctor and you 'a man of the cloth'! You could do it."

"Just like Clyde," thought Blackie. "Clyde P. Impostor, playing doctor," and Clyde's mirrored visage receded into mist and steam and the boys' photo reemerged on the edge of the mirror. "Living the lie and the lay—cutting and trimming and snipping the truth to suit his and everyone else's fantasies. Me a true 'man of the cloth.' Why, what could a priest do under such circumstances? Maybe I could administer extreme unction to the old guy. Death is certainly no stranger to me."

The shave refreshed Blackie, as he knew it would, and he splashed on some Old Spice. Then he was ready again for the sofas and the chairs and the car seats, the covering and sewing and rebuilding and restoration that made up his days. He hoped, he prayed that David had good doctors, real good doctors, and some good luck, and he took the photograph down from the mirror and carefully placed it back in his well-worn wallet, where it fit so easily into its established, special, and habitual nook.

The next call from Brad came much sooner than Blackie had hoped for.

"It's not good news, Father. Maybe you could meet us right away here at University Hospital and give me some help while I try to help Barbara. Her folks are out of town but on their way back. Mom's coming in from Reno. I called her too. And maybe you could give us some support until Barbara's mother can get here. The baby's been transferred to the neonatal intensive care unit, and he's gonna be on a ventilator. It's a problem with a big name: RDS, respiratory distress syndrome. But it amounts to his lungs not holding air. They leak, and air pockets are forming that they have to aspirate periodically. So he's to have some incisions and tubes and periodic X-rays. Lots of X-rays. It's pretty serious, and Barbara is having a hard time accepting this. So am I."

Blackie wasted no time getting ready to go. He had hoped to see his grandson under different circumstances there in the nursery. His two sons had been born at St. Joseph's, and mental pictures of that time surfaced again. He had already shaved, so that cut down on time, but he still had to change clothes. His wardrobe was limited. For dress—funerals or weddings or births—he always wore the same thing: dark gray slacks and a black polo shirt that he liked to button at the neck. He had one elbow-thin navy-blue blazer whose fancy metal buttons he had long since replaced with ordinary dark buttons. He brushed off his heavy-soled black work shoes, picked up the keys to his old El Camino, and was out the door and into the night headed east across town to University Hospital.

Once at the hospital Blackie made his way to the neonatal unit on the third floor. The elevator door opened on the waiting room, a long, narrow area furnished with a couch, some chairs, and plenty of tattered magazines. There on the austere waiting-room couch were Barbara and Brad, and he knew her heartache at a glance—for he had known the same heartache all those years ago, except that then he had been the cause. Only a few hours after giving birth she now waited, even in her dozing, to know any piece of news, any report on the baby's condition. Her room was close by, but the baby was isolated from her. Barbara's body leaned against Brad's, her head on his shoulder, her eyes swollen from crying that had seemingly depleted her last tear, from crying beyond even the ache in her heart and bones. She had cried, he knew, and so had Brad in his way, inside their very souls. Her hair was pulled back into an uncaring ponytail, so that the little yellow elastic band that scrunched all the hanging, oily hair told volumes about her encounter with despair. Her clothes were wrinkled, and she had made no effort to put on any kind of face or presence, other than grief—deep, despairing, painful grief.

The grief Blackie witnessed in the faces and demeanor of his son and daughter-in-law was kin to the grief Blackie himself had known for twenty years. The kind of grief he had seen in the bottles and glasses and cups—even at times sloshing in the palms of his hands—of all the good bourbon and expensive Scotch and brandy, and then the vodka and gin, and finally the cheapest of wines that he had consumed. For one final year it was schnapps—peppermint and peach, terrible stuff, which after his fixation he had taken pleasure in rounding up and pouring down the toilet.

Brad was exhausted and grief-stricken almost beyond recognition. What a change had taken place since the happy wedding times—evidence of how the vows of holy matrimony had a way of forcing people to prove up—"in sickness and in health, till death us do part." "Death certainly parted us," Blackie mused, as he looked at the forlorn pair. Brad was unshaven, haggard, his hair tousled and knotted like Blackie remembered seeing when his young family would do battle for the bathroom on Sunday mornings before church. Before the unthinkable had happened all those years of yesterdays past.

Blackie turned to greet the young couple and whispered, "Don't disturb her, Brad, let her rest there. I'll just sit here and wait with you." And he pulled up a vacant, torn chair that even in his agony and worry he sized up as something he could fix up in new vinyl for about eighty or ninety dollars. He puzzled at how he was programmed to think such thoughts in such dire straits—his urge to fix, to repair, this situation transferred back to furniture.

"No, Father, go ahead in and see David," Brad whispered, trying not to awaken Barbara. "You can see him. Just go through that door. . . . Scrub up good and ask the nurse." Brad pointed to the large swinging doors into the intensive care room.

So Blackie walked through the doors into the scrub room and started mindlessly reading the signs and following the instructions about supply locations, antiseptic soap, towels and sterile gowns and masks. There was a large sink, almost an elevated tub, and long faucets with flattened-out handles so the water flow could be controlled with arms or elbows. He tore open the tinfoil packet as instructed, squeezed out the iodine-looking soap, and dropped the torn packet into the trash can with a light step on the pedal that opened the lid to the waiting congregation of other packets and used gauze and other wastes. The soap was strong-smelling and dark, with a brownish-yellow tint of disinfectant. He let the liquid run through his fingers, turned on the water, and scrubbed his hands and high up his arms, clear to the biceps.

He wiped his hands thoroughly with a white, sanitized towel and then reached for a green cotton gown and a gauzelike mask. He put on the gown and secured it, then placed the mask over his mouth and nose and tied the mask string, caring little how much of the hair at the back of his head he caught in the hard knot he nervously secured. It was flimsy attire but very clean, the cleanest cloth he had ever seen. So clean it appeared synthetic. "Cotton," Blackie routinely identified the fabric, benumbed by the ordeal he faced and trying to preoccupy himself.

"Cotton, an amazingly useful cloth. Now I'm a man of cotton cloth," he thought, and then thought back to Clyde's hospital anecdote and wondered if someone would mistake him too for a doctor. Half wondered if Yvonne Penhurst was still on some adjacent floor. This was the hospital where Clyde's escapades had occurred.

Then Blackie turned and opened the next heavy door and entered a large room where he saw many small bodies, the tiniest of babies, some still almost embryos. They lay encased in glass boxes, in little incubators and open warming cribs surrounded by monitors and screens and tubes and stands, cords and wires and small lights here and there. The room was dark except for the glow from the small beds that created a kind of otherworldly golden light, like little luminous electronic candles, each of them attempting to hold back the unspeakable darkness that threatened the room's tiny occupants.

The nurse on duty approached him, her mask speaking to him in little round, moving indentations, and then, after his mask spoke back to her, she took his arm and escorted him to the far side of the room.

"This is David Blackburn, your grandson," she whispered. "We already call him DG, and he's a tough little guy. He's strong, but I must confess we're worried about him, as I know you are." Her words were muffled through the mask, and Blackie looked down at his tiny grandson and both marveled and panicked. There were three tubes running into the baby's tiny chest. "The doctors can tell you about it more fully. It's a kind of hope-for-the-best-but-expect-the-worst situation. These pneumothoraces, the air pockets, are the big concern—especially if one crowds his heart."

What Blackie saw and felt so deeply at the sight of the special little baby almost overpowered him. There was one thick plastic hose leading from a large machine and passing through an opening in the side of the box. The hose led to a plastic mouthpiece inserted in the small little mouth and taped to David's round, small face—a face that resembled the two faces—the sons, the brothers—in the worn photo in Blackie's wallet. There were also tubes on each side of the small torso, just under the arms, and one tube into the front of the chest. Blackie smiled and in a halting, interrupted greeting he spoke to his new kin for the first time. "Hello, grandson. Hello, little guy. Hang in there. Hang on, Blackburn, hang on."

The little body looked simultaneously strong and weak, perfect and yet affected by these man-made, jury-rigged, plastic imperfections. The boy still seemed up to the battle he faced, the tough fight for life that he was waging. Blackie stood and looked into the light of the crib and said the still-remembered prayer from his first orientation lessons in the church, a prayer that carried with it the hope of a second chance—for the small grandchild; for his dead and long-grieved and honored namesake; for that baby's older brother now a man out in the corridor, waiting and worrying for this little life, and for himself in the hope that he would not see a brother and a son twice dead; and for his son's wife and her shattered life if this long-expected and treasured child should not make it.

"Hail, Mary, full of grace. The Lord is with Thee. Blessed art thou among women, and blessed is the fruit of Thy womb, Jesus." And with the prayer, Blackie said, "I'll be back to see you a bit later, boy. You're a Blackburn for sure, and we love you. Hold on. It's worth it. You'll see. My blessing goes out to you, David George Blackburn. My blessing be with you."

The words were out of Blackie's mouth before he realized what he said. The blessing he had bestowed on the baby, and on the family, on the shared blood coursing through its tiny arteries and veins—the only tubes, natural and life-giving, that it should know. But more than that, it was a blessing on life. He looked around the still dimly lighted room, slowly and deliberately, and silently blessed each of the glowing beds and the small, struggling lives they held, each trying to stave off the besieging darkness. Without knowing it, as if in an automatic action, Blackie made the sign of the cross and announced the name of the Holy Trinity. Vague, tripartite patterns of fleur-de-lis and standing purple iris gave background to the cross motion of Blackie's hands.

From out of the edge of the shadows in the deepening darkness of a distant corner of the room, a young, forsaken-looking couple came to stand by the baby next to David, and the thick yellow light from the warming crib washed over their faces. The mother was little more than a child herself, but with a look of extreme and profound wisdom in her dark eyes—eyes made all the more prominent by the mask she too wore. A piece of cloth keeping her from the warm, tender, human kisses her child so ardently needed. A piece of cloth Blackie suddenly wanted not just to untie and gently remove but to rip away, as he reached up, reflexively, to pull down his own mask—and then hesitated, paused, and resisted at full thought. He had seen the same look in Helena's eyes and in Barbara's vividly anguished face. The years were fusing. He had seen the same look in his own mirrored eyes and in Brad's eyes that he now saw in the dark, sad eyes of the young father—a longing for hope mixed with the presence of terror, an inward searching for the strength and resolve to locate some small shred of purpose and meaning in the torment of tiny lives so scarcely begun.

Neither the young mother nor the young father paid any attention to Blackie and his close-by shadowed preoccupation with them. They stood over their child with their arms and bodies propping each other up, attempting to infuse a mutual and married strength into each other and into their surely dying child. "God be with you, children," Blackie said as he backed away a few steps and then headed out of the room.

The next morning Blackie was at the hospital very early. Brad had slept some, after seeing Barbara settled again in her room, where a sedative had brought her some needed respite. Brad would join Blackie for breakfast after a scheduled 8:00 A.M. examination and conference with the doctors.

Blackie waited in the hall while the doctors checked on David once more, carrying out another battery of X-rays in a side room. Then, while he paced back and forth, unable to concentrate even on the complimentary newspapers just dropped off on the waiting-room table, the doors of the intensive care room burst open.

"Father, Father, you're here! Thanks be to God. Our son has barely made it through the night and has little life left, and the doctor is with him now one final time. We phoned the hospital chaplain, asking for a priest, asking for you. Thank you, Father, for coming so quickly and for the last rites needed now so desperately by our son. You must administer this safe passage to our son. You must hurry, Father. Please, come now. Hurry!"

And the young man he had seen last night, the ghost visage of his younger self when he had carried his own crushed son into the house, hovered before him like a vision, a vision of an all-tender, vulnerable faith waiting to be crushed, obliterated—or raised, reinforced, and given sustenance.

Blackie followed the boy back into the intensive care room, lit now with encroaching morning sunlight. Beside the young husband and wife stood a physician, who simply looked into Blackie's frantic, expectant eyes and said, "There is no hope, Father. I'm sorry. I have done all I can do." And the doctor was gone, back into the middle of the room to talk with the night nurse now leaving her duty. The glow of the pale baby's lighted bed was diminishing with the sun now coursing more fully through the curtains. David's small bed was gone. "But only temporarily, thank God," Blackie said with a start. And the parents misunderstood him and said, "Yes. Thank you, Father. This life is only temporary and soon he, soon we, will be with the Heavenly Father."

These despairing parents had phoned for a priest, and Blackie knew that in his grief the young father had mistaken his dark polo shirt, his blue blazer and dark trousers and shoes for the garb of a priest. Because of his clothing, and probably subconsciously remembering him from the previous night, they now saw in their desperation a real "man of the cloth" standing with them. They believed. He couldn't do it, though—he couldn't deceive them, lie to them. Lie to himself. There was no hope. There had not been hope for him in all these years. Until now.

He would help them and try to give them hope, try to fulfill their faith for them. Who was to know? He could do it, and in the doing perhaps he could absolve and forgive himself as a person and as a father, as a child who had fathered sons and now a grandson. Certainly if there were divine graces, if there was a God in heaven, He would understand these quirks and turns and riddles of events turning back on themselves. God could forgive him. And as for Blackie, he was, most ironically, most fittingly, a man of the cloth after all.

"Let us pray, my children. Pray with me as I now pray for this soul that it may live eternally with God in heaven." And Blackie began, almost as if inspired, and blessed himself on this occasion, in the doing reciting his at-once-remembered-and-invented version of the appropriate prayers.

"Holy Mary, mother of God, pray for us sinners now and at the hour of our death. Father, into Thy hands I commend this young, this pure soul." The nurse knew, of course. She knew, but she said nothing as she watched and listened, ready to leave her shift after having made her reports. When it was over, and Blackie's prayers for the baby were finished and the parents further consoled, she stepped over to console them also. And then she asked Blackie to follow her back to the scrub room, where she slid down her mask and said, "Mr. Blackburn, I just wanted you to know I know. It was a fine thing to do.

"The word is that DG has turned the corner. He's going to make it now. His lungs are clear and the air pockets are gone. But let your son tell you. He's up with his wife now, telling her. They'll be bringing the little tyke back here just for a few more hours of observation. But he'll be fine. He'll be back with his momma by my next round of duty."

Then Blackie smiled and said, "You know, then . . . that I'm not a priest. You recognized me from last night?"

"Yes, I recognized you, Mr. Blackburn." She was untying the strings of her gown. And then Blackie realized that she too was smiling—the most strangely familiar, glorious smile Blackie had ever seen or hoped to see.

Truth or Consequences

Professor Harry Claude Koster had worked hard for his station in life. As a youth in Iowa he had done any number of odd jobs, from having a paper route, to house painting during the hot and humid summer months, to mowing neighborhood lawns, shirt off, perspiration dripping profusely, to shoveling sidewalks and driveways after winter snowstorms, to helping out at the College Hill Pharmacy, a neighborhood drugstore owned and operated by Anton Bergson. "Boy, you are a workin' fool, I do say!" exclaimed Bergson.

Anton was a friend to all, but a special family friend to the Kosters. When the medical bills from Claude's father's chronic illness began to mount, Anton found some new need for a delivery boy. It was in working for Anton that young Claude learned some of life's most valuable lessons, and where he developed his initial interest in medicines and remedies and what could be regarded as holistic pharmacology, the assumption that medicines treat not just the body but larger social and psychological contexts and causes.

You might say that Claude's father, Karl Koster, with his asthma and eventual tuberculosis, and Anton Bergson, in his role as employer of young Claude and as avuncular advisor, pointed Claude toward his eventual role in life—not the expected M.D. in respiratory and pulmonary disease but a Ph.D. in sociology and the professorship he now held, and immensely enjoyed, far away from the lush and humid summers and the icy and subzero winters of Iowa.

The hardworking boy and dutiful son, Harry Claude Koster, was now, and had been for some years, Professor Koster, Department of Social Sciences, University of Texas at El Paso. Among his many lessons learned was that causes have results, that hard work leads to success, that duty and responsibility are more than hollow ideals, and that the somewhat more vague ideals, honor and truth and honesty and compassion, are worthy of one's allegiance.

Those recognizably midwestern values Claude had carried west with him, values made tangible in the person of his wife, Nancy, the once-sanguine Iowa hometown girl, Nancy the neighborhood girl with the smiling face, whom he had married just before finishing his dissertation. She was a delicately built woman, blonde and lovely in her bones, refined, and always socially proper—the perfect faculty spouse—but passionate and loving and affirming of Claude and of life.

But as the shades of the prison house of middle age descended, so did diabetes. Her case resisted treatment, deteriorated into gangrene and the necessary amputation of her right foot. The dance had ended. She was now an invalid, depressed, wan and suffering, her former radiance corrupted by disease into the foul temper of termagant rage. Claude, still believing, at least in outline, in duty and honor and loyalty, had done all he could for her, reorganized the household for her comfort, stoically endured her tantrums, and provided the best medical care available. But he soon found no semblance of Walter Mitty humor in his hellish, henpecked life. Midwestern male stability and virtue drifted into chauvinistic caricature as Nancy's girlish smiles mutated into scowls and one shrewish allegation and demand after another.

Amid the many admonitions of his principled upbringing, Claude had listened to the well-meaning advice of both Karl and Anton: "Go west, young man. Go west, Claude. Go west!" Texas was west. El Paso was the far Southwest. Had he lived, Karl would not only have approved, he would have been living in the dry climate with his son. In fact, the climate just might have saved his life had he been able to head west himself. Short of that, he inspired his son to do the next best thing—westering in his stead.

In one sense, however, Professor Koster was still back on the College Hill of his Iowa hometown, for it was there he discovered both his interest in human behavior and its motives and patterns, its choices and decisions. Claude's idyllic, albeit hardworking, hometown of Cedarloo remained a cornerstone to his personality and his midwestern values—most of which had been transferred from the immigrant beliefs of his grandfathers, and the grandfathers of his neighbors, and of his remnant memories of Nancy.

In another sense, however, the good Doc, as his students either unthinkingly or perhaps affectionately called him, was now at the end of the earth, always and ever interested and intrigued, yet still somewhat bewildered by the alien southwestern border cultures that had—for much of his life now—surrounded him.

Karl Koster had always talked of taking the family someplace out West where the sun and dry air would drive the deadly tuberculosis bacilli from his lungs, but he never made it and was dead long before those dreams could take shape. But the dreams stayed alive in his son, almost the bright and hopeful reverse of the dormant TB, which showed up in annual physicals as small black but contained spots on Claude's lungs. And for the past twenty-five years Claude had been living part of his father's dreams, living in El Paso, just across the border from Juárez. The house he was able to buy with his father's inheritance—relayed later through his mother, Bertha, who survived Karl by only three years—seemed an even more fulfilling completion to the Koster family myth.

But while El Paso represented work and duty and career and profession, Truth or Consequences, the small New Mexico town 150 miles to the north, represented relaxation and freedom and escape from midwestern moral and mental confinements. It was a place where Karl would have thrived, had he only found it, had he been able to shake the dark and stifling shades and shadows of repression and illness.

Claude had considered buying a place in Mesilla, closer to El Paso, and just west of Las Cruces, only forty miles to the north. There was a university in Las Cruces too, and the library there would have made books easier to use, research better facilitated. But Claude was winding down. He found less and less interest in books and scholarship and research. Now he wanted to live life closer to the bone, a life of more passion and heart, a life less cerebral, less intellectual.

Mesilla was a more picturesque village than T or C. There was a plaza there, where on any given day you could hear locals strumming guitars and *viejos* lazily talking and smoking in the sun—hunkering with each other in the most authentic, oblivious sense of *carnalismo* and cultural heritage. But Claude's decision to choose T or C ironically hung on tourism and its ramifications and effects. Mesilla meant tourists who wanted to buy the culture and the climate and the atmosphere. T or C meant tourists more of the snowbird variety, retirees who went there for sun, for the mineral baths, for the leisure and health of the place.

The constant stream of materialistic tourists in Mesilla was just too much for Claude. At least in T or C the stream of curiosity seekers was more seasonal and older, many of them winter escapees from places like Iowa and Indiana and Illinois and Ohio. Perhaps he had rationalized his decision, but Claude considered the Winnebagos and Airstream trailers and other RVs appealing. They reaffirmed the wisdom of his own emigration from Iowa, and his retirement choice of New Mexico over Texas. He hated to admit it, but T or C was more charmingly Hispanic. The border culture of Juárez had a sinister side to it that, at times, despite its theoretical fascinations, wore on Claude. It wasn't racism, exactly. Claude would never accept that possibility. T or C just had a nicer, more comfortable Anglo/Hispanic feel to it—less Mexican and more Spanish.

Tourists were generally hard to take, though, even in T or C. And Claude never accepted, really, that he was anything but a transplanted native son. He had, he felt, left the Midwest far behind, but in truth, his family's summer trips to Iowa's many small lakes had planted and nourished the allure of lakes like Elephant Butte, located just a few miles out of T or C. Tourists in T or C somehow seemed more entitled to be in that place and to reshape it in their own images. Not so in Mesilla, which had become so à la mode that real estate prices had shot up and even the smallest of apartments was beyond the means of a professor's salary.

There were, besides, fabulous mineral baths at T or C, and the lake, Elephant Butte, the desolate but exotic reservoir named for a volcanic rock island shaped like an elephant, was one of the Southwest's premier boating and fishing spots. Its overall ambiance proved quite captivating to Claude, much to his surprise, for about the only thing the lake had in common with the waterways of his youth was the water, and even that was considerably muddier. But then so was life itself—especially the churn and turn of things with Nancy, the once-upon-a-time girl with the laughing face, the young bride now a twenty-five-year spouse, now sour on everything. And understandably so.

Claude rationalized the history and sociology of T or C to be curiously more honest, even respectable, in its goofy transformation from Hot Springs to Truth or Consequences! The town had renamed itself for a radio quiz show as part of its development plan, as if growth and jobs and quality of life were worth any price, even the advertisements and hype of quizmaster Ralph "Mr. T or C" Edwards, even the elevation of a radio personality to founding father. The town's publicity-gimmick change from the more natural and telling name of Hot Springs to the fabricated and abstract Truth or Consequences, held something quintessential about the ethnocentric and capitalistic motives of Anglo-Americanism.

Before Hot Springs the Spanish had named the place too: Las Palomas de Ojo Caliente. And before the Spanish *entrada* the indigenous Indian populations had named it as well: Geronimo Springs. What were the causes, the truths and the consequences, of a name? pondered Claude. Nothing and everything.

Claude at one time thought of writing an article about how a place of healing and neutral resting for indigenous peoples had become the near ultimate absurdity of American advertising: the early days of the name change in 1950, all the celebrity visits, the radio broadcasts generating from the newly christened town, the Ralph Edwards Fiesta. As if Ralph Edwards was some latter-day equivalent of an Apache chief! Edwards brought his nomadic camp of announcers and engineers in an act of debauchery to the natural landscape and those who communed with the spirits of that special place. There were fake fiestas and ludicrous parades and all manner of community celebration. "Hi-ho the American throwaway!"

Truth or Consequences! What a name for a town. What an amazing collection of forces to cause a group of well-intentioned but misguided citizens to invite and sanction such a circus of public relations. Hot Springs had no doubt been a more alluring and authentic place to live, or visit. But there was a kind of perverse attraction to it now too. And there was the lake, after all. Before the dam and the lake had been the river, the Rio Grande. But progress had come early in the century to bring greater irrigation potential to the southern part of New Mexico and to Texas. The devastations of "conservation" and "progress" were powerfully perverse.

So Claude developed a certain ambivalence about his relationship to Hot Springs and to T or C. Just what those consequences would be he had dismissed, caring less and less about them with the accumulation of years since he discovered the place and chose to purchase land there.

The property was actually a space in a trailer park, Casa Algodones, and an adequate trailer, and . . . Irma Apodaca. The good life was finally within his grasp. Claude lived for his trips to T or C and for the new life he had found and was, in his mind, "pioneering" there.

T or C was a reconciliation of past and present for him; easier there to blend in with the snowbirds who came south each winter. They were people like Karl and Bertha—had they been able to enjoy their retirement, even their health. Claude now could maybe enjoy the place for them by proxy. And for Claude at least, there was Irma, wonderful, loving, accepting, sensuous Irma in whom his past hopes and future dreams converged.

From Iowa to Texas to New Mexico. Claude's midwestern, westering life was continuing to unfold. After finishing his doctorate, Claude accepted the offer to come to UTEP. It was an alluring, exotic call and offered much close-by research potential, both in El Paso and across the border, along the border towns and further down into the interior of Mexico, though he never got much beyond Chihuahua and Guadalajara.

That amazing recruitment, a quarter of a century ago now, had been a fundamentally good decision. He had published several significant articles in the area of social geography, the interactions of race, ethnicity, and place—and the social and medicinal uses of place in promoting happiness and well-being, or misery and discontent. He had come to understand the uses of natural remedies, herbs and grasses, and other nostrums, especially water, oils, and perfumes, and their effects in dry and desert climes. And he had come to see the perniciousness of viewing the Southwest as an empty space, a land there only for commercial development.

In his younger days he was quite zealous in leading a charge, almost a protest, against the misappropriation of place. But the momentum for ruination and corruption rather than protection, conservation, and understanding had been relentless and his zeal soon modified itself into compromises of one sort or another, care becoming a kind of carelessness. But his evolving marriage and what had happened to Nancy influenced things. Perhaps had there been children things would have been different. He regretted not being a father. Even that feeling had mitigated itself into a kind of dull disregard.

One year Claude won his department's outstanding teacher award, and he had made some wise decisions in his pension planning and in his investments of his inheritance. As the only child of his father's estate, and then of his mother's legacy, he had a windfall of nearly ten thousand dollars. And that had allowed him to buy the trailer and lot and settle in T or C.

There was some measure of mystery and intrigue involved in Claude's purchasing his hideaway, as he himself liked to think of it. "Harry Claude Koster's Hideaway." As much as Claude knew and understood about collective human behavior and its institutions and rituals, the folkways and mores of human society, he never fully understood or even very much tried to comprehend the real motive behind his desire to keep the purchase of the trailer in T or C a secret—from his colleagues, from miscellaneous friends and acquaintances, and from his wife.

He didn't tell Nancy a thing about it: not about the buying of the property, not about his much cherished and more and more frequent trips there, not about how he both relaxed and carried on (carried on relative to the fashion and inhibitions of Harry Claude Koster, you understand) when he went there. There were the baths. There were the dances. There was the fishing. There was loving time with Irma.

On this particular day when the causes and effects of Claude's life were converging, he was headed north, not to a conference in Denver, as he had told Nancy, but for a long weekend in T or C, and time to fish and recharge with some TLC from Irma and her circle of friends. Irma, a Spanish-American woman in her early forties, nowhere close really to Claude's own age of fifty-eight, was a full-figured and alluring seductress right out of the legendary past of Nuevo México, along the lines of La Tules, the famous and infamous María Gertrudes Barcelo reputed for a time to be the "best" of the Taos prostitutes.

Because of La Tules, the Yankee occupation forces were able to secure the territory—or so went the Anglo histories. Because of Irma, Doc was able to assimilate into the T or C social scene, or her fragment of it. And, like La Tules, Irma had some loot. She never asked Claude for a dollar or a dime. Always paid her own way. They would sit for hours over a beer conjugating *abrazar* and *amar* and *besar,* nursing Corona or Tecate longnecks and cuddling in the corner booth of Rocco's La Posada Rincon. They loved Mexican beer and made something of a game about the various brands. They had met over Mexican beer and Claude would whistle the jingle "*¿Qué toma usted? ¿Qué toma usted? ¿Qué toma usted?* Pabst Blue Ribbon," then always substitute the brand Dos Equis or Carta Blanca or such. It was a commentary on his studies of cultural appropriation. "'*¿Toma tu madre, o tu esposita?*' Doc," Irma would joke with him!

María Barcelo and Irma Apodaca were, in Doc Koster's analyses, merely individualized manifestations of the Spanish and Mexican ethnocentric and archetypal señoras and señoritas who had so motivated all comers over the Santa Fe Trail, and even the many dauntless souls, clergy and others, who traveled back and forth along the passage from Mexico to Santa Fe, up and along the nearby

Jornada del Muerto that coursed to the east of T or C along the Fra Cristóbal and Caballo mountain ranges. Claude saw his more modern passage as a journey of life, headed straight for the loving arms, generous breasts, and silk-smooth desires of Irma.

"Poor Nancy . . . poor Nancy," he would mutter to himself on his drive north, listening to the motor sputtering him along to his newly designed destiny. "She'll have to fend for herself the best she can. As for me, I must reach out for life. *¡Con gusto!*" He searched for the right expression. "*¡Con duende!*" He'd started to keep a renewed, more diligent list of Spanish *dichos* and miscellaneous phrases and terms since he'd met Irma.

"Why don't you like blondes with small tits, Claude? *Díme, ¿porqué, viejo?*" Irma had asked him soon after their first meeting. "*Eras muy rubio cuando jovencito, ¿no?*" He was always sandy-headed, more gray and thinning now, of course. "I do. I did," Claude replied in shameful echo of his wedding vows. Irma had no way of knowing that Nancy was such a woman—reserved and puritanical and even in her laughing youth tempered with a sternness that Claude had never been able to thaw. "I like my women dark and sultry and well endowed, like you, Irma," Claude had countered. And there was never the least bit of bother about such chauvinism with Irma. She was . . . she was just Irma and worth whatever consequence resulted. Claude couldn't worry about it, couldn't overanalyze it. He had spent his life doing that, doing the right things, being kind and considerate and tactful and appropriate in his manner.

He had, however, an amazing ability to separate his professional self and identity from his personal, private one and, further, to run his private life along two tracks, never really attempting to understand why he compartmentalized his life to such an extent. More and more, Claude knew one thing: he longed to go more frequently and to stay longer in T or C. More and more, he thought less and less about his work and his wife. Nancy seemed not to notice that good, respected Claude was fast going to seed. He couldn't blame himself for this. When he thought about Irma and her attention to him and then thought about Nancy and the attention she now demanded from him, it was clear choice and clear sailing . . . all 150 miles of it.

He remembered their wedding all those years ago in Iowa and who he had been, and who Nancy was then and what now she had become. The injustice and the pain of it weren't lost on him, of course: her standing next to him then in the town's all-knowing, all-encompassing, spiritually suffocating Danish and Lutheran church. Their honeymoon had been less than satisfying sexually, but they worked at it and had achieved some pleasures in bed. And now, to think of her alone in her small bed or in her chair, frail and immobile and suffering . . .

Physical pain was one sad, bad thing. Diabetes wasn't pretty, and it had meant a bad turn of luck for Nancy, and also for him. The amputation of a foot and the transformation of an even-tempered woman into a raging bitch were not easy things to witness, and Claude had tried to get beyond them, right or wrong, by seeking solace in T or C. Nancy's transformation was a prime cause, or maybe ultimately an excuse, for him to relocate his center of self, or of selfishness.

Claude had a litany of terms for what drove him into Irma's warm and dark and loving arms. Every time he was with Irma, Claude empathized with what Nancy must have felt—or didn't feel—with her missing foot. He felt it every time he and Irma danced at the T or C Community Hall or Rocco's La Posada Rincon. But he couldn't be held captive to an invalid again. He had had enough of that as the son of a tubercular father.

And now, on this particular early autumn day, advancing in his own middle age, Harry Claude Koster headed for his other life in T or C, his only real responsibility to live out the freedom and the vitality and the zest denied his father and his mother, and his wife. A denial now threatening him.

The Casa Algodones trailer park was located on the east side of town, on Lake Road, and Claude's trailer was the third one on the right just through the entrance arch, a cross-iron, jury-rigged contraption welded together for seeming immortality. When he drove under the arch and by the big cottonwood for which the park was named and which Claude warmed to each time he saw it, it was just turning dark. He had watched the sun go down over the mesa on his drive north and felt anew the sublime quality of the surrounding lava lands and tabletops and felt how fully the life was upon them, the plants and the birds, the darting doves and the lingering crows, and the smaller forms of insects and lizards and the like.

The brakes on his old International pickup hadn't stopped squeaking and the one working headlight hadn't yet lost its glow when Claude, already out of the truck and up the three small steps, was unlocking his hideaway. Irma's dog, a mongrel named Azul, roused himself from the side of the trailer where he had been sleeping underneath a spirea bush. Blue, as Claude called him, was a good old dog, and Claude took the stretching and yawning and slow shake-off of dust as a special welcome, for old Blue moved fast once he was awake and could inevitably make up for lost time and beat Claude through the door before he could toss the keys on the dinette. "Well, Blue boy," Claude greeted his new shadow, "how goes it, old friend? Where's Irma? I thought she'd make up the greeting party. Not that you're not a welcome sight yourself, now."

But as soon as Claude turned on the lights he saw right away that Irma had been there. There, next to the photograph of the two of them taken on the Elephant Butte Dam, standing next to an observation telescope, was a note from Irma:

Querido Claude. There's some Carta Blanca in the refrigerator and clean sheets on the bed. As you might expect, I'm at my sister's house in Belen until Sunday afternoon. ¡Qué lástima, mi amor! It's my niece's first Holy Communion Sunday morning and I'll be back for Sunday evening with you. Blue's there for you. Be sure to feed him.

—Te amo, Irma

The news was tough to take. His sham Denver conference was just a long weekend affair, and he would have to be back at work Monday. So that meant only an hour or so, on Sunday, if Irma returned in the early afternoon, leaving him time to drive the two and a half hours back to El Paso. "Damn it, Blue. Looks like just me and you tonight and tomorrow." And he paused to rub his finger over the glass and the image of Irma.

She was so beautiful to him: her oval face, her eyes dark brown, made even darker and more alluring with the heavy mascara she used—even for outings to the lake. He remembered the day the photo was taken, how she had looked high and low for the scarf and then when she found it how she folded it into the most practical of bandannas for her head. And there she was with him, his arm around her. He was about twenty pounds overweight. His bald spot and receding hairline were converging. But his skin was still tight and clear. He still had some good years left.

They had gone for a boat ride, had a couple of beers and some nachos at the marina lounge, played some Prez Prado tunes on the jukebox, and then gone back home to Casa Algodones and Irma's trailer for a long night of customized New Mexico loving. "*No hay un tonto como un viejo*" was the accepted rule of those days and nights. "*La risa abunda en la boca de los locos,*" she would say. And Doc would ask, "*¿Qué es? ¿Qué dice, mujer?*"

Now, though, Claude put down the picture and checked the refrigerator for the Carta Blanca and found it easily enough—two bottles side by side. And more *viejo* memories surfaced. He had met Irma at the Spanish Kitchen in T or C. She was waiting tables then and joked with him about his order and their own fumbling, teacher-student ways with language: "*¿Qué toma usted hoy Señor?* she had asked. "*A sus ordenes.*" "*Tragame uno Dos Equis, por favor, y la comida combinación número tres,*" came the words as he looked up from the menu to see her smiling.

"*¿Tú quieres uno, dos, o tres, Señor? ¿Cuál quieres exactamente?* two x's? Plus *número tres? Andale pues,* that's pretty confusing. Would you order *cuatro equis* for two people? And don't you mean *traígame* instead of *tragame?*"

The humor and even the grammar lesson had hardly registered on Doc. He was captivated by the face and the smile and the figure before him. She was so refreshing, such a relief after the chains and suffocations and carping, painful demands of sick, pitiful Nancy.

"*¿Cómo se llama, Señora?*" he asked in his best but still very Iowa-Anglo-sounding pronunciation.

"*Me llamo Irma, Señor,* Irma Apodaca, *¿y usted, por favor . . . tu te llamas?*" She replied slowly as if speaking to a child. So he repeated "Irma, Irma, Irma," a few times under his breath after she turned and was walking back to the order window. He watched her reach up and clip the ticket on the chrome cylinder. And he watched her turn and walk over to the bar for the beer. He had always been aroused by the light-skinned yet somehow dusky beauty of Spanish-American women.

In his university classes, in El Paso stores, on his research trips and travels in Mexico and other towns along the border, and in his readings, he had become infatuated with the *Hispana, Mejicana, mestizaje* presence. It was a strange, inevitable kind of attraction. And it, of course, wasn't without its racial and political strife. But Claude, over his years in the Southwest, maybe even in his Iowa boyhood, yielded to the attraction. And as Nancy declined in health and in her looks, the *Hispana*, and to a lesser extent the *Mejicana*, ideal ascended in his mind and myth and heart.

And so Irma came to hold a powerful kindred attraction to his own soul. Her light but dark skin. Her black hair, full flowing or swept back in a ponytail or covered by a beautifully improvised bandanna. Her full bosom. Her somewhat short and squat but still firm and shapely body. Her smile, her long eyebrows and eyelashes, even the dark dusting of hair on her arms—all triggered fantasies and desires and erotic images so intense and surprising to Claude that he felt reborn much beyond his first, and now not-so-ancient, adolescent awakenings and yearnings.

There that first time in the Spanish Kitchen as he looked up at her admiringly, he gingerly took the bottle and then the glass and coated its lip with the wedge of lime and then squeezed the fruit so hard that it popped out of his fingers onto the floor at Irma's feet. And so it began. Irma soon became much a part of Claude's own soul and his soulful feeling about his newly manufactured life in T or C. And now that first intense attraction was months ago. Now Claude knew Irma and she was his lover in reality. She was real, more real than the years with Nancy. More real than Nancy's torturous present life. And yet it was all, even the moment now reading Irma's kitchen table note, like something merely longed for, something invented. Something dreamed.

Rousing from his reveries and seeing the shadow of a shape jump by him, he turned and swatted at the dog. "Blue, get off the damn bed. It's the floor for you, *compadre*. Irma's not here to spoil you.

And I'm not sleeping with you no matter what, *perrito*." Then Claude opened a bottle of Carta Blanca and took a long, hard swallow of the cold brew.

He unpacked his small suitcase and took out his shaving kit; then he turned on the little black and white TV and settled down on the couch intending to watch the weather report. No sooner did the Albuquerque weatherman come on and start to draw his mascot figure, Thermo, than Claude was dozing and soon asleep. He liked to watch Thermo, but the drive and the night and Irma's note and the cold Carta Blanca had been too much. Blue circled once or twice and then curled up on the floor by the couch, not even slightly rousing Claude, who slept through the sign off and the national anthem and the ensuing blank screen that filled the room with a crackling glow.

His sleep, though deep, was nevertheless disturbed, for in his dreams Nancy was back home in the bedroom crying out for Claude to bring her more water and yet more pills from another new prescription. And all he could do was hand her the glass and the caplets and stare at the outline of her stump-legged, footless body beneath the cover. And he started to reach out and slowly pull the bedspread and the blanket and the sheet full over her anguished, grimacing, frowning face and matted gray head. And her once-youthful smile hovered above him in a vanishing mist.

The next morning Claude was off to a quick breakfast at Gabriel "Rudy" Montoya's One-Minute Diner. Montoya had once been a state politician, and Claude enjoyed some of the stories he liked to tell when he could collar his customers. But this morning Claude had no time for chewing the fat with Montoya. So he said his quick hellos, got his usual Denver sandwich and his cup of wake-up java, and coaxed the pickup into action. Blue was seated, panting and enlivened, by his side on the tattered bench seat. They were at the lake by 8:00 A.M. He had his icebox filled with Mexican beer, bologna sandwiches, and some water. He also took along some plastic bags for the fish he would catch and clean, and he threw in a box of Milk-Bones for Blue.

By the time Claude rented the boat and piled his tackle box, dough balls, minnow bucket, icebox, and safety gear into the boat, it was a little after nine. Blue was there too, through it all, barking at the morning and the water and the rev and hum of the twenty-five-horsepower Mercury outboard, as Claude gunned it and charted a rambling course for the deep water just above the dam.

Just past Elephant Butte, which stood out like a sentinel island in the middle of the lake, Claude shouted at Blue over the noise of the motor, "Thermo must have been right about this one, wasn't he, Blue? Sunny and warm and a great day for the lunkers. *¿Verdad?* Let's find those 'cats' you'll enjoy barking at when we land 'em. You like to bark at catfish, don't you Blue? What dog worth his salt wouldn't, eh? We'll catch a big one for Irma."

Claude was in good spirits, feeling the freedom of the lake, the wind in his face, and the rough control of the aluminum boat as it banged and dipped against the waves of the lake and the wakes of other fishing boats he encountered. The morning sun was warm on his back as the professor and distinguished teacher, the long-time husband, illicit lover, student of Spanish, and would-be fisherman and friend headed for the deep waters.

Blue's excitement and confidence excited Claude, too, for Blue seemed almost like a pup again as he surveyed the scene and barked when the urge struck him. Claude had to chuckle at the confused and mixed-up bundle of genes that Blue represented—a miniature, affable Doberman-terrier mix. Now there was a puzzle for you. Claude thought of his life here in much the same way. "Beats being in Denver, or El Paso, doesn't it, Blue?" he blurted out, along with other random observations and testimonials.

He thought of Irma and their upcoming rendezvous on Sunday. How their trailers would embrace them both. How maybe soon even El Paso and Nancy's suffering—for her and for him—would be in the past and he could go out on the lake and buzz over to the dam every day if he wanted to. "Right, Blue? Right, old buddy?"

Soon he yelled out to Blue, "We're here, Blue. *Nosotros estamos aquí, aquí*," as they reached the deep waters framed up ahead by the curving, grayish-white concrete ribbon of Elephant Butte Dam.

He killed the motor and his thoughts drifted back to his Iowa boy-hood: times on Lake Okaboji; times on the Mississippi when one summer the family felt well enough and was prosperous enough to rent a houseboat for a week. He had loved the water ever since. And this desert lake was all the more exciting in its contrasts to what he knew of water as a boy in the Midwest.

"There are some big ones down there, Blue. Let's bring one up, what do you say? But don't bark till I land him. Too much racket spooks 'em, even down that deep." And subliminal flashes crossed his mind, surreal pictures of just how it looked under the water, and where the odd and curious creatures called fish might be at various levels—thirty, forty, fifty, seventy-five feet under—languishing there in the cool, silent, drifting, and pressurized darkness.

The bait was foul-smelling, but soon it was on the hook and the fifty-pound-test line was spinning out from the reel, going down, down, with the heavy lead weights. At about twenty-five feet Claude set the lock and settled back to wait for the first strike.

Old Anton Bergson used to tell him about his fishing trips up to Canada, past the Boundary Waters—up with the moose and the black bears. Claude and his father had always planned to go up to Canada and fish, maybe take a canoe and portage it across those many waterways there in the northern wilderness. But TB put a stop to those plans—and to the trips planned to the Southwest to see the Grand Canyon and the Gulf of California and the Big Bend country in Texas. Claude and his father had gone ice fishing a few times on some frozen Iowa lakes closer to home. Suddenly Claude ached for the days of his childhood and his long-dead parents and for the days working for Anton, and for the people he would see in doorways, grateful for the delivery of their prescriptions and what-ever solace the colorful medicines might bring. "Nature's the best remedy, Blue," Doc observed out loud. And Blue listened to the words as if he understood, waiting rather for "biscuit," or "treat," or some such signaled enticement.

Then Claude's line tugged hard, nearly bending the pole double with the pass and hit and dive of the fish deep down in the chan-neling Rio Grande waters of the lake. Claude stood up, speaking to Blue all the while but not registering what he was saying. He was reeling, hard, hard, and his pole was dancing in the air. And then his foot, or was it Nancy's foot he felt somehow, hit against the tackle box and caught on the life vest he had neglected to put on, and he overcompensated for the stumble and imbalance, and he dropped his pole and fell backward over the side of the boat, not quite believing he was actually falling into the water. And he was immersed in the cold lake water, falling deep, deep down, and he could see in the murky distance of the water his white and red fiberglass Shakespeare pole and oversized, heavy-duty Zebco reel spiraling downward in frame-by-frame slow motion, and when he finally paddled to the surface of the water, exhausted, the boat was distant and he caught a watery glimpse of Blue barking at him, but he couldn't hear him and he remembered the box of Milk-Bones, and his life jacket in the boat, next to the tackle box, and the ice-box, and he thought of the bologna sandwiches and the Mexican beer, and Irma, veiled and at her niece's Holy Communion (or was it at a wedding, standing next to Montoya, with his hands reaching to pull up the veil)—and Nancy swallowing pill after pill in succession, drinking from the lines of countless glasses of water he kept carrying to her. And then the image of his father gasping for breath and coughing pinkish phlegm and fluids flashed across his consciousness, and Anton Bergson was giving him a sack of medicine to deliver to his own house in a swirling snowstorm that had brought the little Iowa town to an icy, desolate stop. And he more vaguely wondered about the big fish with the pole and line dragging behind it, swimming deeper and deeper, and then he thought he saw the smiling face of Nancy blending into the smiling face of an officious and solicitous but sinister-looking Ralph Edwards, with his slicked-back hair and his toothpaste smile, saying with a gurgling voice, "Truth or Consequences. Truth or Consequences."

And Claude, slowly twisting and sinking to the deepest and darkest depths of Elephant Butte Lake, hadn't the slightest awareness of anything at all . . . even while his slowly flapping, open mouth tried to form the name and the word and the sound of the dearest and greatest of all future but suddenly ended expectations.

Nueva Entrada

"What, you've never ridden a horse, Jerrod? Well, if you're gonna live in the West, it's a must. You can't begin to understand this place until you mount up and ride."

The words were those of LaVonne Bishop. She knew New Mexico, horses, and men. And she took every occasion to combine her vocation as a high school teacher with what might ordinarily be regarded as her avocational enthusiasm for western living. "A woman's place is in the West," she would tell her students. And they were convinced as much by the confidence and obvious sincerity of her actions as by her words. Right now that bit of westering gusto and self-reliance entailed her growing interest in Jerrod Templeton and the challenge of conquest he presented as a stranger in strange lands. Gender roles and the "race thing" made the gambit all the more intriguing.

She wasn't quite sure if she saw Jerrod as a black man before she saw him as a man. Her own American Indian heritage made her keen on the power and politics of prejudice. "Just remember, students," she would harp, "the Zia Sun of our state flag shines down on many cultures."

At present her brown eyes smiled across the table at Jerrod, causing him almost to choke—more on the friendliness of the moment than on the salsa searing his tongue. As he downed the welcome glass of water, even the din of the adjacent student cafeteria subsided.

"You're telling me the truth, now—you've never *ever* ridden a horse, not even at a carnival or a fair or something like that? Aren't there horses in Indiana or Illinois or wherever you come from back East? Don't tell me we have a proverbial tenderfoot here? Not Mr. Jerrod Templeton!"

"Well, I walk and run mostly, but if you want to include a Shetland pony ride or a turn or two on a merry-go-round, sure. And it's Iowa—Waterloo, Iowa—not Indiana or Illinois or Idaho. What's so hard to remember about Iowa, anyway? And it's in the Midwest, not the East. Haven't you ever heard the old cowboy song, Miss LaVonne—something about 'a herd of cattle coming down Nebraska way into the state of Iowa'?"

"Yes, of course. You can call me Sue. I remember 'Sweet Sioux City Sue.' But I ain't Sioux. I'm part Pueblo Indian—from Zuni. How does Sweet Zuni Sue sound?"

"It fits. Pretty Zuni Sue—but she's not too good at geography. Anyone who teaches at an illustrious institution of secondary learning like Valley High should know some U.S. geography—you know, the states, the capitals."

"Hey, I teach U.S. history. I know geography and enough history to know Des Moines is the capital of Iowa, and that they make John Deere tractors in Waterloo. But I'm happy with being Sioux City Sue if you're happy with . . . Nebraska Ned or something. Or maybe I'll call you Esteban. He had his ways with the native women, they say." Her voice was raspy and low as she leaned further across the table, and Jerrod, laughing, as if to locate the source of the resonance of her voice, cast an obvious glance along her open-necked white blouse and followed the silver-chained lines of the turquoise pendant hanging around her throat and down her chest, the blue-green stone centered beneath the sheer, soft cotton and between the mounded outlines of her round, dark, and hardened nipples. The stone was carved in the shape of an animal—a bear, it seemed—and he was surprised that it held his gaze.

"Just clear one thing up for me, Jerrod, or Johnny Neb, or Stevie Wonder, before I issue a special invitation. How much do you *really* know about horses and riding?"

"If you start calling me Stevie Wonder or Esteban, I'll really be confused. We don't have the time to get into that game, seeing as how this extremely generous and hospitable thirty-minute lunch period is just about over and I'm due to meet *El Capitán* Mike Graham in a few minutes for grounds duty. And seeing that I haven't yet finished this succulent scorched enchilada plate, I can't give you all the details about my horsemanship. I did just about get trampled underneath some thundering hooves once, under a picturesque Iowa harvest moon. The YMCA had a hayride out in the country for disadvantaged city kids, like yours truly, and me and some pals didn't know enough to stay on the hay wagon, in the hay with the girls and behind the horses. So . . ."

LaVonne laughed. "That story I want to hear about in detail. And I'll tell you about Esteban. But I wouldn't want you to be late for your tour of duty with Meatball Mike Graham, a man whose patience is easily tried. You can tell me the hayride story tomorrow. You *do* know that tomorrow is Saturday and you're coming down to my place? Tell me the whole story when you get there, and I'll introduce you to my remuda and take you horseback riding through the alfalfa fields and along the drainage ditch that runs alongside the bosque and the river. It's really quite beautiful. We can even ride over to a big cottonwood and then, afterwards, to a remote sandbar I know on the *río* there."

"You've got to be kidding me. Your *remuda*? Not your mother or your second cousin? What will your horses say when you tell them, 'Hey, guess who's coming to dinner?'"

"I don't know. Something like 'Hey, hay's for horses, bring it on.'"

"Very funny. But seriously, it would have to be a tried-and-true horse, Zuni Sue, before I could saddle up and ride the fields and ditches with a rodeo queen like you."

"Don't sell me short, Jerrod. I didn't make it to State Fair Queen, but I was a Valencia County rodeo princess. I'm quite the barrel rider, and yours truly, LaVonne K. Bishop, rode right there in the

Queen's Grand Entry entourage. I carried the 4-H flag, too. And for my labors I received a pair of Nacona genuine elk-skin boots and two pair of lady's slim-cut Wranglers! I'll wear 'em just for you tomorrow. And I have just the horse for you. Steady and intelligent. His name is D.J., for Don Juan. Named him after Oñate, you know, the conquistador. D.J.'s a good old horse. Medium-sized and easy-tempered. Just the right ride for a midwestern city buckaroo like you. I'll put the directions in your box and see you *mañana*."

"I accept. But if I leave you now, do you think you can ride through the thick of the table talk here and commiserate with the others about the sorry state of the Duke City public schools and education in this great American Southwest? Chime in with them in calling the superintendent a bigoted, illiterate bastard and why we need longer lunch periods, year-round school, and more equipment and a raise?"

"You mean you don't have adequate equipment, cowboy?" Again the low voice teased and taunted him. "Just turn up tomorrow, Neb, down Bosque Farms way. Or, come to think about it, I *am* going to call you Esteban. Yes, that's perfect."

"You'll have to explain this Esteban name. That completely escapes me."

Lessening his look of puzzlement, Jerrod cocked his head to the side and smiled slowly. Then he pushed back from the table and picked up his tray, which looked almost miniature in his strong, athletic hands. He took a white paper napkin and wiped the chili stains from his mouth in a motion that almost looked like he was seriously signaling for LaVonne to shut up, but he knew there would be no secrecy about a weekend horse ride with her. He moved the napkin slowly, softly to his runny nose. The chili had been hot, and his neck was perspiring and his nose was running, but it was dry, too, chafed and sore.

And he felt the familiar urge. It was part of his lunchtime ritual, this craving beyond appetite. He thought of Iowa and his time there before heading west. Of how, for a month or two in the previous fall, he had thought this new place would give him a fresh start and he could break free. But he just couldn't kick his habit, rid himself of the relentless ache of a deep drug appetite.

Or the racism. It was the same thing everywhere, Midwest, West. He'd seen it all before. The glances, the stares, even now. Black man. White woman. Black boy. White girl. He'd known that taboo all the way back to those hayride days in Iowa when "good faith" attempts were made at school integration and he was in the middle of the experiment. This time the equation was complicated by LaVonne being part Indian. He crumpled the white napkin into a round wad of paper and tossed it in a long arching shot to the large trash barrel just inside the door to the faculty lunchroom. And the whiteness floated on in his mind, so palpable he could smell it and taste it and feel it.

Lost in reverie about LaVonne's brazen laughter and bold invitations, he was all the way through the cafeteria and into the hall when he realized he had forgotten to bus his tray and dishes. How sincere was she? he wondered. Just how far would she take her flirtations? Was she really ready to test the taboo this way? Ready for the talk, the innuendo and outright vilification that would inevitably come her way now that this was finally set in motion. But what the hell, why think of *her* reputation? Who ever thought of him? He'd get what he could while he could.

Maybe life out West here in the Rio Grande Valley was going to be different. Maybe he could get away with it, get by without the hassle. The risk was worth it, though, because LaVonne was tall and supple and alluring with those geometric patches of lighter white skin around her blouse collar and sleeves where the sun had not darkened her skin. He wanted to see the true hue and shade of her breasts and legs, which he supposed were lean and muscular from constant horseback riding. He fantasized about her as a kind of river-riding, funky Indian princess and Lady Godiva crossbreed, riding bareback along the ditches, and the image of a naked, moist, and spraddle-legged LaVonne Bishop merged with the lingering heat of the chili still in his mouth. How would a sauntering horse feel with that precious cargo of mingling moist skin and soft hair? Jerrod would soon see just what kind of a rider she was. He was confident he could handle it. The question was, could she?

There was still time for another lunch hour hit of the white stuff before he met Mike. The whiteness of the powder he craved mingled in his mind and in his nose and loins with the whiteness of LaVonne's skin, and he thought of dusting her with cocaine and sniffing it off of her, head to ever-lovin' foot, and all the mounds and crevices in between. She was in for a ride, all right, the ride of her smiling, innocent, bosque boondocks life. And Jerrod "Esteban" Templeton would be the one to crack the quirt and beat the tom-tom.

LaVonne watched Jerrod, walking out of the small faculty lunch-room. She knew she shouldn't move too fast because it was still his first year, and only her second, at the school, but she had waited most of the year, waited all the way to May and the Memorial Day weekend. Whatever gossip there would be would have time to heal over the summer, if such things ever did heal. Today she had acted on an impulse of long duration, for she could not shake her attrac-tion and ambivalence toward Jerrod and the fantasies about him that had surprised her beyond her wildest knowing, seeing him as a latter-day explorer, conqueror, a companion of Cabeza de Vaca and Fray Marcos de Niza. The others must surely see it, too, see that she was finally beyond superficial friendliness, ready to act on her fantasies and urgings, ready to see just where this crossing over the line would take her. It would be some ride, and she was ready. "Beyond bounds," she thought.

"Hey, LaVonne, do I see what I think I see going on here?"

Slowly Pops Ferrill's cracking voice penetrated her reverie, ask-ing her straight off about what was happening. The gossip was already starting, inevitably, inexorably. Maybe she could slow it down some, but she doubted it. And maybe she just didn't care. Discov-ering what Jerrod was really like would be worth it.

It began last fall when Jerrod first showed up and had the temer-ity to stop and talk and say an extended hello to what the others saw not so much as a person, as LaVonne, but as an *indio*-white woman, a tall, brunette woman that the others had claimed as one of them, yes, but also as theirs to own. She had not been at the school much longer than Jerrod, but they had already claimed her and recognized her as at once taciturn and talkative, reserved and outgoing, coy yet assertive. From Zuni via Grants and Gallup—whatever all the Indian maiden, mixed-breed images added up to. But they thought they knew her, thought they accepted her, and thought they should watch out for her welfare in the threat of the temptations of Jerrod Templeton.

Had she never said hello quite so warmly to Templeton, the talk, the suspicions, the mean-spiritedness, to seek out either her badness or his, would not have been there. But in their benevolence and caring they simply took for granted the inevitable corruption of her tan-colored goodness by his darkness, black invading near-white as if by nature. They had suggested to her, behind Jerrod's back, that he was a druggie and had even been a dealer, though their accusations never were proven. There was something in his record, they hinted, even something in the press about his losing a job and entering drug rehabilitation. But it was all vicious rumor, she was almost certain. He was too vital and healthy to be involved in hard drugs or any other physically harmful substance abuse.

What did they really know of her and her own indigenous, darker-hued ways? Total Americanization, total Anglo social conditioning were things she resisted with a passion. If women were unique and individual beyond stereotype, so too were Indians. So too were Indian women. So too were blacks. So she befriended him, and her attraction and her fantasies grew, and now he was coming to spend the day with her, and she was at once apprehensive and aching, ready for the risk and the ride of it.

"Now, Missy," Pops spoke up again, "you just be sure you know what you're setting yourself up for with shenanigans such as this."

LaVonne just drank the last of her iced tea and looked over the rim of her white paper cup at the old man who undressed her with his eyes Monday through Friday. She'd seen this in Gallup, where she grew up, and certainly she'd seen it in Flagstaff at the university, with all the bleeding-heart-liberal but oh-so-lustful-and-prejudiced professors, and now she was hearing it again here in this petty little high school lunchroom, made explicit and sleazy in the cautioning and oh-so-concerned phlegm-laced voice of Pops Ferrill.

"Now, Pops, don't start getting ahead of yourself in your advice. You know I only have eyes for you. It's as certain as all those circles and line drawings you have your drafting students measure out."

"Sure, LaVonne, hon. Sure thing," Pops said with as much schmooze and sugar as he could muster, between wheezes, and pulled out a pack of cigarettes. He carefully took out a brown-ended cigarette, tapped it on both scraggly ends, raised his see-through Scripto lighter, and flamed up his habitual after-lunch smoke.

"I know you're my gal, sweetie," he coughed. "Old Pops just wants to look after his best gal, is all. I know what all men want from women, and black men like that Jerrod fellow especially. Remember, I'm 1/52 Injun too. We got to stick with our kind, girlie. Just got to."

All LaVonne could really think about, however, was how adept a smoker Pops was and how many times she had seen him execute that complicated motion of hand to pocket to pack to cigarette to lighter to mouth. How much did thirty years of this ritual all add up to? All those expensive cigarettes? And how much did all his tobacco-perverted "American" advice, good or bad, matter to anybody at all?

"Just be sure we don't have to memorialize you and Templeton come next week. He's a bad match, LaVonne. Bad."

"Sure, Pops," LaVonne quipped as she put down her cup and readied her tray to leave. "But what does a wannabe Injun guy who uses a lighter know about matches, anyway? Enjoy the weekend. I plan to."

Jerrod headed out of the cafeteria and down the wide hall to take the needed hit and then meet Mike. Hall traffic was thinning out as the students from the second lunch period moved outside for a few minutes of fresh air. Templeton ducked into the men's rest room and went into a stall and closed the door. He reached into his pocket and found the slide-guitar chrome finger bar that he had capped to hold his cocaine. His daddy had played a slack-string blues guitar and this was what that all-my-hopes-and-dreams-dashed legacy had come to. He removed the base slowly to avoid any suction spill and lined the drug on top of the toilet paper dispenser. Then he removed the top of the cylinder and leaned into it and over the white powder all in one movement. As he snorted the snowy stuff he heard again wailing riffs of his daddy's old guitar, and he thought of LaVonne, and her image slid and melted into the knifed-out, scratchy graffiti sayings and vulgar drawings on the stall wall. He envisioned how it would be to introduce her to the highs of cocaine, how it would be to sniff it from around her navel, her erect nipples, and then, once she was on, how well she would do his bidding. He shook his head, capped the hollow guitar finger bar and put it back in his pocket, and opened the door, seeing slightly double and laughing all the time he rinsed his hands and stared into the floating mirror. He could tell Mike he had already checked this rest room, as usual.

He and Graham had the third and final lunch period and part of fifth period classes to check the rest rooms and the grounds and especially the students who were driving back into the parking lot after lunch at the local eateries. The parade of Valley FFA trucks and customized jalopies, evidence of both teen and ethnic pride, never ceased to remind him that he was indeed in the West.

"This ain't Iowa, is it, Templeton? Or was it Idaho?" Graham would invariably say as they observed the recurrent waves of lunch-period migration.

"No, this ain't Iowa, Graham, and it ain't Idaho or Chicago or Des Moines, Decatur, Detroit, or New York, or any other place I've ever been or seen. You're sure as hell right about that."

Templeton always had to correct Graham, who continually confused Iowa with Idaho and their produce, corn with potatoes. And it was sincere confusion, or ignorance. Graham just couldn't keep the distinction straight. Usually it was just part of the game played by everybody, including LaVonne, a reenactment of the greenhorn-goes-west mentality, except in this instance the greenhorn was black. Templeton was for certain a stranger in a strange land. He could adapt to the ways of the West, but these westerners would maybe have to take on some big-city ways in the process. Corruption was a two-way street, or so he reasoned.

Graham was a large, sandy-haired, big-bellied Irishman who kept his hair cut short, military style, and liked to wear polo shirts, golfing slacks, and tasseled loafers. He portrayed himself as a golfer and talked the game, but when he and Jerrod played at the LaDera municipal course, it was clear he was more puffery than anything else. And for the high school track coach to be bested by an algebra teacher was a blow to the ego, even if the math teacher was a natural athlete.

Graham lived more for golf than he did for coaching track, and he always complained about weekend track meets cutting into his "tee-time," as he called it, arching an eyebrow and raising a little finger in the air. Over the past weeks of spring, through March and April, they had talked quite a bit as they made the rounds—checking rest rooms, hall lockers, athletic fields, parking lots, and the ditch bank that bounded the northeast parking lot.

"You never ran track, Jerrod? No dashes, no relays, no nothing? No field events? ¿Nada? ¿Porqué, hombre?"

"I never played much beyond football, Mike. Some baseball, some basketball. Sorry to disappoint you, coach," Templeton would say time and again, and finally Graham dropped it. His lines of conversation were limited and always focused on Jerrod's being from Idaho and not running track. And he always worked in a free Spanish lesson for the newcomer. Graham dwelled on the negative, on inadequacies and limitations. His own career, such as it had been, was stuck.

Jerrod would almost *have* to get high to handle the grounds duty and the boredom of this dullard's conversation. "What if I could get this big mick on crack?" he would contemplate from time to time. But the risk wasn't worth even entertaining. Jerrod figured he could get by with a lunchtime hit or two mainly because Mike's overall sensibilities were so dull, so unobservant. So he reasoned, the tenderfoot westerner.

"It don't make sense, Templeton," Graham would mutter. "A guy like you, natural-born athlete and all. Just don't make sense," he kept repeating as he smacked his chewing gum and then pushed his heavy plastic-framed glasses back up to the bridge of his nose. They had some dull times on their tours of duty. Truants, loiterers, lollygaggers. Lately they had mostly just been enjoying the spring weather, watching the irrigation waters come to the ditch, catching more and more students leaving their cars to make out in the willows or in the shade of the large cottonwood trees.

With spring and the flow of irrigation waters and the flying of the cottonwood and elm seeds came the visible resurgence of teenage libido. And lately Templeton looked forward to grooving on the associations he had when he was high on the white powder—the flying cotton, the spuming foam in the brown-watered ditch. Today it all reminded him of LaVonne and what it would be like to be with her, alone—except for the goddamn horses. But even they had their flowing, electric natural sexual power. And in his stoned state he coaxed along into a certain climax some beastly imaginings.

This particular tour of duty began as usual. A rest room cigarette or two, some littering of lunch sacks and napkins and unfinished hamburgers. Graham had a few new dirty jokes to tell Jerrod, but they didn't seem intolerable, nor did the razzing or the talk about golf scores or Graham's bragging about how many of the new female teachers were after him, including the new history teacher, the *indio*-cowgirl, LaVonne Bishop. And just as Graham was going into some detail about his exploits with Bishop they reached the end of the last row of cars in the parking lot and approached the ditch levee.

"What the hell?" Jerrod heard Graham say, and then he was running. "Come on, Jerrod, let's move! Trouble up there on the ditch."

Jerrod shook off his drug-induced daydream and saw what his companion had seen through a clearing in some of the ditch bank foliage. A girl with long black hair was lying prone, kicking and twisting in the dirt and dust on the ditch bank. Another student seemed to be holding her down, restraining her.

"It's a goddamn rape or something, Templeton," yelled Graham, his tasseled loafers filling with ditch dirt and his heavy glasses sliding halfway down his nose. "And on our watch, Templeton, on our fuckin' watch! See if you can still haul ass."

"How horrible! Oh, how utterly horrible, Jerrod. Poor thing. Poor thing." LaVonne couldn't stop whimpering, almost sobbing, as she handed Jerrod a plump mug of Saturday morning coffee and slid onto the bench on the other side of the small breakfast booth in the house trailer that was her Bosque Farms home.

"Who was she, and who was the boy, and how did Mike Graham feel, the big lummox? Such a mistake, always thinking the worst. But I guess anybody might think it was a rape or a reaction to drugs. It's just that his mind is always in the gutter. Believe me, I know. He's as big a pothead as any of the kids."

Jerrod let that pass and took a sip of coffee, enjoying the strong, hot black bite of it all the more because of what he saw, how LaVonne's jeans fit, how they held her long, lean legs and her firm, curving hips, how her half-buttoned denim work shirt only partially covered the white T-shirted contours of her small but beautifully pointed breasts. The fetish pendant was still there, still, kinetic. She had kept her promise about wearing the Wranglers, and he noticed every inch of her legs. When she propped one knee up to her chest, Jerrod saw how soft and comfortable and sensible her flat-heeled boots looked. He wondered why all the Indians he'd seen out West dressed like cowboys, wore boots and hats, and drove Ford pickups.

She was, he surmised, the real thing, experienced but with an innocence he recognized and liked in women, a malleability of temperament and personality, an acceptance of people and a hunger for new experience and exploration. She was the kind of tough, trusting woman who liked everybody more than she should, who gave everybody more than the usual benefit of the doubt. He would be able to take advantage of that and play off the complexities of miscegenation.

He had come into something very good here, he was certain. He had felt it on the drive down I-25 from Albuquerque. The sky was high blue and the river bosque green and winding as far as he could see into the south. "What a windfall," he said again under his breath. "Make the best of it, Templeton. Make the best of it. She's like the ditch mud, soft and pliant and ready to shape into what I need. She's ready, and she doesn't even know she's in way over her head. If she as much as smoked pot with Mike or some of the other guys, why, she's all mine."

But as he was thinking these things, he was registering her question. He responded, "Pacheco or Padilla. Sally Padilla, I think. Something like that."

LaVonne smiled at his mispronunciation of Spanish names, but it made him seem all the more innocent in her eyes, especially as she tried to re-create the reality of the ditch experience in his telling of it, how he and Mike had come upon something other than an assault or a rape, a seizure of a different sort.

"And the boy was a long, lanky white kid, a Tom Kern or Curran, something like that. I'd seen him in study hall before. He was the one who more or less saved the day, saved the girl from serious injury, maybe drowning. Kern got there right at the time of the epileptic seizure. He took control of things and put a stick in her mouth and then kept her from falling into the ditch water, which was churning along in full spring flow just a few feet away. She was lucky."

"And just think, Mike almost clobbered the boy. But I guess it was a natural conclusion, that an assault was in the making." She shook her head and sipped her coffee.

"Yeah, I held him back from hitting Kern just after we ran up and Mike grabbed him and threw him off her. I was shaky from the excitement of it all, but I could see what it was, and then this Kern kid started yelling, 'Epileptic fit! She's having a fit.' Then Mike reprogrammed and saw it, and we all just stood there and watched the ugliness of what had come over this pretty girl. The eyes rolled back. The jerks and contortions. It's like a strange demonic possession or something not unlike orgasm. You can see how the old superstitions took hold about epilepsy. Even the nurse commented about it when we brought the girl back inside the school afterward. And the girl was so pretty. Except she has epilepsy and a withered left arm, as if she had been twice cursed or something. But strangely she was all the prettier because of the ugliness imposed on her without any of her doing, just a couple of nature's quirks. And the Kern boy was copping a feel, too. He had taken advantage of the moment, because her blouse was torn and her breasts were out of her brassiere."

"Oh, don't tell me that kind of thing. What women have to endure, even in being 'rescued,' for Christ's sake! It's disgusting how little control we have even when we are helpless and should be totally off limits. You know that the damn conquistadors took great sexual advantage of my Pueblo ancestors."

Jerrod could sense, even amid her anger, that he had her trust more fully now as a result of not just the anecdote but the way he had related it to her, presenting himself as even more chivalrous than Mike, or the Kern kid. For the kid had been a sincere gentleman and honored the girl's person. In fact he was trying to straighten her clothes and cover any inadvertent revelation. But in Jerrod's telling of the incident, he had saved the kid from himself and saved the girl, the fair maiden in distress, and saved even Mike from his meathead self.

The truth? Jerrod had been so stoned on two heavy snorts of crack that he had just hung back when Mike went into action. But women loved romanticized dramatizations. The Kern kid should have been all over the girl before they stumbled across him, and no doubt was. He might have even caused the seizure had he been true to his instincts in forcing her to do what she wanted to do all along, what all women wanted to do—submit to a masterful force, submit to dark and compelling male powers. What had Othello and Desdemona been about, if not that? Jerrod had first encountered *Othello* in college, and now his interpretation of the play and of Othello's character was a universal principle that shored him up in times of self-doubt. Othello was the one wronged by Iago, by Desdemona, by circumstances, but he had conquered even over conspiracy and death. Whatever had happened in reality beside the ditch between Kern and the Padilla girl was now twisted up with *Othello* and with the ubiquitous O.J. Simpson trial and what the media had done to O.J. and to Jerrod, and to all black males in that circus of a trial. Unavoidably, O.J. and Othello mixed in with Jerrod's contemplated seduction of the new friendly white Indian— LaVonne K. Bishop. What happened by the ditch was simply a means to his end, a way to manipulate this situation and prime LaVonne into acceptance of what she was asking for all along.

Jerrod knew the kid was lying. He had to be. You could see it in his eyes, hear it in his eagerness to tell how he had just come upon the girl as she swooned into the fit. He had himself imagined what it would be like to take the girl right smack in the middle of a fit like that, with her helpless arm flailing in the air, and his imaginings seemed so real that he had a hard time distinguishing real time from dream time.

Mike had yelled him out of it. Jerrod knew about liars and lies, knew it deep down in his own self. The kid was hustling Graham and trying to hustle Jerrod, but Jerrod was too smart for him. Mike was too kind and naïve in his own rough-edged obtuseness to know, but Jerrod knew a hustle when he saw one. He was a master at the hustle himself.

Like now. You had to be that way. Women demanded it, wanted it that way. Like yesterday at the lunch table. Like seven or eight months ago and all the times in between, when he met and became acquainted with LaVonne Bishop, with her cordial ways and hokey name games, her benevolent, liberal greetings, her vanity and enjoyment of her own personal charm. "Independent, free-wheeling Amerindian woman will tolerate the black man in front of real white bigots."

And she thought she knew about controlling and training horses and students and men! Well, Jerrod Templeton was a far cry from the likes of impotent old cronies like Pops and the faculty lunch-room crowd, or Mike Graham, who thought he was *El Capitán* and in authority over *soldado* Jerrod Templeton. None of them could begin to know his own private war and how he flared in silent anger against all whites, against all the bowing and acquiescing blacks worshiping at the feet of patronizing, mainstream, white liberal assimilationists. That was part of the fun of his conquests of women like LaVonne. Reparations! There was no free man like a slave, no better master than a servant. Why didn't they, why didn't *she,* realize that?

So he engaged her again in conversation, enjoying his hustle, watching his rap work its spell.

"So tell me about your place here, Zuni Sue," he said, coming out of his silent scheming into spoken sparring.

"Come on, *vaquero,*" she said, "enough coffee and chatter. Time to saddle up. I'll show you the bosque and the river and my ditch. But you have to promise, no fits once we get there—by you or by me. If you can help it, that is." There it was again. Another taunting smile. The promises of her dark Indian eyes. Did she know what she was offering? He was almost sure.

"I've packed a little picnic brunch for us. Just some wine and fruit, and some fresh bagels. And a surprise for the appetizer. D.J.'s all saddled and waiting. Not my big gelding, Bud, but that won't take long. You can watch me and double-check your blanket and cinch and adjust your stirrups. Then it's time to hit the trail at last and see if we can tell the sizzle from the steak."

They left the trailer and walked toward the horse shed and small corral where LaVonne kept the horses. She went inside the shed and brought back a bridle, used but well treated with saddle soap and balm. He watched her move across the small corral to the far fence where one horse was standing, saddled and waiting. Then she opened a gate and stepped into another small fenced area and coaxed another horse, a large bay gelding with a black mane and tail, over to them. As she slid the bridle over the horse's head, she said to him, "Bud, this is Mr. Jerrod Templeton. This is a big day for him. We're gonna take him for a little ride along the ditch." Then she led the big horse back through the gate and tied him next to the smaller horse, a surefooted strawberry roan, though to Jerrod it was just a horse. "D.J., meet Jerrod. Jerrod, meet D.J. Better check the cinch and stirrups while I get old Bud saddled up."

He was quick to learn, although he pretended not to understand how to buckle the cinch and lace the stirrups, in a very successful move of getting LaVonne to come over and show him how to do it, her hands on his. She was more than willing to touch him, inviting his touch, he could tell, and when once she turned, laughing, over her shoulder, hands entwined on the roped cinch of his saddle, he felt her linger, looking for him to kiss her. But even as her flirtations sought immediate resolution he resisted, carrying out his own teasing game of control. "There will be time at the ditch, much better time ahead," he thought, given over to the larger ironies of the moment, the larger scheming of the day.

The ride took them out of the alfalfa field of her property along a dirt and gravel road that stretched east toward the river and the bosque, past other alfalfa fields and the small irrigation ditches that crisscrossed the landscape. As they rode, LaVonne recounted the actions of her life that had led her to live in a trailer on an acreage with horses in Bosque Farms, New Mexico, teaching high school in Albuquerque, and to this fated horseback excursion through the fields and over to the river bosque with Jerrod Templeton.

Naturally enough, her commentary led her to the history of the Southwest. The Spanish *entradas* and their effects on the Pueblo peoples fascinated her the most, and as she spoke of the history of the little ditches, the *acequias,* and the larger ditch, the Acequia Madre that ran parallel to the river where they were heading, her fervent love of the place, the *río abajo,* and its people showed through. She alluded to the Rio Grande's magnificent geological and historical meandering and how she felt a land determined a people and was determined by them in turn. She recounted the myth of Cibola, the Seven Cities of Gold, and of Cabeza de Vaca and his companion, Esteban the Moor, and his adventures with Fray Marcos.

"He was a fascinating figure in a strange land, just like you— this Esteban. Legend says he was irresistible to the Pueblo women and held them all in thralldom. Though the assumptions and accuracy of that legend are suspect these days, as you might imagine. But it is an interesting instance of a myth with a black hero—or villain, depending on your perspective. Esteban was a black man, in an exalted position. He even jerked poor Fray Marcos around and was very independent in his ways. But the Indians, the women, were in danger of greater servitude than the powers of Esteban's legendary charisma and allure. Why were the conquistadors called conquerors? That's very problematic, you know, in the long scheme of time. Who rules who and what the land has to say about it, what time and history have to say about it."

"This Esteban fellow seems like a guy I could identify with in more ways than one."

"Well, yes, but not to draw any analogy to too fine a point, things ended badly for Esteban, you know. He was sacrificed for the Spanish, killed for his transgressions of native ways."

The slow-paced walk of the horses and the hot morning sun and the rhythm of LaVonne's talk took Jerrod's thoughts more into the next few hours than back through the centuries of Nueva Granada and the temporary conquests of the Spanish explorers. His future was to take control of LaVonne, and he knew she was leading him to that moment, that place just up ahead in the coolness of the river waters and the bosque shade. He would conquer her and take her into this thralldom, take her much further into his control than she in all her willingness could ever anticipate. Yes, she was consenting to more than she knew. He checked his back Levi's pocket for the needed supply of cocaine. He knew she would consent, and then she would be his, physically and mentally, and through any blackmail he could bring to bear on her reputation and responsibility—that and what he could soon tell others, discreetly, of course, about her wild, ecstatic sexual appetite for him. "Blackmail," he smiled to himself. "Blackmail funk. Blackmail fuck."

Thinking through his two-tracked consciousness, he focused on LaVonne's firm, rounded butt moving in the saddle ahead of him in counterpoint to the gelding's strong, alternating haunches, and asked, "What did this Esteban do, exactly, to get murdered?"

"Oh, I don't remember all the details. There are several versions. Fray Marcos never reached Zuni Pueblo, the actual pueblo with the sunny walls mistaken for pure gold. You know how motives can distort perceptions of *reality*, and part of the good friar's reason for turning back at the last minute was his fear, his failure of nerve, when he received the news that Esteban, as an advance scout and messenger of sorts, had been killed by the *savages*. As if savagery doesn't come in many guises, right, Jerrod? Apparently Esteban was as arrogant as he was handsome. The Zuni thought him a shaman at first, what with his imposing presence and physical stature and great good looks. But he brought some wrong paraphernalia and confidence with him into that new land. Some unknown items and some alien gourd rattles, of all things. And he wasn't as knowledgeable as his puffed-up cockiness led him to think."

Jerrod looked toward the bosque and the ditch only a few hundred yards in front of them. It seemed more remote and wilder than the ditch he and Graham patrolled at school, where yesterday's unfortunate incident had occurred. But it was essentially the same terrain, and he thought again about what he and Mike had come across with the Padilla girl and how he had hesitated and watched those lingering minutes as first the Kern kid, and then Mike, and finally Jerrod himself had their way with the girl, all of them sadistically laughing at her tears and gagging her attempts to cry out for help. He could see it all vividly.

But had that really happened? His imaginings were so strong that they blurred reality. They had all had their way with her, taking her in the damn middle of an epileptic seizure and then actually pretending, as far as the girl knew, or the world knew for that matter, to help her. Placing her soft white young breasts back into her brassiere, sliding her panties and her skirt back over her scuffed, schoolgirl saddle oxfords, tucking her blouse in gently, as if they had never gang-bang fucked the ever-lovin' sense out of her while she was hopping and twitching around and trying to swallow her tongue and the stick and whatever else got in the way. Then they just kindly helped her into the nurse's office. It was perfect. The boy wouldn't tell, and if he did nobody would believe him. And if the nurse found clues, Jerrod and Graham could just point to the kid. Who would bother with DNA in such a trivial instance?

But now there was the reality of the ditch up ahead and LaVonne and what she would be like out of those tight jeans and crazed in her passion for him and begging him to tell her just what pleased him the most and then how she would do it without ceasing. He could feel the hard leather of the saddle rocking, pressing between his legs. And his memory panned back to the time as a boy when he had watched a drunken man and woman, late at night in a Waterloo alley under the shadows and silhouette of a dust-coated streetlight fumble and fuck, oblivious to his wide-eyed presence. "You want it, mama? You want it? You want it, baby?" the guy kept saying, slurring his words as he thrust time and again between the woman's raised and open legs. And she kept saying in chorus, "Give it to me, my man. Give hot old Mamma Rosalee what she wants." And her words piled into each other and groans and panting, and the Padilla girl's mumbling had sounded much like that, too.

And then he heard his own voice surfacing again and saying, "It pays to keep a low profile and learn the local customs first, I guess."

"Sure. That's your philosophy out here, too, isn't it, Jerrod? Just do your job. Adapt. Try to fit in. I understand. But you shouldn't be out riding with me then, spending this nice morning with Mother

Nature and talking in and around the long shadows of Moorish hero-villains in Southwest history. It'll go hard on you if people find out, especially if this leads to anything else."

"I know, but it'll be worth it, Zuni gal. I've got something I want to show you. Something I want to give you. Something I want you to do for me, LaVonne. And trust me, you'll like it."

LaVonne reined in her horse and stopped, waiting for Jerrod and Don Juan to pull in adjacent and close. And then she leaned over toward him, balancing herself with one hand wrapped around the saddle horn and one arm on the black man's shoulder, and she kissed him, her tongue playing with the inside of his lips and mouth.

"You think I don't know what it is? Just up ahead in the shade of that cottonwood. That's where I can see what you have for me. I planned to ride straight here, you know. I have something in this canvas bag for you, too, more powerful than wine, more enchanting than any common fruit you've ever known."

Then they had tied the horses and were standing close, under a gigantic cottonwood that may have been alive when the conquistadors established the *estancias* along El Camino Real. After she had consented, only flirtatiously feigning surprise, to try the powder, her new nakedness more fantastically, shockingly strange than he had imagined, he tried to impose his complete will on her. She asked for another hit. Then she pulled at him, pinching and squeezing his arms, biting his full mouth, sucking his nose and eyes and lips, obsessed with them.

"Do you like this, Jerrod? Do you? Would you like to put a stick in my mouth too, like the Padilla girl? I know Sally, Jerrod. I know her!"

What she was saying didn't fully register. Everything seemed syncopated, delayed by a beat or two. Just as she was about to bend lower to the subservient ecstasies he desired most, she said that she had a request, too, and she reached across his pounding chest and into the canvas satchel. And she handed him two or three peyote buttons. He looked at them in a daze, preoccupied, even distanced from what was happening to him. She showed him how to bite and eat one. He followed suit. The taste was totally new, bitter and transporting, and he could not only feel the heat and friction on the metal slide bar and hear the bending blue notes of his father's old twanging guitar, he could see them! And then the fragile silver necklace hanging down from LaVonne's throat grew heavy-chained and the turquoise blue-green bear started to open its mouth and move toward him, and he saw his own head as a cactus button and the bear fetish was about to maul and consume it, growling with the same deep, unending hunger Jerrod could feel exploding inside his chest and stomach.

Very soon, LaVonne sloughed off her worry about him eating too many of the cactus buttons too fast, and the next thing he knew his hands were secured behind him and she was having her way with him, and he wondered at the intensity and the mystery of it and the sudden release and strange calm.

Then he heard first the hooves of the old hayride horses coming on him fast, almost on top of him, and he tried to roll out and away. And the thunder of the hooves turned into the rhythms of rattles, primitive, indigenous, and the muffled pounding of drums, and he heard thunder and saw flashes of distant lightning in the blue sky beyond the green leaves of the cottonwood tree. And in the cracks of lightning he saw a large man, a Moor, dressed in bizarre animal skins and traveling through the wildest of lava landscapes. He was being pursued by Pueblo people—men and women and children. And the Kern kid was in the procession, and Graham, and the school nurse, and old Pops Ferrill. And the lard-assed cafeteria cook, Alice, was lifting a long, sharp-tipped spear.

And then the tall black man turned to face his pursuers and raised the red and white gourd rattles he was carrying in little withered hands. He raised the gourds high and shook them in frantic motion above his head. Then the spear rammed hot and hard into his body, and he felt a pain like he had never known seize his chest and he heard faintly voiced words calling to him. It was the Padilla girl now become LaVonne, and the words said, "Jerrod, Esteban!"

But he couldn't respond. The pain took him away—all the way past Zuni and the pueblos to Sonora and Mexico, all the way back to Spain, all the way to earliest deep and now eclipsed and darkened Africa.

¿Quiere Combate?

"Hey, Gillie, what do you think those little black things are, man, in the cafeteria pickles?"

"What do you mean, Jesus, black things, where?"

"In the pickle jars, man. At lunch—on the tables. You know, floating around there with those big round pickles, *los pepinos, los diablillos.* You know, the ones with the warts on 'em."

"Oh, Jesus, *claro,* man, that's the spice, the peppercorns, I think they're called. Don't you have peppercorn in your mom's spice rack at home?"

"*¿Las chilitas de maiz?* Those things in the pickle jars may be spice, but not from *mi casita*'s spice rack, *tonto.* You know what makes the pickles so spicy, though?"

"No, Jesus, what makes the pickles so damn spicy, other than the sting of the pepper?"

"Well, I'm going to tell you . . . in a minute, man . . . just as soon as I see what's going to happen to Jonesy. It's his time to bat, man. *Mira, alla.*"

Both boys looked up from their hunkering and their talk and cast a long, watchful eye toward the baseball game in the near distance. Jesus was Chicano and Gilbert was Anglo, but each had assimilated into the other's culture in the South Valley. Spanish, English, Spanglish—it hardly mattered. Both boys switched back and forth, homeboys enjoying each other's company. A larger drama was taking place on the same rocky dirt that extended all across the vast school playground where the two friends crouched talking in the shade of several elm trees that helped define the third-base line of the baseball diamond. There, two ragtag pickup teams held forth on a warm, southwestern Sunday afternoon, many of the players wearing long-tailed Hawaiian sport shirts or else cotton T-shirts.

The rough playing field was situated between the stand of elm trees to the south and, to the east, the back wall of the long, gray stucco school building. A tall chain link and lead pipe backstop angled one of its arms toward the third baseman, a vigilant, lithe Chicano with a blue bandanna folded neatly across his forehead. The more easterly arm of the backstop pointed in the direction of the first baseman, who was standing with his legs spread apart, socking his trapper glove with his left fist. He was positioned almost halfway between first and second base, which like all the bases consisted of a pile of rocks and other debris.

The first baseman, a neighborhood guy named Pablo Benevidez, wore an oversized white T-shirt and a pair of khakis with the cuffs rolled high over his black canvas Converse shoes. A silver-chained crucifix dangled outside his shirt, and Gilbert saw that, simultaneously with Juan Vigil's first lobbing pitch to the batter, the first baseman took care to place the chain and crucifix again under his shirt. It was a habitual motion, repeated just before almost every pitch, and with each repositioning of the crucifix came a mumbled, muted prayer. Between prayers, Benevidez always lifted his face to the wind, wrinkling his nose. Whatever the reason, he had an uncanny sense of where the ball would go.

Gilbert didn't know everyone on the field, but all the players, both infielders and outfielders, between the encompassing arms of the backstop were either Chicano or Mexicano. Most were in their late teens. One or two were in their early twenties, except for the catcher, Little Joe Cisneros, who was younger—about fifteen—and a schoolmate of Jesus's and Gilbert's. He was not only catcher but, given the forcefulness of his commands, the self-appointed captain of this particular team—shouting orders and giving out assignments of field positions with each new batter. Little Joe was calling the pitches and coaching Juan and the other players with his own stylized but rather obvious hand signals and exhortations. The other players humored him in his presumed veteran air of expertise.

Cisneros loved baseball and was a good player, although not quite as good as he perceived himself to be. His big hope was to get some South Valley merchant to sponsor his team and get his *compadres* some uniforms. He had almost sold Lopez Opticians on the idea, and Benjie Olivas, the proud proprietor, sole owner, and manager of the Sugar Bowl Pool Hall.

Part of Little Joe's love for baseball came from his father, Chickie Cisneros, who had played semipro ball and passed his love of the game along to his son. In raising Joe, Chickie took him to every home game of the great Albuquerque Dukes, and when Little Joe was old enough, Chickie pulled some strings and got his son on as the Dukes' batboy. Little Joe was small and fast, really built to play shortstop or maybe second base, but he thought of himself as a catcher. Maybe it was because he saw the best of all panoramas from behind home plate, and maybe that was why he never wore a catcher's mask—although he did reverse his cap. Little Joe hung out with the pitcher, Juan Xavier Vigil, whose greatest passion was pool at the Sugar Bowl—and gardening: the care and cultivation and marketing of marijuana. In these endeavors, as in pitching, his middle initial stood for "Xpert." Sometimes they called him "Super X."

"Jesus," Gilbert said, surfacing from his musings and interrupting his own thoughts about the game and his friend's concentration on the athletic action to ask again, "What do you really mean about the pickles and the peppers? Tell me what's on your mind, man. I'm curious now."

"*¡Espérate, Gilbert!* Watch Little Joe work on Jonesy."

Jonesy, a redheaded Bosque Farms fellow, dug his boot heels into the dirt and swung hard at Juan's first "Xpert" lob—and missed clean, losing his balance and falling back into a little shuffle. Little Joe taunted him a bit, holding the ball high in the air and shoving it under Jonesy's nose, saying partly to Rudy and partly to Jonesy, "*Ese,* bro, that's it. That's the pitch, *hermano.* That's the one. The old sucker pitch for Farmer Jones. He's a big boy with a little bat. Right, Jonesy? How long is your bat, bosque boy?"

Jonesy's team was all Anglo, mostly cowboys from down Isleta Road and along South Second and further down Los Lunas way, around that part of the Rio Grande Valley known as Bosque Farms. Jonesy himself was a farmer boy from not too far down the Valley, along Mushroom Road, just at the outskirts of the zone that determined the district and attendance for Ernie Pyle, the high school where Jesus and Gilbert, Jonesy and Little Joe, Pablo, Rudy Olivas, the second baseman, and some of the other players had just started school that September under the tough-fisted principalship of Thadeus Gurle.

Gurle was a debonair, virile man of mixed Hispanic and African-American heritage. He was bilingual, as was required for such a Valley school, and had the reputation of handling tough schools. He was rough with the students but charming with the parents. He had intense brown eyes, made all the more intimidating by his heavy, thick-lensed horn-rimmed glasses. His mode of operation was known as glasses on, tough; glasses off, charming. "Beware the glare" was the word among teachers and students. *¡El mal ojo!* Gurle let it be known that he wanted everybody to get along at his school, and he would tolerate no bigotry or racism or prejudice— no "bickering," he called it. He meant "no fighting, no scuffling, no arguing, no fighting," period! He used an old flea-market fraternity paddle to enforce his rules.

"Hey, Gilbert," taunted Jesus, "looks like you gringo stompers are getting stomped yourself today. The shit kickers getting the shit kicked out of them and off their boots! That Jonesy swings like a rusty gate, man. *¡Bateas como viejita!*"

"Come off it, Jesus. Just finish your story and stop the 'you and the gringo stompers' shit, man. Jonesy and the boys can handle themselves, plus *todos los Chicanos.* The trouble with you guys is, when you start some story like the spice and the pickles stuff, you take forever to finish it. Just tell me the straight shit, man."

"*Orale, buey.* Okay, okay. But I've gotta see Jonesy go down for the count, man—three strikes, man. Just like that. *¡Mira!* See, see, here comes another of *jota* Juan's Super X *pelotas pedrudas. . . .*"

This time, however, to the disappointment of Jesus and some disguised pleasure of Gilbert, Jonesy hit a long ball deep to left field, with a trajectory right into the irrigation ditch that functioned as the farthest left field boundary of the makeshift ball field.

"Gringo, *falló!*" Jesus yelled. "Foul ball! Foul ball!" he shouted, rising to follow the arc of the ball through the sky, over the willows and into the ditch water. The Bosque team cheered and shouted and taunted Little Joe and Rudy and Orlando Savadra, the left fielder, who pulled to a screeching halt just short of running into the ditch.

"Jonesy can hit, man! That bruiser can hit the long ball. Did you see that, Jesus?" Gilbert gave his friend an elbow nudge. "It's far from over, just like your friggin' story, man. The pickles. What's all that about, anyway? Pickles and spices, spices and pickles. Pepe Pepino, man."

"Okay, pickles, cukes, and chukes. I'll tell you while Savadra fishes out the ball. And the *chingada* throw better be good, man.

"It all has to do with old man Gurle. You know, his tough-guy way to run the school. You realize that his father is brown, a Mexican, and his mother is black, African, right? Well, she gave our man Gurle here the magic recipe for the cafeteria pickles. And it's said that his *mamacita* came north from Belize or Haiti or New Orleans, and that's where she learned voodoo—you know, the black arts that the Caribbean people practice with dead goats and chicken blood and mumbo jumbo and frenzied dances. *¿Sabes?* So she teaches her son all these things as he grows up. His father doesn't mind. I mean, he's something of a *brujo* himself, man. So they pass their ways along to their *hijo*, man. Gurle can cast a spell, man. Gurle *era el duende*. He can conjure. And that's just what he's doing with the pickles—conjuring, man."

"Come off it, Jesus. You think I'm crazy enough to believe this bullshit? Where did you hear such a cock-and-bull bunch of stuff, anyway? You're hitting foul balls yourself, amigo."

"No, Gillie, listen, it's true. So, anyway, when he was young, all he thought about was girls, see. You know, GIRLS, and what they did and what he did and how they could do it together. Man, look at that throw! Orlando's got an arm, man—¡*tíralo, tíralo!* Thataway, bro. ¡*Qué bueno,* bro! Good job, Orlando! And the ball is wet, man, soaking wet, and heavy."

"Jesus, he's just throwing back a foul ball. It doesn't count how he throws it or how he gets it back. Get back to Gurle and the girls and the pickles, man. What's the goddamn point?"

"You haven't figured it out, then, *vato?* Voodoo, girls, the pickles?"

"I don't know what you're talking about. This game and this story are going nowhere fast. Hurry up with the story. Eugene's coming up to talk with Jonesy. He's telling him where to hang the next one. Look, Little Joe's getting worried, man."

"Now who's drifting away from the story, Gilbert? Let me get back to fill in some of the details so you can figure this thing out and I can watch you try to handle the shock of it. *Tengo miedo, hombre.* It's more serious than you realize, man.

"Anyway, as a *chapito* Gurle liked the girls, see. And you know what cucumbers remind you of, right? You know pickles can give you a hard-on just looking at them. And girls really like pickles, too—the big ones especially. I mean, you look at those long ones, *los grandes,* and they give you the hots, man, *verdad?* But a whole jar of cucumbers standing tall, man, a whole damn jar of 'em. Just think. But what's a pickled cucumber anyway, but a cucumber in a damn pickle, *sabes?* I mean, that thought can calm you down, too. You get excited, then you calm down. Just think of the contradictions in one jar of pickles. Sweet and sour, fire and ice. ¡*Los diablillos, los adobos!*"

"You're pathetic, man. You can't tell a story worth shit. I don't want to hear anymore. Let's just watch the ball game and not say a word, okay? I mean, if you think I have to sit here and listen to this crazy *caca,* you are yourself *poco loco en la cabeza.* How a guy can look at a jar of pickles and see it as some concoction of Spanish fly and saltpeter is beyond me."

"Listen, Gillie! As part of his *sota*'s love potion in reverse, you know, to calm her son down from all his interest in what boys do and what girls do and what they do together, Gurle's mother started feeding him special pickles. They were sour, but Gurle still liked the juice and the cool, round feel of the pickle in his mouth, the bumps and warts on them sliding rough through his lips, and the crunch and bite of them. And he started carrying around a little jar of pickles and giving them to all the girls. And the girls would take them and run away, and then he would go watch and eat more pickles while he watched. See, you're getting the hots just as I tell you, right, man?"

"You are one sick *vato*, Jesus. Really sick. Watch the game, for Christ's sake."

"No, listen. Gurle liked the girls even more after his mother started feeding him her pickles. And what was worse, he started liking the boys! You know, the boys! *Los muchachos. Chapitos.*"

"*¡Basta!* Look, Juan is starting his windup, and you can start your shut up. You're way out in left field on this one, man. Cock and bull become cocksucker shit. *¡Cállate!*"

"No, no! So his mother had to take extreme measures, desperate remedies, you know. She had to modify the potion. So she put in those black things, told him what they really were, and scared the piss and vinegar right out of him! No more interest in girls, man. No more interest in sex of any kind with anyone, *mujer o hombre*. Not after she told him what they really were, those little black 'pepper' things, you call 'em. He just got meaner and meaner and meaner."

"*¡Qué loco! Cállate*, here comes Juan's wet-ball pitch." Everyone on both sides was watching that pitch. All the players, Rudy and Pablo and Orlando and the others, and especially Little Joe, were watching it. And in the mesmerism inspired by the slow, spinning, waterlogged, arcing ball, Little Joe extended his glove and moved in a bit too close over the plate. He didn't notice. The others didn't notice. Nobody noticed until that loud split second of collision when Jonesy's powerful swinging bat hit Little Joe, crack, full on the head.

There was a terrible breaking sound, and Little Joe fell down fast and hard. Everyone was horrified, at first frozen and then yelling and crying and running toward home plate. Little Joe's left foot covered the base, almost as if he had slid into home and was lying on his back looking up at the sky in some moment of celebration.

Except his head was bleeding red from under his black hair and blood was coming out his ears and his nose. And his eyes had rolled back white and twitching in his head.

"*Está muerto. ¡Venga la mujer muerte! ¡Madre de Dios!*" Jesus said softly under his breath. "Joe's gone, man!"

"Jesus, Joe! Son of a bitch!" Gilbert gasped. He'd seen what a bat could do to a piñata, crack and split it and generally knock the stuffing out.

Jonesy still held the bat, but he was clearly stunned and shaken. He stepped over to Joey in one big loping stride, and Eugene raced up to Jonesy's side and placed his hand on his shoulder as they both looked down at a kid everyone thought was dead, or soon would be. The rest of the Bosque boys moved toward home plate from the sidelines. By the time Rudy and Pablo and the other in-fielders reached Little Joe, Orlando and the outfielders were al-ready crossing the bases, converging on home plate, moving scared and angry and fast.

Gilbert saw everything in grainy slow motion, all movement and sound subdued against the whizzing swing and lingering crack of the bat on Little Joe's head. He suddenly thought of Chickie and how he had seen him one night at a Dukes game, smiling, drinking a beer and enjoying himself, watching Little Joe, his son, take care of the bats on a nice summer night while Ricky Sanchez, the home-town pitcher, hummed a no-hitter and the Dukes beat the crap out of the Pampa Oilers. And some inebriated fat fan took down his pants and mooned the field, saying, "Kiss my pimpled New Mexico ass, Texas! Kiss my pretty pimpled, chili-peppered New Mexico ass!" And then all the Dukes fans went crazy and picked up the cheer.

As Gilbert moved with the rest of the crowd toward home plate, he heard out of the blurred motion in front of him on the field the words he had heard all his life, dreaded words, but ones he knew were as important as any words could be. "*¿Quieren combate? ¿Quieren combate, gringos?*" Rudy and Pablo and Louie Lovato were squaring off against Jonesy and Eugene and Lyman Overton. Russell Birdsall was ready to go at it with Orlando.

"Goddamn fuckin' A! Fuckin' asshole, right! Come on, you chickenshit hophead greasers!" Russell was shouting. Jonesy and Eugene just stood there, big and barrel-chested, ready for any comer.

Pablo put one hand on his crucifix and the other in his pants pocket, feeling for the ridges of the stag handle and the cross-shaped S-curved hilt of the four-inch lock-blade knife he always carried. Rudy's eyes were tight on Jonesy's hands, watching the whiteness of his knuckles around the bat handle. He knew Jonesy could crack two or three more heads in the blink of an eye.

"*¡Trucha, carnales! ¡Mucho ojo! Mira la batea, cuidado.*"

Beside him on the sidelines Gilbert heard Jesus shouting, "Fight, man, fight! There's going to be a big fight! *¡Chingao!* We'll have to take sides, Gilbert, if we go over there. I'll have to fight for my *primo*."

"But it was an accident, Jesus. An accident. Jonesy didn't plan to do that. You know Little Joe, how he gets gung ho and creeps up on the plate. Catching *es su mole*, man. He'll reach his glove out and then scooch up closer, way too far over the plate and into the batter's zone, man. You've seen him do that before. This was just the wrong time and the wrong place for him, Jesus. You know that."

"*Claro que sí, hombre.* But it means a fight sooner or later, a fight for sure. *Listo o no listo.*"

When the two boys reached the others, the hostility was heavy, primed and ready to explode. There was pushing and shoving and one verbal accusation after another. Little Joe's teammates had raided the rock pile bases and held the stones and clods like so many adobe-brown mortar shells ready for delivery.

"Give him some breathing room, man, give Joe some room," Jesus spoke up when he reached the crowd.

"Somebody bring a car over here so we can take him up to Bernalillo County Hospital," came a response from Gilbert.

Little Joe looked like he needed a hearse more than anything else—looked like he was dead. But he was still breathing, somebody determined, braving the pool of blood that now outlined Joe's head like a martyr's halo.

"Yeah, bring a car. He's still breathing. The little fucker's still breathing!"

Floyd Rafferty, one of the Bosque Farms crowd, offered his pickup. But by that time Robert Avila was pulling up, and the crowd was making room for his Chevy Bel Air. It was baby blue and white, and they all called him "Dydee" because of it and his baby face.

They opened the door and lifted Little Joe, limp and bloody and still bleeding, onto the backseat.

"No se preocupe. Llavarlo después," Avila volunteered.

"Give 'em plenty of room," Jesus kept up the directions, and then he turned to Gilbert. "Man, look at that poor guy—bleeding from his ears and his nose and the side of his head. If he's not dead *ahora,* it won't be long."

Pablo crossed himself, and Jesus and the other *carnales* followed suit and each said a soft prayer. Jonesy and Eugene offered to follow Avila to the hospital, but Pablo spoke up, directing his comments to Jonesy especially. "Monday after school, shit kickers. *¡Aquí!* Monday! And you better bring more than your bat with you *caca vacas. ¡Pélame la verga! ¡Vete a la verga!"*

"Bite me, Pancho! We'll be there," answered Russell. "We'll be there!" Just as his words trailed off into another taunt, someone threw a rock. It flew right toward Gurle's office window, breaking the glass into a clatter of small pieces. For a second, they all remembered the sound of Jonesy's big bat cracking Little Joe's head, and they were silent.

"See," said Jesus, looking at his friend, "I told you it meant a fight. And now old Groucho Gurle will want to know who's been breaking his window on a nice Sunday afternoon. And he's already after me, man, for what I did in that *runca* Spencer's class when I hid her roll book in the trash can. Let's get going, Gilbert. Nobody can help Little Joe now, not even a voodoo doctor with special remedies and herbs and chicken blood recipes. Gurle'll get plenty more of the *chingada* little black things for his evil pepper pickles now."

"What? The pickles again? Jesus, I just don't know what the hell you're talking about and what a softball through his window and a kid with a broken head has to do with it. Gurle'll be mad as hell, sure, but . . ."

"You'll figure it out. Monday, you'll see firsthand how really mean that bastard Gurle is. He'll get wind of the fight, *qué no. ¡Qué cabrón! ¡Qué pinche mal suerte! ¡Vámonos!"*

Gilbert could tell the fight was on as soon as he got off the school bus. The words *quieren combate, quieren combate* still hung in the air. Fight it would be. He could tell. Students were grouped along the chain-link boundary between Kit Carson Elementary School next door and Ernie Pyle High School. Even the Kit Carson kids knew. They could feel the tension, and they imitated the impending combat in a kind of pygmy pantomime, jumping and horsing around and wrestling each other to the ground.

There was the usual rush of parents dropping off their children in front of the Kit Carson doors, but even more cars came this morning than usual, slowing the high school bus traffic to a prolonged and frustrating stop. It was a yellow-and-black traffic jam, knotted and twisted by impatient, honking bus drivers—old guys with grizzled, stubby beards and no teeth; dumpy women in caps, chewing gum, the flesh of their arms waving with each turn of the big steering wheel. Even the crossing guard was out of sorts, blowing his whistle fast and furiously.

When Gilbert stepped down from his bus and walked toward the concrete benches under the portico of the school entryway, he heard the words again.

"*Combate, combate, ellos combatan* now, *poco mas tarde, a tres* or *cuatro, ¿quiere combate?*"

"Are you gonna fight, too . . . ?"

Again and again, in any number of voices, "Fight, fight, *combate, combate.*"

The words kept coming, reverberating, everywhere in the air. *En toda la escuela, en todo el mundo.* It was an incantation, a whispered chant, distorted, unbalanced, out of sync, but building to some greater unison and climax.

"Fight, Fight, FIGHT! ¡*Combate, Combate, COMBATE!*"

The message reverberated with such force and volubility that it seemed Ernie Pyle himself might return from the grave and try to cover this story of imminent warfare. The school was an impending war zone, the South Valley school grounds and baseball field and irrigation ditch now being reconnoitered and zoned by the generals of both sides. Jonesy's forces were clustered next to the elementary school fence, and Little Joe's forces, led by Juan, gathered around the chain-link backstop and spread out intermittently along the ditch bank. Two armies glowered across the rocky playground.

Gilbert sat down in the neutral territory of the entranceway. He usually met Jesus at the bus drop, but today was different. Some other decisions had to be made. Maybe Jesus was already over by the fence with his *primos y hermanos*. Gilbert could see Avila hunkering down next to his Bel Air, drawing lines in the sand with a stick. The blue-and-white car seemed positioned like part of a colorful military motorcade involved in delivering top brass to the command post.

"Hey, man," he heard a voice say behind him, from the direction of the fence. Jesus was there for the action of the day. "Hey, man. It's gonna happen. Today's the day, just like they promised. It's really goin' down today."

"Yeah, I know. And so does everyone else. *Las palabras de combate están en el aire*. Where's the chief, old Gurle and his bodyguards?"

"*El jefe* Gurle, he's patrolling the whole walk around, both sides, man. He's no *idiota*. I saw him talking to Jonesy when I got here. Now he's over collaring Juan and some of the others. Old voodoo man Gurle wanted to know if I knew anything, if I was here yesterday. I shrugged and headed over here. Juan was looking my way, man."

"Say, Jesus, how's Little Joe doin'? What's the news?"

"Bad injury for sure. A double fracture or double concussion or something. They had to open up his head in surgery and relieve some pressure caused by the ruptured blood vessels. They say he's alive and conscious, but he can't see right, and he can't talk. A nurse told Pablo that Joe's head must feel like every piece of fireworks that ever exploded on the Fourth of July, man. He might never be the same again. And Chickie, man, he can't handle it. They had to give him some sedatives or knock him out somehow, too. What a *chingada* mess, man. You saw it. Like hitting a watermelon."

"*Claro, exactamente.* I just keep hearing that cracking sound, and then it shifts into the sound of people saying *'combate.'* It's hard to believe all of this started on a nice leisurely weekend and us just telling wild stories."

"*¡Qué vato!* You still don't get it, not yet? It'll hit you like a sledge-hammer, man, when you figure it out. I hope I don't have to spell it all out to you. Have you heard anything from your side? Did you talk to Jonesy?"

"My side? Are you going to fight? Are we going to fight?"

"It looks like we might have to, man. This is major shit, Gilbert. Big *caca!*"

"The word on the bus, from Yaples, Jonesy's cousin, is that Jonesy's really sorry for what happened, but he won't back down. He's no coward, as you know. And Eugene keeps him stirred up with all his anger and hatred. Just look at all the shit kickers around the back steps over there. I mean, there are some tough motherfucker bas-tards over there. Moose is there, and David Lowes and Lyman Overton—the angel of death, man. I mean I've seen those guys do a hundred push-ups and never blink—fifty friggin' push-ups per arm!"

"Shit, man, speak of the angel of death, here comes the devil of death, *el diablo* himself, right now. Old man Gurle. Watch your *pepinos*, man. Watch 'em!"

"Boys, good morning—and let's get right to the point. You recall we worked out the fight you two guys had the first week of school. Some talking. Some negotiating. Some persuading. Some com-mands. We worked it out, right? And I need your assistance in this morning's situation. You two boys can be my intermediaries in this rather tense, distressing fight situation that's percolating here this morning, to think of my morning coffee, which I sorely need, yes, I sorely need. *¡Mi cafetita!* Be in my office right after homeroom. I'll inform your teacher—who is it, Mr. Foster, in U.S. history?"

"No, sir, it's Mr. Sandoval, and we have wood shop first hour."

"Thank you . . . , Gilbert, is it? Yes, thank you. Not fat-face Fos-ter but Señor Sandyballs in shop. I'll tell him. You bring your friend here to my office first thing after homeroom."

Gurle turned and walked back into the building.

Jesus cringed with memories of his last visit to Gurle's office and with rekindled realization of just what measures Gurle was capable of going to as a devil incarnate.

"Damn it, Gilbert! Damn it all to hell. Remember that shit I told you about the pickles. We've had it now, man, from all sides. You've just gone and pickled our pricks, man. Just wait until Juan and Jonesy hear about this. Intermediaries, my ass!"

"What was I to do, man? That was an order from the supreme commander. He'll have our ass any way he wants it, whether we cooperate or resist or whatever."

All through homeroom Gilbert thought back to his first visit to Gurle's office, the fight and why he had been taken into the office with Jesus. They'd been playing basketball. There was the drive for the basket, the blocking of Jesus, the hand slipping off the ball and into his face, the body contact of chests and legs. The words echoed in his head again from now and from back then, "¿Quiere combate, gringo cabrón?" There was Jesus's quick punch to Gilbert's nose and the stars—oh, what must Little Joe have seen and felt— and the tears and the blood. And then, then, the wild swings and blows back, hitting Jesus high and low and in between in a windmill of flailing arms and fists. Kicking and stomping, shit-kicker style. Charging and holding and wrestling, ready to bite and scratch and pinch and punch—whatever it took, just like he'd been taught by his cuñado, Billy Bert, in the backyard.

Then the march into the principal's office to see the tall, dark man with his hand-tied paisley bow tie and his heavy-framed glasses, the man who turned out to be Gurle, the voodoo man. And him standing over the boys and staring at them, staring at the blood all over Gilbert's yellow wool sweater vest and the sleeves of his neatly ironed white shirt with the starched creases that his mother took so much pride in. Gilbert didn't remember what Gurle had said, just the quick whacks of the paddle, down from the wall. First him, and then Jesus. And that was that.

Except that then he and Jesus were friends, and Gurle was the enemy. Gurle had brought two fighting boys, gringo and Chicano, together in mutual resolve against a new enemy. But Jesus was still somehow separate and apart. Take the damn pickle story, for instance, about Gurle at the root of some sinister plot to poison the school and spread his inclination for whippings and beatings and blows, for violence to bring peace. And Little Joe and Jonesy, just catcher and batter and one mistake, and a war was pending. It didn't all add up for Gilbert. Not yet.

Gurle's office was just like Gilbert remembered it, except for the broken window that had just been discovered that morning, slivers of glass still sprinkled and scattered on the floor like so many hardened crystalline tears.

There were the same manipulative questions: "Now, boys, tell me, just how did my office window get broken? How and who and what do you know about all this? From the top, now. Let's hear it from the top."

The two boys looked at each other with a shared stubbornness born out of their past visit here and the time they had spent, almost always together, since then. And Gurle knew something had changed. He had not seen this bond between the boys before the instructive paddling. Silence—but with an echo of the remembered slaps of the board, the thump of Jonesy's bat on the head of Little Joe Cisneros. And there was the paddle, displayed like a trophy on the wall. Where was Jonesy's bat now? Gilbert couldn't help wondering.

"Come on, now, boys. I know about Cisneros—his injury—and Rusty Jones and this big fight that's supposed to take place sixth hour. Well, it ain't gonna happen, boys, not on my watch. Besides, what's a little smack on the head, eh? The little guy will be okay. Maybe a little punchy, but okay. And I'll bet he doesn't want to play catcher for a while, though. But back to my window—tell me, who threw this rock?"

And Gurle tossed the round gray stone up and down in his hand, taunting the boys with the testicular heft and feel of the stone. "Some nice little *pelota* here, right, boys?" Jesus and Gilbert squirmed with the feel of old Gurle placing their own balls in the vice grip of his hands. "Come on, boys, have some *cojones* and tell me. Cough it up! Spill the beans! I'm gonna find out soon, and it can help if you tell me now."

Jesus cast his eyes over Gurle's shoulder and pointed faintly to Gilbert with his chin, drawing what he thought was subtle attention to the photograph of an old woman. There was a space clear on the bookcase that looked somewhat like a family shrine—not so much a place of acknowledgment or recognition or honor as of dominion. A kind of altar to some overweight goddess! And then Jesus mouthed the word "mother" to Gilbert, pointing again with his chin to the photograph.

But Gurle noticed. "What did you say, you little *pendejo*? Say that again a bit louder, and I'll paddle that skinny ass of yours so hard that it'll collapse and take your little shriveled-up pecker with it. But your dick won't be able to hide anywhere, because I'll smack it right back out of your asshole, front and back, going and coming. Just say that again, you little peckerface!"

"He didn't say anything, Mr. Gurle, honest, other than wanting us to say we weren't even around the school Sunday. Not here, anyway. We were . . . we were at my house. And we're sure very sorry about Joe and your window and this fight that's brewing."

"You lying little *pinche cabroncitos! ¡Quítate!* Get out of here, the both of you. I'll get to the truth about this in good time, and when I do it's good-bye to two little lying turds I know."

The rest of the morning was slow, ever so slow, in passing. After shop the two friends went into separate classes but agreed to meet in the cafeteria.

"For *lunche,* man," said Jesus, rubbing his stomach. "See you in the line first lunch period. I'll buy you an Eskimo pie. I owe you one. Cuts the spell of the pickles, man."

Gilbert was late for lunch because of all the gossip and rumors flying up and down the hall and in the classrooms. By the time he met Jesus, he was full of news about the plans for the fight and the odds on who was going to win. As he crowded in line with Jesus, warding off the grumbling complaints of his classmates, he turned somewhat out of breath to brief his *compadre.*

"They say Juan asked Jonesy to square off with him. Just the two of them, no holds barred. But then, they say, Pablo challenged him, too. Weapons of choice, Jesus. Weapons of choice! That means *las navajas,* knives, man. Pablo's knife is wicked, man. I've seen it."

"This is going to be very brutal. There will be casualties," Jesus said as he picked up his tray and a plate of enchiladas, Spanish rice, and pinto beans, and an extra Coke. "*Dos manticados, por favor. Dame dos.*"

The sight of a tall Anglo cowboy and a stocky Chicano rummaging their way to a table for lunch looked even more unusual today than in previous times. Gilbert wore Levi's and roughout boots now slick and blackened around the heels and toes, and Jesus wore khakis and sharp-pointed, highly shined black boots that zipped up the sides. Gilbert was blond, with a heavy shock of hair cascading over his forehead; Jesus had glistening black hair, long on the sides and cut into a flattop with a single curl flipped down in front. They were the epitome of two cultures coming together out of ancient rivalries, friendship out of their own shared suffering and individualized but mutual respect. They took a table midway down the large room that served as a lunchroom at noon and as the study hall in the afternoon. Today it was a segregated lunchroom—divided along ethnic and racial lines rather than age and gender and grades, as it was ordinarily.

By the time Gilbert followed him to a seat, Jesus was handing him a Coke and separating the table's condiments and furnishings. He slid the bowl of whipped honey and peanut butter, the chrome, diamond-embossed napkin holder, and the large tin salt-and-pepper shakers to the center of the table for sharing. But he pushed the notorious jar of pickles far down to the end of the table, as much out of sight and use as possible. Isolation made the pickles all the more sinister.

Jesus was the first to speak over the cafeteria noise. "Two times now in this guy's office. Thanks for the help. He must have thought I insulted him and his mother. You saw it, though. You saw the picture I was pointing to. Well, she's the one. She's the *bruja*, man. The old mother witch of his childhood who taught him all the incantations, the rituals and fetishes and trances. All the whole bag of shit, man. Even how to get the stuff in the pickles."

"What's the big deal about the picture? A guy's entitled to have a photograph of his mother or anybody in his office, I guess."

"I tell you, she's the one who taught him, man. The one who started him off on mean street. It's her recipe, don't you see? The little black balls in the pickles. See 'em floating around still in the jar? I just barely moved it down to the end of the table and all those black things are sailing around in the juice. And didn't you see the stuff around the picture frame? The different kinds of objects and dried herbs and stuff around the base of the picture? I pointed it out to you, man."

"Look, Jesus, we got a very big fight coming this afternoon, re-member? We have to choose sides or be in big trouble, and you keep talking about pickles and a picture in Gurle's office. I didn't understand your story yesterday, and I don't understand it today. You're acting more afraid of that pickle jar down there than you are of Jonesy or Juan or Eugene or Pablo, or even Gurle and what he can do with that paddle of his."

"Don't you see, it's Gurle, it's him, he's the cause of all the trouble—the accident yesterday, the fight this afternoon, our fight playing basketball. He's not only bad luck, he *creates* bad luck. He's evil itself. *Cabrón mala suerte. ¡El demonio!* Only our friendship can ward him off, but that's just what he wants to destroy. Friend-ship. Love. Beauty. Fun. All the good things. He's poisoned all of us with his goddamn pickles. *¡El diablillo!*"

Between bites of lunch and intermittent greetings with other friends of both Little Joe's and Jonesy's, and between talk about what would and wouldn't and might and might not happen at the fight after school, Gilbert looked around the cafeteria and tried to take count of just how many people were eating pickles. He couldn't believe he was doing it, but he was. Jesus's talk was finally really starting to frighten him. He kept thinking of the strangeness of it all. A jar of pickles on every table in a school cafeteria, and the unusually large number of black peppercorns floating around in each jar, almost as if they had a life of their own. He had never eaten a peppercorn as such, except maybe by accident. He just assumed they gave the pickles their strange contradictory taste. And this school obsession with the pickles, which he realized weren't like regular store pickles. Not as refined, more primitive, closer to home-canned pickles or pickles from a large barrel in a delicates-sen or a country store.

While Jesus and the others rattled on in their excitement, Gil-bert became mesmerized by the little balls of hard blackness bounc-ing off the long, firm, yellow-green pickle shanks. Through the cafeteria noise and clamor, as if drawn into the floating, murky liquid of the pickle jar and the past, he heard Little Joe's head crack again and saw him spread limp on the rock-strewn ground. Gilbert felt a strange urge to get up and eat the whole jar of pickles and then run through the room and smash everything in sight, to yield himself over to the strange hysteria. He was starting to believe that this strange mood of violence was due to Jesus's persistent talk about the pickles.

If only Gilbert could smash all the jars on all the tables, maybe then Jesus would give him some relief from his crazy sense of constant, never-ending suspense. Always spinning out the story, saying the same things, never really progressing. Why the fuck couldn't Jesus tell a simple story and end it? What were these dark floating beads of blackness, anyway? What the hell were they?

And Jesus, who was he but a damn greaser Chicano? If he wanted to fight on the side of the Chicanos, his own kind, let him. He would go up against Jesus, too, if he had to. It was hypnotic, this violence. He too would butt heads, throw blows, risk knife wounds and the bittersweet, pleasurable pain of giving the hits, taking the hits and the blows that would come to his own body in just a few hours.

Little Joe wouldn't be the only one to get his head busted. Gilbert would bust a few. He would join with Jonesy and the gringo stompers—his kind. There was really no other choice. Jesus would choose his kind, do what he had to do. Gurle could try to stop it, but he would get his head busted, too—maybe with his own damn paddle.

"Hey, Gilbert, where are you, man? That's the bell." Jesus had his hand stretched out across the table to tap Gilbert's hand and get his attention again. "Fifth period already. The count begins. Preliminaries are just about over. Almost time to fight. *Queremos combate, ¿no?* Let's go. You can't sit here dreaming of what it would be like in some backseat screwing some *wisa*. Who you gonna be fuckin' with in the fight, man? *¿Quién quiere, hermano?* I'll try to find you by the baseball field again, Gillie, by the backstop where Little Joe got it. It's gonna be bad, so take care, man. Stay away from any knives, and don't let them stab or cut your chest. That's the first rule. Dodge any thrusts to the chest. *Hasta el combate que viene. Buena suerte, amigo.*"

Gilbert, with the sound of the bell, and Jesus's good-bye, slowly roused himself from his reverie. Then he picked up his tray and walked to the end of the table, where he picked up the jar of pickles for a long look at the contents. The jar was warm and slick in his hand. The black balls seemed like bullets, and the pickle shafts like spears. The whole mix felt ready to explode and vomit forth in putrid green volatility.

When the next bell rang Gilbert hightailed it down the hall to the back of the school. He wasn't alone. A mass of students crowded down the hallway with him, and when he pushed through the heavy double doors and passed under Ernie Pyle's aluminum-lettered name, many students were already formed into camps. They were easy to identify. Avila had pulled his blue-and-white Bel Air around and parked it right beside home plate. All of Little Joe's buddies were massed along both sides of the backstop, backing up to the Chevy. Jonesy and his friends were settled throughout the outfield, spilling over into second base and the infield.

A third group was gathering under the line of elm trees where Gilbert and Jesus had hunkered just a day before, talking and telling stories, *cuentos y chistes*, and watching what they thought was just the fun of a Sunday afternoon softball game. Other students with other motives were there now—standing and squatting and taunting anybody who looked their way.

Gurle and a bunch of his teachers, including Foster, the shop teacher, Chavez, the history teacher, and two tough *pendejo* coaches brought in from Pittsburgh to teach soccer, of all things, were working with little effect to disperse the crowd of milling, angry students.

Gilbert headed for the stand of elm trees again. Around the front corner of the school he could see the dust of school buses coming back down the road to pick up the Kit Carson kids and any Ernie Pyle students wanting to avoid combat. He could see, in his mind's eye, the parents in their cars, coming innocently to the elementary school at dismissal time, and he imagined their little reunions along the lines of his own past gatherings with those sent to pick him up after school. Such distant, naïve days they seemed to him now. The pieces of paper with proud, large-lettered printing and crayon colors filling in the blue mimeographed lines of daily lessons. In the distance he could hear the motors of the buses and the bells of the elementary school ringing high on the adobe-brown stuccoed walls. Fights back in elementary school, such as they were, had seemed so much fun. This fight promised serious injury.

"I made it, man. I made it." It was Jesus. *"¡Estoy aquí!* Some battlefield, huh? We're gonna play hardball now, man! Who's gonna call the game? This ain't no Sunday picnic, *¿qué no?"*

"What would Little Joe think now, if he could think . . . if he could see this?"

"Yeah, if he could still see at all, right, man? I hope Juan nails Jonesy's ass and that Pablo gets that loudmouthed rabble-rouser Eugene."

"And you? You gonna fight? You want to fight? *¿Quiere combate, amigo?* Are we gonna walk out there and choose sides before the fight begins or wait or what? You against me? *¡Qué lástima,* man! Too bad. Us fighting again like before, like the last time."

"We'll have to, sure. *Seguro,* man. But I just want to try and watch for awhile, don't you? We can't stand here on the sidelines too long, though, like we're here forever. I mean, really on the sidelines here with the *wisas y runcas y viejitas,* man. It'll have to be blows for us, too, Gillie. *"Nosotros también, juntos."*

"Pues, pienso que tú tienes razón. Not that there aren't enough people to fight without us, man."

"Fight! Fight!" someone shouted from the outfield. The cry was taken up by the crowd by the backstop, and in an instant the words were bouncing off the building walls and resonating with the final, dying school bells and the grind of the buses pulling away from the front of the school.

"Fight! Fight!"

"¡Combate! Quiere combate. Qué combatan. ¡Qué comenzca! ¡Adelante! ¡Santiago!"

"Charge the motherfuckers!"

And then the two groups were converging, mixing together, duking it out, kicking and scratching and swinging. Violence was upon them with vengeance.

And there in the middle, lost as if in some wild stampede of bison on the prairie, were Gurle and his teachers. Gurle had his hands and arms up, protecting his heavy-rimmed glasses and his gleaming bald head. Then Eugene rushed up and pushed him, and Gurle's glasses were knocked lopsided for a fraction of a second before they fell to the ground. And then it looked like Jonesy stomped on them and both sides cheered. And then they were all up and on Gurle and his henchmen, hitting them and kicking them in frenzied revenge and blind, mindless hatred.

The third group of spectators were screaming, and one girl's voice could be heard in a combined yell and whimper, "No. Oh, no! They're killing Mr. Gurle and the teachers. Help him, someone. Help them!"

And then another volley of voices shouted, "Kill the bastards! Stomp them to shit. Hit 'em and slice 'em and cut 'em to pieces."

Gilbert looked at Jesus. Jesus looked at Gilbert. Then they were running, too, heading for the ditch, not the center of the fight. Running, running, out of panic and fear and revulsion at anger become evil, at wickedness gone wild. Running away from the destruction of it all, from their old and present hatreds. Running toward their hard-kept friendship. "To the ditch where we had the clod fight," Jesus yelled, between huge gasps of breath. "To the ditch!"

When Jesus and Gilbert reached the ditch bank, they crossed the wooden conservancy bridge and reached the maintenance road along the top of the levee. They ran until their sides ached, and then they slowed down and finally stopped to look back across the steady-flowing, muddy ditch water, at the school and the warfare going on there.

The fighting was spreading into the buildings, where they could hear windows shattering. The boys stood there, aghast at the commotion of it all. They gasped for breath and bent over, spitting out saliva and bile, trying to catch their breath and ease the pain in their sides.

Gurle was down on the ground, curled into a dark little ball, and everyone was taking turns kicking him in the gut and in the head and face. All the two friends could hear was the roar and screaming of the crazed crowd. And the cracking and thud of the blows.

And then Jesus blurted, "You shouldn't slice off dead people's nipples, Gilbert, and put them in pickle jars. Not even if your mother shows you how."

Gilbert drew in his breath at the gross horror of it and at Jesus's superstition and the mystery finally told. And he wondered, amid his shudders, whether even Ernie Pyle himself in all his wartime experiences had ever, ever heard such an explanation of the world run amok. The world in such a fuckin' goddamn *pepino* pickle.

Time Tagger

The softness of the cement surprised him. The stick penetrated the still-wet grayness and slid down and around and back up to the top in looping, glistening strokes—like the track left by a slow-marching snail. The imprint of the letter was rough and deep. Along the canyon-edged walls of each letter, miniature boulders—pieces of tiny gravel in flecks of light tan and coral red—shifted and tumbled into the carved crevices, connecting little turns and twirls and swoops etched by the stick he had picked from the debris at the edge of the driveway. Two-by-four pine forms outlined the newly poured and finished cement, its smooth, even surface just beginning to set up and cure.

He had walked by the same driveway, before this recent transformation, for the past year or two, but it had never called out to him like now—now with its wet, gray, placid pool-like surface. But the slip of the surface was deceiving, he knew, for beneath it was a base of stone and gravel and oozing, watery concrete, waiting to set. Waiting for some signature, some mark of that time and that place and his passing through it like a latter-day Oñate coming across the lava malpais to El Morro.

The driveway until now had been a hard-packed white caliche road giving access to Abe's Autos. "New Used Cars for YOU" was Abe's motto, and in an obvious play on Uncle Sam, he had a picture of Emiliano Zapata, the Mexican bandit king, pointing out of a sign, and from behind his bushy mustaches and *bigote,* at potential customers.

Abe had always waved and smiled at Richie. He would point at people just like his picture of Zapata, like pointing a make-believe pistol, and the boy would turn off the cement sidewalk up the bumpy *caliche* surface of Abe's driveway to talk with the used-car salesman. Once in a great while he was even allowed to sit in Abe's newest used car or car-truck acquisition. "*Orale, jovencito,* this Camino is one good *truka-coche,* bro. *¡Qué bueno!*" Caminos and Rancheros Abe would take in trade, but he stopped short of any full-sized "truck." Autos were Abe's thing. Not trucks.

"*Primo,*" Abe used to call him. Or "*Cuate,*" or "*Choppo,*" or "*Joven.*" Or some other slightly disparaging but kidding term of acceptance.

"Hey, *Primo,* how's it hangin', bro? How's the old set of wheels holding out, bro? When you gonna trade up, *ese* bro? *¡Cuatro ruedas sobre dos son mucho mejor, muchísimo mejor!*" And Abe would give Richie a special, cool Chicano handshake, clasping all fingers and then touching thumbs, and the boy would beam and maybe get a cold Coke from the old red machine and "hang" with his *cuñao,* his *compa.*

Abe had a wonderful '59 Chevy drop top, red and white, with a blunt nose and rear fenders that flared out flat into wings. He kept it in great shape, smart and sassy, complete with its own special license tag: ESEBRO.

"Dumb *caca* gringos, man, they think my name is Esebro, *carnal.* Can you dig it, *ese vato,* can you dig it, bro?"

Richie loved being hip and in the know with Abe and loved trying to make his bicycle as cool as Abe's Chevy and some of the other cars in the lot. He added handle-grip streamers—especially chosen red and white in honor of the '59. And there were white rubber mud flaps with the round chrome-ringed red reflector positioned smack on the back and squarely in the middle, again in honor of the '59. There was a genuine saddle-tan leather seat and a horn and light and compass, all bolted onto the handlebars. There were stabilizer bars that ran from the handlebars down to the front axle sprocket, and there were precision-cut leather straps around each axle that bounced and turned and shined the chrome with every rotation of the wheel.

Richie had a little license tag behind the saddle that he'd found on a revolving stand at Woolworth's. His was a California tag, and it said "Richard." Not quite as cool as "Richie," but better than "Dick." He had spent some minutes hoping to find "Ricardo" but soon knew all the names were in English. He had never really minded his name, Richard Hardesty, but he didn't like to be called Dick. At times, resisting the nickname meant a fight. "Little Dick," "Dick face," "Dick breath," "Dick stick." He even loathed the name "Dickeys" on jeans. "Richie" was what he had written in the fresh cement. It was a matter of identity, of pride—his name as he wanted it. His mark. His time tag.

There was a new owner now at Abe's and a new company name painted over Abe's sign. A new driveway, too. Cement. Solid. *Firme* . . . harder than the caliche and soon to be more fixed than even Richie's hanging with Abe. But for the moment the cement was subject to change, subject to shaping.

COUSIN CLIFF'S TRUCK AND CAR CORRAL, read the new sign. This guy Cliff was stocking farm trucks, of all things. He deserved to be tagged. Unlike Abe, this Cousin Cliff guy had no class. How would Abe find out about it, anyway—Richie's name carved in the new cement? And what would he care? And so what if this Cliff guy saw it? Maybe Abe had a bundle of money now. But Abe should have told him something about an impending sale of the lot. Maybe old *Esebro* Abe was already south of the border, cruising his Chevy down the Baja coast. ¡*Orale, buey!* ¡*Firme! La vida buena.*

Right now, Richie had the concrete to deal with, and Cousin Cliff had his crappy Car Corral sign to look at every day. The newly poured cement driveway was setting up into something so hard and final that the good *primo* days with Abe would soon be forever covered over, and nothing short of a jackhammer would be able to redeem the white pureness of the caliche beneath. But his letters, round and running through the soft gray concrete, could hold and mark something of the compulsion of the moment. "Richie *y Esebro*," he had written, and then with a slow, ornate flourish he signed his initials, RH, and underlined them forcefully, deeply.

At first Richie had avoided the urge of the concrete. He knew it was wrong to spoil its smooth, glistening surface. But he knew too that he must write his feeling of right and wrong, his feeling of friendship and loyalty for Abe and for their joint claim to this corner, this neighborhood, at this time. New cars and customers might pass by Abe's auto tag and all that it meant for those who knew what it meant to be a *primo*, a *hermano* to a classy guy like Abe. "*¡Qué Vato!*" he always said. "*¡Qué buen vato!*" They had been here, both of them, here on Calle Puente between Terrill's Variety Store and Farmers Oil Company, and it had mattered and Richie had marked it so.

Now at dusk his bike leaned low, slanted on its kickstand, the handlebars drooping, bowing as if in homage to Abe and the sacredness of the time. A handful of letters, and then the initials. "Richie Hardesty," he thought as he watched his mark begin to cast itself in stone. No one would see the results of his artistry until next morning. The secrecy of the doing was his alone. The revelation of now, for the future. The tagging.

So, amid such thought and motive, he had picked up the stick, a small, strong, crooked piece of old elm branch, and he had knelt down and carved out his message with criminal care. Defacing private property. Trespassing. The *E* was a balanced trinity. The *S* was magnificent. The next *E* added more balance and symmetry. The *B* was full and matching in its bubbled, connected extremes of the *E*s. The *R* was kindred to the *B* and the *E* but straddling, standing tall and round and ready to run. And the final *O* was full and complete, ending in beginning, encircling and open all at once.

With each careful letter Richie's reveries grew and expanded into associated shapes and meanings. He thought of landforms and how the river and mountains and mesas and the volcanoes on the West Mesa defined his days and his life. Those geological and geographical forms and patterns were reflected in the shapes and process and meanings of his tagging. His today.

For a long time he didn't hear the honking and yelling. His dream writing had transported him across space and time, and his ears registered nothing but the scratches of the stick as it carved and scraped its way around his marking. But finally his thoughts were gouged by the cacophony of a blaring truck horn and a strident, nasal yelling and cussing. The soft calls of swooping nighthawks writing through the darkening sky with their wings were drowned out by the siren screech of the intruding, harsh-worded voice, and the whistling sound of traffic behind him became background for the voice calling out to him, cursing him in the very holiness of his written tribute to Abe and their block, their road, their world. *¡El Valle!* Someone was yelling. Yelling angry words that arrowed through the dusk air at him.

"Hey, you goddamned kid! Stop that, you son of a bitch! Stop writing in my new cement!"

The sharpness of the words awakened him, shocked him into panic. Stand up, move, run confused into the chilling, darkening evening air. He caught sight of a white Eldorado Cadillac convertible with a set of longhorn steer horns mounted on the hood and two long air horns, taken from an big tractor-and-semi rig, mounted on the fender. A fat-faced, red-faced, gutty guy wearing a curled-up cowboy hat was leaning over the door and yelling between passing cars while he slowed down to wait for oncoming traffic to pass so he could turn and pull up in front of the new driveway of Cousin Cliff's Corral. And Richie knew this was Cousin Cliff himself come to catch him and turn him in, sending him straight to hard time at the juvenile home in Springer.

His bike? How would he get away on that now? But what would it mean to leave it? The hell with it. Maybe Cousin Cliff would impound it as proof of his identity. What the hell! What the hell! He was running even as he thought it and said it, as if the words were spilling out into the thickening night air. And then he was running from the charging white Cadillac with crazed Cousin Cliff at the wheel. Running down the side of the long, newly poured cement driveway. Or he was trying to run. He didn't intend to step on the fresh cement, but his frantic staggering veered him into it. One, three, six, nine, twelve, and more squishing, sucking steps. His scruffy Thom McCann brogues sank all the way to the ankles, over the laces in the front, almost all the way down to the old caliche base. Both shoes sucked up a wet, globby, bubbly coat of gray, water-weighted cement.

The yelling kept coming, but Cousin Cliff had stopped short, hitting a mudhole, slamming on the Eldorado's brakes and splashing gray, hard-cement water along the fender. The car's weak shocks rocked the long body up and down for what seemed an eternity. Richie felt like he was trying to run on the ocean depths in giant lead diving shoes. Then he was free of the sticky, grasping cement and on the caliche shoulder, hightailing for the back of the trailer that had served as Abe's office.

Cousin Cliff, high-stepping in his Tony Lama iguana boots, had slowed down when he saw the footprints in the cement leading up to his new "corral."

"Oh, shit! Look what the hell you did, you goddamn teenage delinquent. I'll have your ass for this. I'll have your fuckin' ass." But his voice and words faded into Richie's running and his recurrent flashes of reverie and worry.

His father would find out, and there would be a talking-to and probably the razor strop for this. The strop that could raise welts of his father's angry signature on Richie's own butt, jeans or no jeans. It would hurt like hell.

Richie ran ever faster, feeling the imagined whacks of the strop. The yelling faded further into the street noise and merged with the rhythms of "run, run, run, run" that kept coursing through his mind and down to his churning legs. He ran past the trailer to the garage where Abe had worked over his inventory of cars—washing, waxing, tuning them—then along the east side of the stark concrete-block wall, the large cinder blocks whirring by to mark his rapid passing. He had to make it behind the garage and then over the high block fence that separated his own house from Abe's Auto. From the Car Corral, he corrected himself as the jumble of letters tossed around in his brain and in his new artist's eye.

He was the one corralled now. He would have to climb over the wall, or else he'd be caught like the dead bull that had given up its long, curving horns to decorate Cousin Cliff's Caddie. He hated to see Abe sell out to cowboy capitalism. But maybe Abe had to sell, or maybe they had confiscated his business. Some of his cars had been very hot indeed. Even Richie knew that, though he and Abe had never talked about it. He'd heard his parents and others talk about Abe's shady business dealings.

"If I can make it over the fence," he kept repeating. "Over the wall." Then he could hide in the pump house or in the narrow crevice between the wall of the pump house and the long wall of their house. He had helped his father build the house and the pump house too. He remembered the trip with the truck to pick up the heavy two-hole cinder blocks and the fun of mixing and carrying mortar to his father's masonry, the leveling and troweling, the stacking of one block on another, the long trough where he mixed the cement, sand, and water, the back-and-forth sweeps of the hoe with its own two holes that matched the pattern in the blocks, the lettered shapes that impressed these patterns on his mind and gave him a liking of masonry and flat work and a feel for the accompanying hard labor of preparation and transport.

Those were good times—holding and settling the yellow guide string, checking the level, helping to lift and position and tap the heavy blocks into line. The circular pump house took shape and seemed a special sanctuary for him, cool in the hot summers and cozy and warm in the winter with its heavy insulated door to keep the pump from freezing. He had helped build the wall, too. The wall he now had to cross.

It would be better to make it over the fence and into the dark safety of the pump house than to hide in the trough between the two buildings. Cousin Cliff might find him there if he took a flashlight and looked deep enough into the shadows amid the discarded oil cans and other automotive debris. He couldn't hide between the walls, but he had to pass along their entire course, and the pits and craters and gouges in the surface of the blocks jumped out at him as he ran along. The jagged crevices snagged his T-shirt, his shoulders, and his back when he rotated sideways to work his way around a protruding reinforcement column. Then he was free of the narrow space between the buildings and running on toward the final wall.

He saw it, the wall with the plaster lipping over the top. He and his father had plastered the walls of the house and pump house in textured tan swirls of plaster. The cinder blocks had welcomed and held the plaster on their pitted surfaces. He had even tagged his own wall with his initials, lovingly, beautifully. And those markings looked for him now, just as he looked for them.

First, however, he would have to cross the raised dock where Abe used a block and tackle to lift the engines out of his cars for overhauling. Richie knew he could use the dock and the big steel dunking vat as a platform to scale the wall. Maybe even swing out and over it like Tarzan, vaulting it with the help of the hooked and clattering chains. A quick grab. A fast hoist. Richie was on the dock. But then he slipped. The dock was slick from countless dousings with oil, grease, and solvent. He held on to the chain and steadied himself, waving and sliding as he maneuvered his way over to the large metal vat that sat flush against the wall. It would work as yet another platform to boost him over the wall. Crankshafts and an old engine block or two littered the dock, ghosts of past attempts at renovation or perhaps the remnants of stripping and chopping stolen cars.

The heavy-hinged lid was closed over the vat, but when Richie stepped on it full-footed for his thrust over the wall, the vat lid caved in and gave way. And he went down waist deep, splashing in the black, burning sludge in the vat. He reached up to clear the sting from his eyes but succeeded only in transporting more of the viscous liquid to his face and eyes. "Run! Run!" switched over in the channels of his mind to "Out, out, get out fast!" He struggled to reach for the still swinging chain, but it was futile. He was barely able to raise one heavy, sodden leg over the edge of the vat and then lean out and over, dragging his other leg behind him. His skin was on fire. His T-shirt was splotched in black circles, and his jeans hung heavy, laden with globules of grease and gunk and dripping the foul-smelling moisture that seemed to be growing from his shirt and pants and shoes, accompanied by a noxious mist. His right shoe was gone, lost in the bottom of the vat, and his other shoe groped desperately for a hold on the slick surface of the dock. In his fear and trembling he fell again, crashing his head on the side of the vat and pounding the palm of his right hand into the unyielding concrete of the dock. He was stunned and started to whimper and then cry, fearful of the red welts and small blisters that were starting to form on his bare foot and the backs of his hands. He had to make it over the wall and get to the pump house. He had to get to the water hose and wash the stuff off.

Cousin Cliff, once he stopped examining the damage to his precious new driveway, lost himself to his own anger and abandoned the pursuit. He was not the culprit now. The real culprit was the fluid that soaked the boy and was eating into his skin, burning it, pricking it, gouging it, scarring him, writing its way into his skin. It occurred to Richie that he might walk deformed and disfigured for life.

Finally Richie shimmied out of the vat and off the dock. He hobbled far down the fence, remembering a passage just at the corner of the wall that would take him onto Heartline Road so he could double back through the gate. By the time the gate slammed he had pulled off his chafing, blistering jeans and shorts, his T-shirt, which tore off like a rotten rag, his one cement- and oil-laden shoe—his now worn-out shoe. The brass, round-spoked faucet handle was turning, and he heard the electric pump motor click on; then the cold water was flowing over him head to toe, coursing over his chest, up and down his legs, and dousing his raw private parts. But the solvent resisted and retained its coated adhesive hold, and Richie was frantic in his cold trembling. He squatted down to turn off the hose, which was shaking and curving now around him into a chaos of twists and contortions. He needed the water pressure inside the house, the soaking and scrubbing power of soap. Naked and shivering with pain and cold, he made it to the back door of the house and ran dripping through the laundry room and into the bathroom and the waiting tub, to the cleansing power of total immersion.

Lying in the tub, he knew he would be found out and labeled as a destroyer of property. The trail of his crime was clear enough, and there was, of course, his bike, no doubt now in the trunk or backseat of Cousin Cliff's convertible.

After the soaking and toweling he rubbed on some soothing lotions. There was a knock on the bathroom door and his mother's voice. "Richie, Richie, are you in there again? There's a man here to see you. Says he found your bicycle. He's waiting in the patio just inside the gate, there on the porch. You go talk to him and then tell me what's going on. Have you lost your bike?"

Quickly he pulled on a fresh T-shirt and jeans and a pair of old loafers—no socks on his sore feet, no underwear on his sore skin. He rubbed more lotion and cream on his blisters, then walked out of his bedroom and into the patio to face the music, face the cowboy who caught him tagging his new cement driveway, the fat fart who had chased him to this uncomfortable moment of reckoning.

"Impossible!" Richie said under his breath as he broke into a smile. It was Abe, not Cliff, standing there next to Richie's bike, leaning just as he left it by the fresh cement driveway only an hour or so ago.

"*Esebro*, Richie," Abe said. "*¿Qué pasa, hombre?* Lose your wheels, *cuate?*"

"Abe, you?"

"Yeah, that *pendejo* Cliff called me, mad as shit. But I told him I'd handle it. I knew it was you, bro, when he told me what the kid wrote. I told the lard-ass *Tejano cabrón* not to sweat it. I'd pay to have it repaired and finished again. We know, here, man. We know," and he touched his chest with a fisted hand.

"*¡Qué muchacho,* Richie! *Qué carnal.* Take care, man. Take care." And he made his hand into his familiar make-believe pistol and blew an imaginary puff of smoke off the barrel before he turned and was out the gate.

As Richie listened to the motor of the Chevy revving and then pulling away down Heartline, he heard his father, an undershirted silhouette behind the back screen door, ask, "Wasn't that Abe Gutierrez? You know he sold his car lot just in time and moved away? Someday they'll catch him, though. He's a suspicious character. You're lucky he brought your bike back. I'm surprised it's not on the way to

Juárez with some stolen cars. And I'm surprised he's not doing time in the state pen. We're lucky he's out of the neighborhood."

"Not so. Not so at all," the boy countered under his breath. "He's a friend. A real friend. And he's here to stay." And Richie brought his own solvent-stinging hand to his chest. "I'll see to it somehow," he whispered. "*¡Esebro! ¡Qué viva el Valle!*"

Neighborhood Watch

Not everyone sees things in quite this way, you understand. You can talk to people all along the street here, and they would all account for it in different ways. All I can say is that the way I see it, it's not so much a question of the evil in him or the things he did, but of how evil coexists with goodness and can, in different ways and degrees, overcome goodness—can corrupt it. Corruption and rot and decay are not necessarily evils, to be sure. If some things didn't rot away, then where would be the good? But what he did, and what we did in response, is a little more serious than mildewed food in the refrigerator.

I'm sure that he willfully sought to corrupt me and my family, whether or not he sought to corrupt our neighborhood, all our lives and our day-to-day doings, or whether his inherent evil (for I do believe he was evil incarnate) just brimmed and bubbled over—like some putrid witch's cauldron of animal entrails and carcasses.

The corrupting influence of his presence in our midst wasn't immediately apparent—rot never is. He was at first just another neighbor, his family just another family. Maybe I was the first to feel it in our earliest front-yard hellos, our small smiles and next-door-neighborly exchanges, but pretty soon we all felt it and saw it in our lives and in each other. As you got to know him and his family, you got to know his evil and its feeding, decomposing power. This goes much beyond saying he was a bad influence. I mean, he was pure waste, rotten shit, and he brought the worst of it down on us. But in the final tally, we rose to the occasion, and in that sense I guess he brought out our best selves.

So, say what you will, I'm glad I did what I did, glad I led the others to rise up against him and cast him out of our lives, the lives he was so miserably changing into the purest hell of corruption. I'm thankful, finally, that we broke his spell. That's what it was, too, a spell. The evil eye. *El mal ojo!* And he had one, let me tell you, an evil eye. It watched over all of us, affected us all deeply and forever.

His obedient wife didn't see it, or didn't seem to, not at first, when we were all friendly and blind to it. But if he corrupted us, how could he not corrupt her? The photographs proved that. His daughter, his diabolical little girl, didn't see it, though she probably inherited some of his demonic legacy, since his bloodline contin-ued into the child's. But you could see his evil manifesting itself physically in the little girl, in her poor, pale skin and her strange, pinkish, sensitive, darting eyes. You know the whiteness of rot? Her skin was a similar hue.

How can I make you comprehend the real nature of his corrupt-ing influence? Seeing how it spread far beyond me and my family is the key. Yes, that's what I want—to make you see the big picture, the unfolding of his plan. If somehow the neighborhood itself could talk about it, had a choral voice to tell you all that it collectively saw of the corruption, then you would know. A street, a neighbor-hood, a row of houses, trees, lawns, and landscaping and pets and cars—all these things build up a spirit, an embodiment of who you are in the place where you live. Want to know about the powers of place, the spirit of places? Watch then thy neighbor—watch and listen.

Yes, that's what William Walters did. He watched. He interrupted, he violated our homes, our hearts, our sense of who we are, and of why we are who we are, even of who we think we are. In doing that, he changed us, corrupted us. "Who do you think you are, anyway?" I remember him asking at one point. "Just who the hell do you think you are?" Well, we knew who we were—until he came into our midst. And in spite of his corrupting spirit we rallied. I rallied. We showed him what we were made of . . . finally, in the apocalypse that was his end.

I liked him, at first. We all did. We began by welcoming him, accepting him and his curious family and tastes and style of living. But I see now that was part of his plan, part of his influence. But you need to see how I saw it, how I perceived it and how, all together, we yielded. And then, just in time, just teetering on the edge, we resisted.

The house he bought was at the very end of the street—our street, Calle Bonita—in a peaceful, picturesque little neighborhood in the great American West, in the state of Nuevo Mexico. We had all moved there seeking our westering dreams, our nest somewhere out in the West where we could live and let live. His was a house much like mine, some tract builder's version of paradise, except the house he bought was severely run-down, a "fixer-upper," in real estate terms. It had sat vacant for maybe a year or two, after the mortgage company foreclosed on the previous owner, a wheeler-dealer who was never there. So we were all glad to see the house sell and to see Walters take an owner's pride and interest in it right away.

First he cut down the encircling weeds, mostly Russian thistle, and raked up the dead tumbleweeds that kept catching on the barbed-wire fence marking his property line and the termination of the street. It was a dead-end street, like I said, butting up against a large vacant patch of land bounded on the far east side by a long, wide irrigation ditch. Each evening at dusk he'd be out there working into the darkness of the night, cutting and raking and piling up those weeds, making his zombie wife hold supper.

Then every weekend, usually on Sunday evenings when we were all settling in to watch *The Andy Williams Show* or *The Ed Sullivan Show*, or read the lingering, floor-strewn sections of the morning paper, or just rest up for the shock of Monday morning, Walters would start his bonfire. And it would be a big, billowing bonfire, what with a week of drying and dead weeds and thistles that he was trying to get ahead of. If you've ever seen a pile of dry tumbleweeds burn, you know what I mean. When they ignite it's like an explosion. The flames and the sound whoosh up into the sky, and the little sparks and ashes caused by this thermal ascension dance skyward toward the stars and past the face of the moon into the darkness. It's hot next to those fires, but Walters didn't seem to be bothered by it. He kept throwing on more and more and still more tumbleweeds.

He wore rawhide work gloves, blackened and glossy with soot, so he could pick up those clumps of thistles and throw them into the raging, flame-dancing fire like a cosmic bowler. Sometimes he used a rake or a pitchfork to twirl and thrust and scoop and spin those weeds around and feed the surging, crackling fire as if it were a voracious maw, ever hungry, ever waiting to reward the one who sustained it.

We would all back away from our television screens with their reflections of burning columns of flames and smoke, turn and look out at the blaze, close any windows if the smoke lingered and drifted our way, and try to control the kids. Because all the neighborhood kids—mine especially, since we were Walters' next-door neighbors— would run from whatever they were doing—homework, supper, washing dishes, whatever—straightaway out the door, to stand as close to the blaze as they dared and stare, spellbound, into the hot, glazing glow. It was as if Walters were some kind of hellish Pied Piper.

He would laugh, enjoying the spectacle of what he had caused— the fire and the attraction of the neighborhood to it. And he would exaggerate and stylize his gestures, clowning around in a frenzy of tossing tumbleweeds to fuel his fire—antics that would alternate between loud laughing and silent, glowering frowns at all of us, parents and children, each spellbound, whether beside the fire or hidden behind our curtains.

After a few weeks he caught up with the weeds, but there was always debris of one kind or another for him to burn: trash, errant food wrappers, drifting newspapers, leaves and sticks and branches. The end of the street was soon scorched and blackened by his fires, and so were the walls and the windows of the houses closest to his—all in the name of cleaning up his yard. You could see his plans take shape. He burned off all the Bermuda grass around his house—front, sides, and back. "Best thing to make it grow is to burn it and kill it back," he said. "Make it crawl around more and spread out further and further." But what spread out mostly in those moments was ash, ash, and more ash. The kids' shoes tracked ash all over the neighborhood.

"Need a rock garden in this kind of arid country," he told me one Saturday when his landscaping and rock gardening project became apparent. He kept hauling in rocks, really big rocks, from the lava beds on the mesas west of the river. He had a homemade trailer he had welded together in his garage, a garage that soon became a virtual welding and metal shop, what with his torches and hoses and tanks of acetylene gas and the welding goggles and helmets and masks he hung all along the edge of the rafters.

At first I just watched with neighborly interest. It was all happening more or less simultaneously—the transformation of the yard, the conversion of the garage into a welding shop. And then he started the roof work. What was going on inside the house was hard to tell, at least at first. His wife and daughter held forth there in their domain, or so I imagined. He hitched up this makeshift trailer behind his old rusting-out Dodge Power Wagon and went up into the malpais around the extinct volcanoes west of town to collect lava rocks. He loved lava rocks. You've seen them: black rocks with pits in them from the gas bubbles blown out of ancient heat. These were what he used to craft his rock garden and the borders around his driveway and around the flower beds. That was his idea of planting a garden—collecting rocks from the four or five defunct volcanoes where people went to shoot and dump their trash and screw and who knows what other mischief. Word had it that some animals had been sacrificed in the dry core of one of the volcanoes. They were damn spooky places and most people didn't want any part of them.

Soon his goddamn yard started looking like lava land itself, and I started to cringe each Saturday morning when his rattling, creaking trailer and tappet-clattering truck pulled out, and then returned with their weekend cargo. I mean, it got on my nerves in ever-increasing bouts of tension and anger. Even Glenda, my wife, started to complain. "For Christ's sake," Glenda would say, "not that home improvement bastard again. He's ruining that house, just ruining it, and the neighborhood with it. Jesus Christ Almighty! Every damn Saturday! Each and every one! Besides, he's starting to give me the creeps with the way he looks at me."

You could see her impatience growing into a kind of all-out moodiness that would last until noon and then the whole day and then the weekend. Finally it turned into full-blown bitchery. I didn't blame her. But then we started arguing about why I didn't do something about "that son-of-a-bitch Walters."

Let me tell you, it wasn't home improvement we were watching at all. Don't you see, the evil SOB wasn't really cleaning and building and sprucing things up—his house, the street, the neighborhood. It was home destruction! Neighborhood corruption! Disturbing the peace and quiet and harmony of all our lives through the visual pollution he was bent on.

A couple of months after he moved in, which would have been late summer or early fall, he started making his wrought-iron fence and windows. And the ladder. The goddamn ladder. The wrought-iron fences and windows were easy enough to figure out, but not the car wheels and the ladder, not right away at least. Now, lots of people do decorative work with wrought iron in this part of paradise, and at first we thought he just went overboard, fencing all around his lot and placing bars over all his windows and the front, back, and side doors. He turned the bars out like magic, working there in his garage late at night forging and spot-welding, producing shaft after curving, rippling shaft of black wrought iron.

The transformation took a more maniacal turn when the guy started welding old automobile wheels together. I mean, this was bizarre—colorful and rather ingenious, I admit, or so I first thought when I saw what he was piecing together, but very bizarre. And not very pleasing to the eye. He started at the back fence, but he worked fast, so the wheel fence started to spread across the entire back length of his lot, about two hundred feet, and then up one side, next to the open field. It was like Bermuda grass, growing, spreading.

The wheels would surely stop the tumbleweeds and the litter; in fact, the fence he was assembling would stop trespassers of any kind. And there were some rather hard-up, hungry people living on the next street over, the Truesdales and a couple of other black families in particular, who were always suspect when anything unusual happened on our quiet street. But these people were a blessing compared with Walters. His fence could stop them—like Gargantuan chain mail, his fence could stop a tank—but what could stop Walters?

The whole neighborhood gawked and gasped when we realized his design, such as it was, wheel next to wheel, wheel on top of wheel, all of them spot-welded together stronger than strong. I mean, how would you like to start each day looking out to see the sun and finding the ugliness of a fence made out of car and truck wheels, red and yellow and black and green and who knows what other loud, soiled, clashing color? Even wheels of uniform size and color welded side to side and top to bottom would have been hard to accept, unless you were some motor-head punk who grooved on kitsch. It was all very gross, very damaging, and like I said, corrupting to the neighborhood sensibility. You can see that, can't you?

Walters watched it all too, of course. He watched us watching him and watching each other. Then he topped off the wrought-iron work and the automobile wheels with the most ornate iron ladder you ever saw, and he mounted it right on the west side of his garage, the side of the house that faced me and Glenda and our once-upon-a-time happy little brood. We had a high cement-block fence for privacy around our patio, where Glenda liked to sunbathe topless and where the kids kept their innocent little plastic wading pool for skinny-dipping. It was really a comfortable, nice little patio. We had our lawn and our flowers, some nice roses especially, and our Weber grill and our picnic table that I had assembled out of two-by-six pine planks and chrome lock-washer bolts. And we had some upholstered lawn chairs that a friend of mine had redone for me and even a special chaise lounge that set me back a cool hundred.

I mean, you can see the contrast, the nuisance of it starting to develop. Here's this comfortable, unassuming, typical middle-class house, not much out of the mold of the rest of that tract of flat-roofed, pueblo-style homes. And somebody moves in and starts to construct a fortress, a friggin' cornball iron junkyard, a combat-ready compound, right next door. Well, you wouldn't just sit back in your quality lawn furniture, sip your iced tea, and take it, would you?

Now, this transformation was not some overnight surprise. It was happening, day by day, right before our eyes, right under our collective noses. We were all talking among ourselves about it, and we were all talking to Walters about it, after a while, when the home improvements started to get noticeably out of hand. But somewhere between the cleaning-up stage and the "what do you think about how he's fixing up the place?" stage, the neighborhood cold shoulder started to develop. It took me a little bit longer to get hostile, actually to turn from friend to foe. That was part of his penchant to corrupt, don't you see? To turn well-meaning, neighborly, helpful folks into an angry mob. From the stage when he started burning tumbleweeds to when he built the ornate, oversized ladder leading up to his rooftop, and then when he started building a damn lookout tower and bunker up there—that all took some time—over a year.

He started changing his appearance, too. At first I thought he was just an average-looking, blue-collar, hardworking guy, but after a while I noticed he had developed a scaly case of eczema, and his eyes started to bulge out, and then a small goiter cropped out; both his bug eyes and bumpy neck were from a thyroid condition that he started to complain about. Then other things happened, like severe hair loss. I mean, whole clumps of his hair dropped out, making him look like the product of mange or some worse canine condition. He started to lose weight and in general just scared the spectral hell out of all the kids and the adults, too.

I mean, when you have an ugly, ill-looking neighbor who has barricaded his house and clambers up on the roof at all hours and looks out at the whole street through nine-power binoculars, then things have gone too far. But these were mere externals, don't you see? The corruption, the pollution, the evil went further—into the morals and the bourgeois values of every good neighbor on our pretty little street, our Calle Bonita.

There wasn't a man, woman, or child on the entire street, and even some, like the Truesdales, on the next street over, who he didn't know something about, who he didn't keep some kind of a log on, as we found out later in the debris. He would sit up there on the rooftop in his observation post made out of old tires and lava rocks and take out his binoculars and monitor us, licking his lustful, evil chops. Or he would walk around the edge of the roof and watch us—stopping sometimes to spread his legs and cross his arms and just stand there, staring into our patio, watching the kids swim, watching for Glenda to flop over and expose her breasts, and him staring deep into our shivering, soon simmering souls.

I mean, I'll admit I helped him at first. That was how he started taking us over, invading our lives, consuming us. Like the others, I first thought he was a little strange, an old hippie maybe, a Dead-head bent now on saving the environment, on ecological purposes like preserving energy, saving and reusing things, trying to be self-sufficient. I helped on most of his projects, if you must know— and he helped me in turn with some of my little handyman attempts.

We built a sidewalk together in front of my house and then over and along in front of his house. Together we put up a two-box mailbox stand. You know the kind, supported by a heavy welded chain curved in a kind of S—at least that's how he insisted we shape it when I helped him weld it one night in his garage. And, yes, I helped him burn some of the tumbleweeds and haul lava rocks and carry trash barrels to the county landfill. I even helped him with some of his iron fencing, helped him transport and stack some of his many car wheels, and I packed some of the old tires with mud and cans after he got them circled on the roof of his house. But things were deteriorating fast, thanks to him—relationships, friendships, marriages, families—all the while he was "building."

Then one Saturday, after finishing the front cement walk, when we were having a beer and discussing his crazy plans to build a retrograde bomb shelter, he pointed to a pile of old magazines over in the corner of the garage by the water heater, which was wrapped and duct-taped and insulated with fiberglass fur. The magazines were neatly tied up with yellow carpenter string, like we had used in building the walk, and standing in two tall stacks.

"I've got some magazines you might enjoy before I drop them off for recycling. Feel free to browse and borrow."

Well, I like to read, as do Glenda and the kids when we're not watching TV. But like most people I can't work my way much beyond *Reader's Digest*. I like the local newspapers. I also like *Consumers Digest*, that kind of thing. I would read *National Geographic* if I could afford it. So I said, "Sure, Walters, sure. What you got available?"

"There's some pretty good stuff in there, Harrington. Old *Playboy*s and some men's magazines and the like."

So we talked some more about the Cold War and finished our beer, and I got up to leave. "Don't forget your magazines, fella," he spoke up to remind me. "Better not let Glenda see 'em, though, not the little missus, at least not right now."

The magazines were like nothing else I'd ever seen or heard about before: graphic, sleazy pictures with terrible titles and shocking poses. Photographs of what I thought couldn't and shouldn't be photographed. I mean, if you could see it you would agree. It was terrible stuff. And with the magazines, get this, was an envelope of Polaroid pictures of a couple that resembled Walters and wife having sex—and a note: "This might be fun for you if you have the right camera." Well, my first thought was to call the authorities, the sheriff or the police, and turn it all over to the vice squad, but this guy was my new neighbor. So, being a good neighbor, I didn't say anything much. Except, over the next few weeks, I returned time and again to borrow more magazines and look for the envelopes of Polaroid pictures that would turn up between strategic pages of the magazines.

The pictures were soon arousing interests and thoughts much beyond my control, conscience, or even good sense. Walters had succeeded in corrupting me—and for better or for worse, I was enjoying the magazines and photos, just as Walters said I would, although we never talked specifics. I was bothered, though, by the guilt of the new and visible corruption in myself and the new control Walters had over me. And when I returned the magazines to him and asked to see some of the others, he just laughed his knowing laugh. "They're kinda fun, aren't they? Some pretty pictures in there. Think about that Polaroid idea and let me know. Haven't talked it over with the little lady yet, have you? We might work on a group photo." So, soon I was seeing poor innocent Glenda in the photos, imagining how I would get this pose and that one. It was dirty stuff.

And all the while Walters was constructing his bizarre fenced fortress, his ladder, and his rooftop observation post. I mean it was like he was not only observing all the chaos and pandemonium he was causing in his remodeling ventures, he was controlling it, too. His wife started making forays over to see Glenda, to borrow some canned milk, perhaps, or some eggs or powdered sugar, a lemon, some of this or some of that which she urgently needed. Once she asked Glenda if we had any extra Polaroid film!

And their strange daughter started getting even stranger and began walking over to our old dog, Chano, and just standing over him or beside him and staring at him. Didn't pet him or anything. Just ran her darting, jumping eyes over him. Then pretty soon Chano was starting to follow her from one room to the next and then outside. She never did pet him or whistle to him or hug him or say a single word to him, but Chano, for all purposes, became her dog. It broke the heart of our little Joanne. Ricky outright challenged the little witch for the dog—and lost. It was like Chano was some darn fickle house cat lured over with magic victuals.

We'd had Chano since he was a puppy, and he was a good old dog, never caused any trouble. But the Walters girl changed that in stealing him away from us. He refused to come into the house, wouldn't follow any commands, and started to range wide and far through the neighborhood, which he had never done before.

Then dead chickens started turning up in the backyard. I buried a few of them because of the feathers and the stench, and out of guilt from trying to deny any responsibility, any possibility that the good old family dog was all of a sudden a chicken killer. I guessed whose chickens they were, too, but I wouldn't admit it. I'd take the shovel and dig the little graves and then pack the dirt down and kick at Chano and yell at him. "All right, get the hell away from here, Chano. Stay away, too. Take your dead chickens next door if that's where you want to live."

Then one late afternoon after I got home from work, this young black kid, David Truesdale, from the house one road over and behind us, knocked on our door. Little Joanne answered and called me to the door. He was a tall, gawky boy and very shy, wore overalls and oversized shoes and an oily cap. I'd talked to his father, who was a church deacon, a few times, at school Parent-Teacher Association meetings, and in the neighborhood, or at Lalo's grocery store over on Gonzales Road. We knew the Truesdale family, you could say.

"Mr. Harrington," David said, "your old dog is digging into our chicken coop and killing our chickens. Daddy told me to ask you to keep him home."

Over David's shoulder, standing on the sidewalk, I could see Walters, and just past him the *brujita*, Valerie Walters, with Chano standing obediently by her side. She was looking at me and the Truesdale kid there in the doorway, and I knew, even as I was talking to him and acting shocked and denying it, I knew that everything was due to that miscreant of a girl and her father.

And sure enough, when I walked outside with David and went around the house to check the backyard fence line, actually walking over the damn ground where I buried first the hen and then the Plymouth Rock rooster or whatever the hell it was, I felt more eyes on me. I looked around, and there was Walters on his ladder heading for the observation post on his rooftop, ready to train his binoculars on me, and his damn confederate-in-arms daughter was with him.

Then the Truesdale boy and I found another dead chicken right by a big hole where the posts of the wheel fence and my back fence converged. The chicken had maggots riddled through it, and I realized it was one of the chickens I had buried myself, now dug up again by good old Chano or maybe even the little child witch herself.

"See, Mr. Harrington, see?" David said and pointed at the chicken carcass with his thin, dark finger, extending from a hand as long and bony as the Grim Reaper's. "See what I mean? This is—was— one of our chickens."

So I took Chano, the family dog, much loved by Joanne and Ricky and Glenda for all seven years of his life, and I called the humane society to come out and have him destroyed. When they brought him out front for me to sign the final release and say my teary good-byes, I saw the strangest reddish-black star pattern in his brown eyes as they darted over me against the pull of the attendant's leash. Then they put our faithful family dog into their cage-partitioned truck and carried him off to the ovens of oblivion, with Walters and his daughter watching from their rooftop.

Somehow that set off a kind of chain reaction of uncommonly frequent deaths and accidents in the neighborhood—all up and down a street that wasn't pretty anymore. Ricky's pet gerbil, Cosmo Medici, died of suffocation when a tarp was "accidentally" thrown over his cage, "accidentally" left out in the sun. Next, the postman accidentally ran over the LaRoccos' big collie right in front of all the neighborhood kids, including Valerie Walters, of course . . . all of them encircling the big, glorious, white and tan animal there on the asphalt, lying still with its back broken and its guts pushed out of it. Then little Gilbert Ramos ran through a sliding-glass door and nearly severed his arm at the shoulder. Then old man Baines had a stroke and died, leaving his poor wife, Erna, all alone and loony with grief for the loss of her lifetime companion. Next, the Garcia boy freaked out on drugs and started burglarizing houses. Finally, in one of the worst turns of tragic fate to descend on our little neighborhood, he broke into the Baines house, right next door to his own, the house of his mother's friend, and high on dope, he beat old lady Baines senseless. And through all of this, through it all, there was Walters, leering, staring.

The neighbors started to talk, started to put two and two together. We realized. The logic was easy. We were happy before he came. Everything was peaceful. After he moved in we were unhappy and troubled. I mean, the man and his family were very bad news. Good-bye, happiness. Hello, evil!

But what tipped the scales for me and forced me, finally, to take matters into my own hands was what happened to Ricky, my son. When he was very young, five or six, I'd build him a kite, tie on the right amount of tail, rig up a nice spool of kite string, and we'd get it up there, really high, darting and scooting in the March and April winds, all of us cold and laughing and invigorated, huddled together feeling the tough tug of the kite and the power of spring blowing into our world, coming new to our neighborhood. Later, as he got older, he'd fly his kites alone, out in the big field beyond Walters' house.

Somehow, that last spring, April 1, actually, Valerie Walters accompanied Ricky on one of his kite-flying expeditions. When I got home from work that day, the house and the neighborhood were in a panic. Ricky was missing. He had not been seen since dusk when Valerie Walters came in to practice her piano and get ready to eat dinner.

"He was still in the field flying his kite, just watching it soar," was her version of things. "He had two spools of string out, and it was high and I got cold and Mamma yelled and then Daddy yelled me in to practice."

But Ricky wasn't in the field, and his kite was caught in the utility lines and was by then whipped into shambles by the winds. I rushed straight over to Walters and asked him what he had seen from his rooftop—him and his always vigilant, nosy looking out on us. "Last I saw he was headed for the ditch, just trying to reel in his kite as he walked. But then I called Valerie and I came down for dinner."

But Ricky didn't make it home for dinner that night. We found his body by the flumes, his face cut and bruised by the churning spring waters intended to bring renewed cycles of life to the valley. So how did he get to the ditch—and why—with his kite now hanging from the wires close to his home?

That's how far Walters' evil, corrupting ways extended—so far as to turn life into death. We knew then what we had to do. I, of course, had the pleasure of lighting the first match. I set the conflagration and saw to its snapping, popping, fiery conclusion. We all did, one after the other: Glenda, Joanne, poor Erna Baines, the Garcia and Ramos families, the LaRoccos. All of us participated together. We saw to it that no one escaped from the house, not Walters, not his fat-bellied, Polaroid-posing, sex-enslaved wife, and most especially not his witchy, evil little girl with her darting, transfixing eyes.

As we piled every tumbleweed and piece of dried-up debris we could find on the inferno that engulfed his kitschy house of horrors and whipped the thermal gusts higher and higher, I cursed the black-souled, evil-hearted son of a bitch and cheered with every dancing flame. And all the while, through the hour or so it took to destroy the place, Ricky's tattered kite whipped wildly from the high electric wires. And there among the glowing lava rocks, the poker-hot, wrought-iron shafts, the paint-blistered fence of welded wheels, and the encompassing smoldering smoke of the last burning rubber tire falling through the collapsing roof, a piece of kite twine floated peacefully to the ground while the whole neighborhood watched.

Code Three

This made the second time. The first time he quit was during the war, after a couple of quarters of hard courses in engineering and not very good grades. So he joined the Navy and went to Korea. This time around, he wanted it to be different, but just three weeks into the fall quarter, with the same hard courses, the same difficult time studying, the way was clear—quit, go home, work in the family business. Who needs to be an electrical engineer, anyway?

So that day at the end of September, Daniel Turner ended his college career for good. He went to the administration building, withdrew from his heavy load of science and technological classes, checked out of the dorm, packed up his things, got in the new two-tone, two-door Ford Fairlane, paid for with some of his Navy Hospital Corps earnings, and headed back to the Central Valley. So long, Central Coast California State University dreamin'; hello, eight-to-five small-town Tules, California, reality.

It was Friday, just before noon, and Daniel was the last student to carry out any transactions at the registrar's window before it closed for lunch. He barely made it to the cashier to turn in the withdrawal forms. Then he headed south down California Street and saluted good-bye to the two rows of palm trees that lined the west-side entry to the campus. He'd grab a bite to eat in Paso Robles, maybe check in with a buddy at Cholame, then drive on to Tules, population 7,569.

He hit Highway 101 at the Apple Farm, pulled into moderately heavy traffic, and began the long ascent over the Cuesta Grade. The weather was warm, and he rolled down the windows and sped past the reservoir on the eastern edge of town feeling a sense of regret and loss at the finality of his decision. But it was good to be on the move—if only for a couple of hundred miles, heading home once again, another chapter of his young life closed. He just wasn't made for college.

He punched in the Paso Robles radio station he liked to listen to, which served as a kind of homing-in point on his trip home, and turned up the volume to hear Dion confirm many of his own feelings. "Call me the wanderer, yeah." He had felt that way most of his life, ever since high school, even during the war, even now. Except now he was wandering home to settle down, if he could.

All the talk at the university was about midterm exams. They were just a few weeks into the quarter and pressures were already building about midterm exams! He had tried to study, especially for the engineering orientation class, but he wasn't getting it—neither mechanical engineering, which was his first choice, nor electrical engineering, his second.

He remembered, just last weekend, meeting some of the guys at a bar called the Library, in San Luis Obispo, and boasting to the ones he also knew from high school, a couple of them now juniors or seniors, almost ready to graduate—guys he still saw from time to time just to have a beer and talk. "Hey, guys, you can see I spend lots of time in the library. Maybe not the campus library, but a library nonetheless. I've got it aced this time, anyway," he boasted. "I made it through two quarters in college before the war, guys. I'll make it this time. Don't worry."

The whole table had given a hearty, high-pumping lift of their mugs of Lucky Lager and cheered him on: "Here, here! Here, here!"

Ronnie Bledsoe, the guy they all called Moose, chimed in, "Yea, *here's* to Danny boy's straight 2.0 GPA." And they had all laughed and looked at each other. Moose reached over and grabbed his friend's neck in a vice grip that reminded Daniel of their times as teammates playing for Tules Unified High School, all those five years back, which seemed like just last week.

He started to feel the cool coastal air warm up as he cruised up the grade toward Atascadero and Templeton and Paso Robles, and he drifted back to those times playing football with Moose. They had been pals ever since, even though life was taking them in different directions toward different versions of success and failure— speeding on and stopping cold.

Moose was almost ready to graduate, with a degree in physical education. Everyone thought he was the least likely to succeed, but he had been plugging away all this time. He had a line on a job in Arroyo Grande as a high school coach.

As for Daniel, in Korea he had opted for trying to save lives rather than taking them. The war, a war which saw hundreds of thousands of casualties, had convinced him to stay with engineering. Whether in times of war or peace, only the machine would rule supreme. Dropping out of school the first time and being in the war had just reinforced Daniel's need to get back to the practical, "hands-on" education offered by a polytechnic school. It was all a struggle, but he had thought the second time around that he would be ready. He reasoned that he didn't want to live in a small farming town all his life and drink away his days with his cronies. But it was harder, not better, the second time around.

High school days, war days, work days, college days. . . . Was there no end in sight? It would be nice just to drive around California all the time. Like today, like this moment. Now he was headed back to Tules to tell his parents he had dropped out. He didn't want to raise his dad's ire, not now. What would his dad say? His mother? His friends? And Julie—even though she had tired of waiting for him and married on the quick? She still wrote to him. She still cared about him.

He was almost at the top of the Cuesta Grade, on the 101 up-swing. Things in his life had once been on the ascent, too, full of expectations and hopes and dreams. Maybe they still could be again, even on the down slope, even in the leveling off of the Valley itself, and Tules. There would be the weekend explaining, the walks, the meals, the coffee, the accommodations, the anger, the disappointment, the considerations and commiserations—all extended to him, since he was finally coming home, not a hero but a college washout, a failure by some standards, a flawed and faulted failure.

When he was in high school his mom never minded much about his triumphs or defeats, whether he got into trouble or stayed out of trouble, came home early or stayed out late. She didn't seem to worry as much as his dad. They were good parents, just tired from working all these many years. Not at all like the sappy shrew-and-milquetoast pair in the movie preview he had seen the previous weekend at the Fremont Theatre in San Luis Obispo. Talk about the idle rich living in Los Angeles! Yet there was something he could identify with in the troubled son of those parents—his longing, his ache to believe in something, even the code of playing chicken, even in his black '49 Merc.

Daniel's own dad, as dads went in the hinterlands away from Hollywood, always got up at the crack of dawn to open the family lamp-and-lighting store in Tules. Turning on all those morning lights in the store was a carryover from the times, before he gave it up and moved back into town, when he worked on the Jack Ranch in the Cholame Valley. Whereas Daniel drove a snazzy new Ford, his dad had ridden horseback and in pickups, leading the life of a modern cowboy.

As he felt the horsepower of the new car and the wind blowing through his hair from the top of the Cuesta Grade, Daniel thought of how different the rural life he and his family had known was from the California portrayed in movies. No knife fights for him at Griffith Observatory, no drag races over a cliff to the death. Once over the grade and through the mountains, there was just the wide, rolling countryside stretching out from Paso Robles through Shandon and Cholame and Ketterman City and Straford—north to Fresno and south to Bakersfield. This was the country that defined him. And of course the land around Cholame and Parkfield, which was determined largely by the San Andreas Fault. Earthquake country.

He was heading into that country now. After Templeton and Paso Robles, their vineyards and wineries, he would be back in that country where his dad had taken him and told him about the quakes and some of his times on the Jack Ranch. Then he would be home amid the farms of the great San Joaquin Valley. He turned off the radio and looked out at the country spreading out before him. He thought again of the car in the movie preview and the talk it had brought with his college friends.

"What about that guy's Mercury, man? Only in Southern California and only around Hollywood. But it was a cool car—and so was the girl, Judy. But that little weird guy, John, or Plato. He's supposed to have gone off the deep end and shot some puppies. Why did they call him Plato?"

"He was always reading. He was a philosopher. You know, the weak, intellectual kind that needed protection, mothering from that girl and all. But he wasn't as weird as the moon people in the main feature—with their blind, staring eyes. That's what the future holds, guys. Maybe some space travel and then atomic war and then back to the caveman days. But say, did you know that the father in that movie, Mr. Stark, is Jim Backus, the voice of Mr. Magoo, the little blind guy in the cartoons?"

"Well, knucklehead, did you get that joke about Magoo's voice, when the new kid on the block imitates him and says, 'shoot 'em like puppies'?"

"How do you catch all that from a five-minute preview, man? I was still trying to figure out the main feature."

They had all exchanged opinions about the movie they had seen, and the upcoming previewed movie, digressing here and there about whether they had seen the actors before, arguing about people and happenings in the past of high school and the present of college. Then they were saying their good-byes and heading off into the night.

And Daniel recalled that at that moment he had been hit by a familiar wave of depression and a hollow feeling that maybe nothing really mattered, and then he had remembered that at least his car was there waiting for him as he left his friends, a shining new Ford, the same year as the ones the cops used in the teen film. And he remembered the satisfaction he had felt unlocking the door and smelling the fresh upholstery, and how the white hood shone under the street light. He had pulled out into the street, wondering about what he should do. Should he quit school? Where should he go from here?

College was tough. Life was tough. He didn't much miss the high school days. Emotions had run hard then, and it had been tough for him to fit in with the hip and cool crowd. And there were always parents and their prayers and ambitions for their kids, and the guidance counselors and their encouragement and eternal optimism about one's potential to try—and eventually succeed. But keeping one's nerve, keeping the will to go on, was tough, especially if things didn't really matter and if hoped-for successes turned to failures right there before your eyes, as if on some big, urgent, real movie screen of your life. "You can face the lion's den, Daniel. You can tame the wild mustang of college. You've just got to be motivated." Those counselors, just like cheerleaders, jumped for joy even when the score was hopeless.

But you can't cheer your way to success. Things happen. Look at his friends. Look at what happened to Julie. All those plans and now she was married to the Farmersville postmaster, drunk Andy Bowen, swaying and staggering his way to sorting out the mail and putting letters into post office boxes while he gave her his own little special delivery every fuckin' night, signed, sealed, and delivered.

Daniel passed through Atascadero. He was getting hungry, and the 101 Cafe menu tempted him on to Paso Robles. Just south of Paso he slowed down to the proper speed as soon as he saw the highway patrol station on the first frontage road. That's all he would need to add to his list of disappointments—a speeding ticket to cancel out his tuition refund. He drove on into the main part of town and headed straight for the 101 Cafe. He saw immediately that his intuitions were working overtime, because parked right in front of the cafe were two big-ass CHP Buicks, freshly painted in their distinctive and formidable black and white. Their radio antennae extended long and high off the back.

The 101 was a great cafe, verified over and over again by the number of highway patrolmen who ate there. They must have had a special arrangement with the owner, a tall, skinny guy from Texas. His name was Ervin Coover, but everybody called him Lightning because of the speed with which he filled short orders. Some people called him the Duke of Paducah, because that was his hometown, Paducah, Texas. He made a hell of a good assortment of Tex-Mex dishes and a scrumptious plate-lunch special.

"At least my way on into Tules should be clear," said Daniel to himself as he locked his car and headed into the cafe. "Once these CHP guys start chowing down, it takes 'em forever. And then they get drowsy." He visualized the road before him stretching on through Whitley Gardens, Shandon, Cholame, and then Cottonwood Pass. Once he made it through Cottonwood Pass and on across Highway 5 he'd be home free. All he would have to do then would be to come up with some heartfelt justification.

"Take it from me, these Central California boondocks are better than the big cities. Better here in Paso Robles or Atascadero than L.A. or Frisco. I started out in Los Angeles, and believe me this area is the place to be. Can't beat this country—and the people. Avocado orchards. Beautiful vineyards and mountains. And very little crime. Minor stuff. All we have to do is wait for the earthquakes, pull our Mid-State Fair duty, and keep citation books handy to issue tickets to the stream of cars coming over from Fresno and Bakersfield and the rest of the Valley for their weekend coastal capers around Morro Bay and Cayucos and Pismo Beach. How many have you nailed so far this morning? Just wait until tomorrow morning. Saturdays are always the heaviest, as if you didn't already know. Come on, put 'em on the counter. How many this morning?"

California Highway Patrolman Fred Freyling put his coffee down and reached over to tap the cover of his citation book. He was talking to a younger patrolman, Bill Pappas, and they were comparing Thursday night and Friday morning ticketing statistics. It was a game they played, and they always played it at the 101 Cafe as they talked to Lightning Erv over either a late breakfast or an early lunch. Their meetings were ceremonials with explicit and implicit professional, practical, and personal purpose that they both realized as such—and needed.

Freyling had been with the CHP since the late 1940s, when he joined after serving as an MP during World War II. Pappas was new to police work and to California. He was a big man, tall and muscular, but no dumb hulk. He was intelligent and sensitive. He liked the ladies, and they liked him. He missed Eugene, Oregon, his hometown. He had seen action under Iron Tits Ridgeway in Korea and was hospitalized for a time. It was part of Freyling's role to mentor his new colleague and guide him through the first uncomfortable stages of the new job. He tried to play down the ugly and gruesome potential of police work on California's highways.

Part of Freyling's plan was to convince Pappas that there was more to police work than the tension and trauma and soldiering of the military. There were cruelty and crime and accidents; there was enforcement, but there were also service and public relations. Freyling was headquartered in Paso and Pappas at the Atascadero station, but they patrolled some of the same portions of Monterey and San Luis Obispo counties. It was a large area to cover.

Freyling loved his work and was confident that Pappas would make a career patrolman. He had the abilities and inclination, if he could just make it over the rough spots, especially the apprehensions of this first year. They had new patrol cars—big-engined Buicks—and they could cruise the blacktops riding proud: handsome tan uniforms; black leather, basket-weave accessories; sunglasses; lights and siren, and the crackle of codes coming over the radio from the dispatchers sending sovereignty, authority, and orders their way. Pappas had confided in Freyling that he worried about not being able to handle anything really serious. Too many ghosts were scattered around the hills of Korea, ready for resurrection in California.

"Hell, Freyling," said Pappas, "I've got you beat so far this whole week, and you know it. Friday along the fault line! Things are shakin' out there in earthquake country. You think I need convincing that we got the big city brights beat out here?" Pappas spoke between bites of apple pie and a second cup of coffee. He liked to linger over dessert. "Nice dry, open spaces, Freyling! Who needs the green of Eugene? Plus I have the added bonus of your company. Do you want the numbers for just today, last night, or the entire week? Take a guess?"

"No, just the numbers. I call."

"Well, let's see, I got a call from the Branding Iron Bar-B-Que in Templeton. Some missing tri-tips. And the Pozo Saloon called in for me to keep the peace. Two rowdy aggie profs cutting loose, up from Santa Margarita. Then there was a drunk in an oil-drilling truck running cars off Highway 58. Or was it speeding tickets only you wanted? I don't have a single one of those. Waiting for the next Labor Day weekend for that. I topped you first of the month, re-member."

"No contest now, I guess," said Freyling. "How can you eat your damn apple pie with all that cheese?"

"You know what they say, 'Apple pie without cheese is like a kiss without a squeeze.' And Betty over there is getting close to the squeezin' stage. I've just never had it so good as out here in para-dise, Fred."

"That's true. Right, Erv? This guy's pretty damn lucky to have not just his pie but his cheese and his squeeze to go with it."

"You got it, Captain. He's livin' at the top of the ladder where them apples is hard and ripe. Sure as hell beats Dalhart and Amarillo."

Freyling paused to take a final sip of his coffee and caught a glimpse of a skinny college guy getting out of a new Ford and coming into the cafe. He took a stool at the other end of the counter.

"I've got to check with headquarters for traffic estimates. Post–Labor Day doldrums, you know. Then I gotta hit the road, Pappas. Take your time there with dessert—and Betty. I have to drive over East 46 to Cambria and then circle down 1 and back over to Atascadero on 41. Will I catch you around here again this evening?"

"Maybe, Freyling. Better have your numbers up by then. I'll be in touch."

"Bye, Erv. Bye, Gaye. Bye, Betty," he said to the cook and the waitresses. "Don't spend this guy's tip all in one place." And the tall patrolman put on his cap, adjusted his Sam Browne belt and his .38, and headed out the door.

"I'll have the huevos rancheros, I guess. And a Coke," he heard the college guy say.

The agent's voice came raspy over the phone. The handsome young man in black turtleneck sweater and gray flannel pants had to cover one ear to hear over the noise in the garage. His glasses were pushed back on his head.

"Listen, Dee, you know it as well as I do. This one will make you, kid. This one will secure you as a star. I've assurances already we can more than double your quote on the next one—it's points we're talking, major points on the gross. It's the big time for you, kid."

"Sure, Manny, that's fine. Listen, I can't talk long. My mechanic and I are heading up to Salinas for a race. And I've got some other calls to make. Just wanted to check in. When's the release date for the teen film? Any PR for me to do after the release?"

"I'll check with the studio publicist. But I think the big PR push should come for this Texas one. The releases will be timed just right. The release day for *Rebel* is in just a few days, October 2 or 3, next week. You'll be back, won't you?"

"Yeah, I'll be back. This is just a weekend deal."

"Okay. I'm sending you a good mystery script. It'll be waiting for you. Just be careful racing. It drives us all nuts. You're too valuable to get skinned up. Be good to yourself, and to me!"

"Relax. I'll see you in a few days. Get me as good a deal as you can on the next one. But remember, this one isn't even edited yet. Stevens keeps insisting the rushes are a bit quirky."

"Word from the execs, Dee, is that they've upped the advertising budget already. So if they give you any crap about being too moody or hard to work with, send 'em to me, laddie, and I'll lay out the figures."

"Good, Manny. Keep it up and maybe I'll buy you a new Mercedes to go along with my new little Porsche here. Catch you later."

The young man hung up the phone and ran his hand partially

through his errant brown hair, not so much to groom it but just because he enjoyed the sensation, almost to the point of habit. Then he pulled his glasses back down over his squinting eyes and ran his finger down to the next number in his address and appointment book. He found it and began to dial. He had a lonely, boyish look about him, and standing there against the service counter in the sports car garage he might have been taken for a young Stan Laurel quizzically scratching his head and smiling. But there was something more brooding and volatile in his demeanor and overall presence as he glanced at his expensive Swiss chronometer and pushed his glasses back on his head. He had a special style and flair that, even had he not been an actor, would have distinguished him as compelling and charismatic.

Listening to the dial tone and cradling the receiver between his head and shoulder, he picked up a caved-in pack of Tarreytons, fingered out one of the last couple of cigarettes, and put it in his mouth to light. He used an expensive gold Ronson. The phone rang five or six times before another young-sounding voice answered on the other end—clear across the country in Manhattan.

"Hey, Sal, how's New York? Thought I'd try to catch you and compare notes. Wanted to call you before I headed out to Salinas for a race."

"Good. How are you, Dee? Where are you in the shoot?"

"It's a wrap, thank God. But I don't want to talk about that. My agent says our release date is next week. What did you really think of the screening? You like it? What's your guess about the box office response? Critics are good so far as I've heard."

"It's good work. I think we can all see that. You're special. It'll be a big one for you. But I'm satisfied with what I did. The trailers are getting good response, my agent tells me the studio tells him. You saw the full board sign on Sunset Boulevard, didn't you? The trades liked it. The *Reporter* review will be out Monday, but advance word is very positive. Want to talk next week? I'll be back then. What's all that background noise, anyway?"

"I'm here in the garage, Competition Motors. I've been doing some commercials for Champion plugs. You should see the Porsche—a new 550RS Spyder. It's a beauty. Call it 'The Little

Bastard.' Number 130. It'll eat anything in its way. The prototype finished first *and* second in the Pan-American race two years ago. Took its class in the Mille Miglia last year, and the same class win at Le Mans for the past two years. Set me back seven thousand big ones. Okay. I know you're not that interested in cars. I'm just glad I finished this latest picture. Stevens is hard to take, but I made it through. You don't have to know the motivation for every single line, do you? Jett Rink or no Jett Rink. Same with Jim Stark."

"They're lining up for you. I should be so lucky. But, hey, guy, you be careful with all this racing and speeding. Keep it on the track, okay? I'd like to work with you again one of these days."

"Like I say in the PSAs 'Drive safely. The life you save may be mine!' You know me, I'm a survivor. I'd never do that bad boy, rebel stuff on the real highway of life, Sal. You know that."

"Sure, Dee, I know that giggle of yours, too. You'll be racing up to Salinas before you even pull out of the garage there."

"Well, I want to live to see what the result of these two pictures will be. They'll bring momentum. You'll make it big, too, Sal. It'll be a fine debut. The work is already coming, right? This one will make you a star. Will you be back for the release? Should I call you at the Sunset Marquis next week?"

"Yes. See you next week."

"Okay, Sal."

The cigarette burned low in the caller's fingers and he took a final drag and snubbed it out. He started to pull the final smoke from the crushed pack, then he glanced again at his watch and repeated the ritualized combing of his hair with his hand. His mechanic was pointing to his own watch and motioning that it was past time to leave if they were going to make it to Salinas for the kickoff party and some good booze time with friends who knew how to enjoy life in the fast lane.

Daniel ate his chilied *huevos*, hot and tasty. He listened to a couple of songs on the jukebox, eavesdropped a bit to hear what was going on between the cops and the waitresses and Ervin, and then paid his bill to the strains of the Everly Brothers singing "Bye-Bye Love." He left the cafe to head out of town to the 46 turnoff to Fresno. He had hoped that both patrolmen would stay in the cafe until after he left, but the older one left first. Daniel watched him through the reflection in the mirror behind the counter as he pulled away in his patrol car. Even so, he knew he would have the road pretty much to himself. When he hit the 46 turnoff he wondered whether the other patrolman had headed this way or whether he was heading back north. If he was ahead of him, he would have to take it easy, keep an eye out in case he had parked someplace, waiting for speeders.

Daniel marked the familiar mileage sign: "Cholame 28; Fresno 60; Bakersfield 110." He would hit Highway 41 just outside of Cholame and then be into Tules in a couple of hours. He had time to stop in Cholame and talk to Bob Terrill's brother, Sparky. Bob had played halfback on the Tules football team. He was Daniel's age, and he had been killed in Korea. Sparky somehow knew how to handle it, and he could give Daniel advice on how to break the news to his folks that he had just quit school. Sparky had always been a kind of big brother, ever since high school days when problems with football and Julie and his parents had seemed without solution. He ran a junky little welding shop, but he knew how to give advice and calm a fellow down. When Bob had been killed, his brother kept it in perspective but moved even further into the boondocks in Cholame and became a kind of desert sage.

The road opened up into earthquake country, dry and spacious and filled with the potential for chaos. It was a feeling Daniel knew well—as if his whole world had crumbled once, was shored temporarily, but was finally, once and for all, quaking and tumbling and crumbling around him. Only the Ford was a great comfort in the precision and order of its newness. As he drove east out of Paso Robles, past the vineyards and wineries, the stillness of the land rose up out of the afternoon. In its extreme stillness and in the highway stretching out across the remoteness of the land Daniel faced the loneliness of his own doubts as to whether he would pull it off this second time around. Quitting again.

With each marking of mileage there was a choice. He had made a choice, set a course, and now he was following it to its conclusion—open road, junction, or dead end. He carried that silent bur-

den with him now. But this day's stillness was special, almost fore-
boding. It was the stillness of pending quake and collision. This
was earthquake weather.

It was the stillness of memory and dream and anticipation. Daniel
thought again of the movie preview he had seen last week, of him
somehow being in the film himself, of his life as a movie. Of him as
the kid in the red jacket, white T-shirt, jeans, and engineering boots.
And of being in the car hitting the lights, waiting for the chickie
run, waiting for yet another test. Go straight, full bore? Or jump?
When to jump? When not to jump? Courage? What was that? Did
he care? Was courage fighting in combat or being on a hospital
ship taking care of the wounded or taking care of those who took
care of the wounded? Was courage staying in school, or dropping
out. What mattered, anyway?

He had felt meaning in the land, first as a boy, when he knew
there was something changing—the land still but ready for commotion. And he had told his father, and his father took him out on
the highway in his truck. He remembered riding somewhere near
Parkfield, and his father told him about the valleys and mountains,
and the space that was near the Howard Jack Ranch, where he
used to work as a cowboy. They walked to a large ravine, and his
father said, "This is it, son. That ravine, there. See how it curves
and courses wide and gully-like. That's the San Andreas Fault. We
can actually see it here, but the fault runs deep and far, and it can
shift and crack and open at any time. But especially on days like
today, son. Quiet, quake-time days like today. This here is an
earthquaking, shaking day, and you can feel it in the air, feel it in
the very land. The animals feel it too, and they act funny, son. Like
now. No noise. Listen. No birds. No nothing. Except the silence.
But they'll all be chattering just before it happens. They'll tell us.
They know. And there's nothing we can do about it. It's part of
living here. The big one's inevitable. It's bound to happen. Waiting
out there in the future, mine or yours or your kids', son.

"It's waiting, deep in the fault there, and there ain't no remedy-
ing or stopping it. The fault is deep and powerful, like the very
gates of hell, and it scares the hell out of your mother. But this is
where we live, son, and there ain't nothing, nothing, not one good
goddamn thing we can do about it, 'cept run—or live with it.

"The scientists come here in droves, son. They set up their instruments and gauges, and they make their drawings and calculations and guesses. And they know it will happen one day. Some day. They know it will happen for sure. But when? And how big? It will happen here. They know that, and they think they know about this place. How it came to be. What it looks like deep underneath these hills and mountains. Deep, deep under this fault which bears a saint's name, San Andreas. The saint associated with salvation, and now, disaster. The fault which bears his name, which he carries like sin itself, a scourge of nature, of God, on this apparently peaceful valley.

"It's a special thing, son, this fault. But it drives your mother to worry, and in its way, over the years, it's been driving us apart in the tension of it all—like two of them shifting, opposing portions of land the scientists tell us about. It was behind her wanting me to leave the ranching and cowboying and move back up to Tules and go into this business we have providing electric wiring and lights and fixtures. But they'll all break and flare out when it comes, son. There won't be no power for people other than nature's awesome, quaking power. Always has been that way. Always will be that way, son."

Daniel could see it all again stretching out before him, over the monotonous hum of the Ford, over the wind hitting him in the face through the open window. He could see himself standing beside his father, and he could feel the land and its power and his father's feeling and his own small-boy feeling. And he looked up and down the ravine and away into the larger valley and the encircling mountains, and the word rumbled—*Fault.*

A fault in the land, a fault in this place where they lived. He had heard the word all his young life. Fault. Finding fault. Mother with father. Father with mother, with work, with the government, with other people. With him and what he thought he wanted to do, wanted to be, but couldn't really be sure. His fault. His knowing but not knowing. Quaking. Splitting. Cracking open. Gaping into fault. Now this day, like all others, flawed and faulted in its potential. And he thought of all of his own faults and all the baggage of blame he carried and knew about in the finding of fault and in the flaws and failings of men and women, of parents and friends and teachers, and of his very self—at home, at work, in school, in the war, in his love of Julie, and in her faults and how she had not waited long enough for him and had married that loser Andy Bowen and how that union itself was faulted.

It was like this before, too, the day his father first explained about the San Andreas Fault. Earthquake weather like this had come upon the land, and the land had rumbled and growled. Tables and desks were tossed around and tipped over, windows had shattered, buildings had cracked, and the old Parkfield Bridge had bowed right there on the Carissa Plains where Wallace Creek boomerangs out and back with the tensions of thousands of years of subterranean stress that radiates right up through the lives of the people who live there.

There at that bridge the two great tectonic plates meet, he had later learned. The Pacific plate on the west, the American plate on the east. Daniel remembered marveling at what stayed strong and what crumbled and broke, what stood and what fell, and how he first heard people praise and blame the engineers and architects who designed the structures and the buildings—good and bad, right and wrong, near-perfect and flawed. And he knew it was important to engineer things the right way. And he had decided to become an engineer. But it was harder than he realized, too hard. And his efforts had failed, just like a failed building or bridge or machine or electrical circuit.

Come this Sunday, after he told his folks he had quit school for the second time and was home for good, he would go to church with them, and then they would come home and eat the usual Sunday meal of roast and potatoes and carrots. Or some tri-tips, cooked outside with Santa Maria beans and hot salsa and home fried potatoes. Maybe some devil's food cake and homemade ice cream and plenty of coffee. And he and his father would talk about the next step, how to get on with working in the family store, and things would be okay. And maybe Julie would divorce the dead-letter postmaster she had hooked up with too soon, too much on the rebound of Daniel's first going away. She could understand failure now. Hers and his. But would things progress that way? Would they?

Freyling checked into the Paso Robles CHP headquarters. He kidded with Harriet Culver, the dispatcher, and did the necessary midday paperwork.

"Don't you long for the busy days of summer, Fred? I do. Didn't see your pretty face nearly as much then as I do now. Do you ever patrol anymore at all?"

"Harriet, I'm almost out of your hair. It's Friday, and there's a wine tasting at Martin Brothers—and one or two other wineries. So there'll be some work in store with the tipplers. The vino and the Valley traffic will be flowing some this weekend. Nothing like the fair or Labor Day, but busy. So don't worry, sweetheart, you'll be rid of my smilin' face around here."

"But what about your pretty voice? Promise not to pester me with tourist tips and updates?"

"You got it, dearie. It's a deal. If you hold back on any airwave girl talk about plans for Sunday dinner or the latest movie."

"We don't like the same movies, so I've given up talking about them with you. Saw a good preview the other night about a teenage rebel."

"Anything with Charlton Heston or Gregory Peck is okay by me. Hear about any good westerns, let me know. Until then, I'm long gone."

Freyling pulled his report from the gray Smith-Corona, picked up his cap and some papers, strolled down the hall and out the door into the warm California sun. As he walked over to his Buick, he reviewed weather reports and road conditions and mentally traced out his patrol for the second half of the day. Weather was clear and supposed to hit the high sixties or low seventies. He could check out West 46 over to Cambria first. He wondered what Pappas was doing. Probably still shooting the breeze with Erv and Gaye and Betty.

Freyling said hello to Nardo Bustamonte, the fleet mechanic, and asked if he'd already filled up the tank and checked under the hood. *"Listo, Capitán. Todos están bien."* Freyling kicked the tires on the Buick, nice, firm, new Firestones. He got in and turned the key and thrilled again to the purr and power of the big V-8. "Capitán

Freyling. *Buen viaje, hombre,*" Nardo yelled and waved as Freyling pulled out of headquarters and accessed 101 off the frontage road, headed north, back across town to the 46 turnoff toward the coast and Harmony and Cambria. It was one of the prettiest patrols he had, and he looked forward to it. The traffic on 101 wasn't exceptionally heavy, and as usual, people started slowing down as soon as they spotted his patrol car, which he kept right on 65 miles per hour. All these people, coming and going between Frisco and L.A. He reached over and picked up the radio to call Pappas. "I'm rolling, Pappas." There was no answer. When he wheeled by the 101 Cafe again he saw Pappas's patrol car and knew he was still having his dessert and talking to Betty.

The silver-bodied Porsche pulled to a quick stop at the intersection of Highway 46 and Highway 33 in Blackwells Corner. The car was like no other car ever seen in that remote part of the Valley. The young driver revved the motor, enjoying the loud, rough-throated sound of the engine behind him, ready to launch him forward as soon as he released the brake and engaged the gear. The sleek body rocked slightly with each new infusion of fuel into its pulsing, six-cylinder engine. The car could outrun anything on the California highways. Built for speeds over 120 miles per hour, it seemed to ask only to fulfill one purpose—race and win. Torque, RPM, horsepower—they all waited, ready to interact at the higher ends of the mechanical spectrum of automotive manufacturing.

Had the two people in the car chosen to continue on Highway 99, they would have passed through Fresno and other smaller Valley towns, where people like Daniel Turner and his family carried out their daily lives, oblivious to such speed and style and awesome high-tech power. But the car, its handsome driver, and the strange-speaking passenger were headed for Salinas, ready to rendezvous with yet another race.

The stop at the Blackwells Corner intersection was merely a recurring pause for fuel—fuel for the hungry racing car and food for the racers inside its aerodynamic aluminum hull. The Porsche had run raw over the past hour or two. The car was all power and pure machine, animated almost mystically into a vitalistic embodiment of motion. The transmission and gears were smooth in progression, at one with the motor and the suspension system, and the feeling inside the car as it cornered or just growled open and sustained along the road at the highest of speeds was one of attempting to harness and control a force so calculated out of chaos as to seem sublime—much beyond the young driver's rational knowing.

He sat low in the bucket seat, looking out over a short and sloping hood, testing the limits of possible ways to pass along the surface of the land. The rear weight of the motor was something to reckon with on sharp turns, though, and the driver enjoyed tempting the limit of the car's tendency to fishtail and spin out at highest speeds. But the vibrations of the road, coming up through the positive-action rack-and-pinion steering, gave him a pleasure akin to that of a cellist feeling his instrument's resonance and resiliency through its gut strings.

The young driver felt as much as thought about his own motives and movements—either initiating or reacting to the machine as though it were an extension of himself or his own being were an extension of the machine. He felt as if his touch infused this wheel and the steering column with some of the same nervous feeling of his own spine, and he thrilled to the feel of the control arms and shock absorber struts and longitudinal torsion rods. The reciprocated response of man and machine was exquisite. The two friends smiled at each other in their rebellious uncaring and pleasure of living in that moment and in that way.

There had been cars to pass, highway patrol cars to avoid, but near Oak Flat the driver was spotted and pulled over. He reached out to sign the ticket, reconciled to such small fines, and anxious to run the Porsche through some more of its paces before the next day's race.

"Just another autograph for the fans, Jimbo. They're already beginning to line up. Won't let you be," the passenger had said, flipping a cigarette up and out of the topless car and watching the butt arc through the blue afternoon sky, hit the ground, and roll off the shoulder of the highway. He watched for some small combustion in the dry grass, but there was none.

As the driver turned the ignition switch and started the engine, pulling out slowly behind the departing patrol car, he squinted again behind his glasses and mimicked Mr. Magoo's voice. "Shoot 'em like puppies, eh, Rolf?"

"Did he recognize you, do you think?"

"Naw, he didn't know who I was. Probably thought I was that country singing sausage king. A patrolman's life is the highway, man. I started to sign the ticket "Jim Stark" and tell him we were on our way to a chickie-run visit with destiny, but hell, the movie hasn't even been released yet. Not 'til next week. Then he'd know me—maybe."

The patrol car was behind them now, way back down the highway. And this stop they anticipated being someplace where they would eat. At the single swinging traffic light blinking red at Blackwells Corner, the driver turned right, pulled into what looked like the only service station around. He came to a stop before a young kid, who seemed not to believe his eyes, as if a UFO had landed right there in an obscure Union 76 station, on his very shift.

"Fill it up with high octane, kid," the driver said to the attendant, who was nervously rubbing his hands with an oily red rag.

"Where's a good cafe?" asked the passenger.

The kid's face went pale, and he didn't answer right away. He was suddenly humbled and hesitating.

"Just down there. Down this same street, sir. Next block," he was finally able to articulate. "It's him," he thought. "Damned if it isn't him. The guy in the preview I saw. I know it. I know it," he whispered to himself as he turned the crank and cleared the old gas pump. Nozzle in hand, he searched, open-mouthed, for the gas tank of the aluminum apparition before him. Then the passenger walked toward the back of the car and swung open the whole back portion of the body to expose the gleaming, still whispering engine.

"Isn't that the guy in that Eden flick they shot up in Salinas?" the attendant asked the car's passenger. "He's in this new teenage film about L.A. It's him, isn't it? What's his name?"

"No, he's just a guy, like us," said the tall passenger, stretching and yawning. Then he looked over the car with a knowing gaze. He knew he had adjusted the valves just right, and he had the timing just like he wanted it. He marveled at the method and mind and sight of it all, what he called "loose precision." Then he hollered out to the driver, who was going into the rest room. "Hurry up, let's get over to that cafe and eat something. I'm starving."

"What might have been and never will be . . ." thought Daniel Turner as he drove late in the day toward Cholame and a brief talk with Sparky Terrill. He would make it to Tules about suppertime, if he didn't dally too long with Terrill.

"Julie has her life now, and the child, and even if I were the father, what could I do now, for either mother or daughter? Andy Bowen probably doesn't care one way or the other. But do I really want to get involved in a divorce this way, the way her letters suggested?"

Thoughts of Julie and the possibility that he had a daughter drifted through his mind as he looked out at the rolling hills around Creston and the wide, tree-lined riverbed. Soon that would be replaced by the barren bed of Cholame Creek. As he enjoyed the remaining trees he was reminded of the cottonwoods around the Salinas River near Paso Robles, and the mistletoe in the tops of the trees, and had a brief memory of Christmas at home, where he was going now, once and for all time—if anything was for all time anywhere. Especially here where shifting and changing and quaking was the name of the game.

He was back in the earthquake zone, and the San Andreas Fault was nearby. The land was nothing like the lush fields in the Salinas Valley. The hills were beginning to narrow on both sides of the road and would soon funnel him right into Cottonwood Pass. The air was beginning to cool, and his thoughts took him back to country rides on late afternoons like this, heading for a dance or a game or a movie. And he and Julie had stopped more than once near Cholame, coming down Highway 41 going into Paso Robles, or they had cut over to the coast for a picnic in the Los Padres National Forest.

Once they had stopped at an old woman's house near Parkfield, right near the fault line. The sign by her mailbox had announced

Birds for Sale—all kinds of birds: doves, canaries, cockatoos, fan-tail pigeons—and the woman said they were good alarms and would tell if there was going to be an earthquake. They had admired the birds and talked with the old woman, but then drove on to their picnic . . . and lovemaking.

That would have been about the time, if he really was the father. He remembered that, like now, he had felt something special out on the land. They had joked about feeling the earth move for them in their embraces. He had kidded her about starting a quake, about setting the fault "right" and ironically causing the Big One! The one that would rumble and reach out all the way north to Monterey and San Jose and Frisco, and down south to Hollywood to tumble the big sign from the hills and cause all the stars to come out of their Beverly Hills mansions and wonder how two kids from a small Central Valley town could be at the emotional and geographical center of something so powerful and cataclysmic as a roadside kiss.

And his imagination got away from him and he saw all of Holly-wood in chaos falling off the edges of the giant fissure. And now there was only an ever-widening chasm spreading out into the Pa-cific and back to the Grand Canyon, opening up a wide rift across the continent. And there was no need to worry about responsibili-ties with Julie or his parents or professors, or promises to do this or that, or even to follow a speed limit sign like the one up ahead. And nothing would matter—school, job, marriage. Everything would be meaningless, like it pretty much already was anyway. There wouldn't be questions about success and failure, a bright future or a dismal one. The future wouldn't matter at all.

Then the big Aleanthus tree up to the left of the highway caught his attention and brought him back to the present and his arrival at Terrill's place. So he slowed down and signaled to turn, even though there were no cars in sight, and pulled up in front of the old com-bination wrecking yard, welding shop, and store. He honked, and out of the back of the building came Sparky Terrill.

Sparky could cheer him up. The big, toothless fat man shook his hand and offered him a Coke from the old red vending machine. Daniel told Sparky all about his situation, about not being able to hack school after all, about the letters from Julie wanting to see him and make things like they once were. And about his worry in telling his folks about everything, about being ready to work in the family business.

Sparky listened, occasionally shaking his head or smiling briefly or rubbing his stubbled cheeks and chin with his hand. And after what felt like a couple of hours, Sparky finally said, "Hell's bells, Danny, ain't much you can do about anything but roll with the punches. If they get you on the ropes, take a breath and stagger back. If they knock you down to the mat, just take the count. There's always another fight, always another day as long as you're alive. That's what counts. That's all old Bob would wish for now if he could. Just being alive. That's what counts." When Daniel left Sparky, he felt better. He was alive. He knew he could roll with the punches.

It was near dusk when he got back on the highway. The 41 turn-off to Tules was a mile or so up ahead. He could see the road sign and the black line of highway angling off to the north, and he thought of dead Bob Terrill and all those other guys who didn't make it out of Korea alive. His problems now seemed minor ones. So what if he dropped out of school? So what if he would be late for supper? What was to be would be. And then he was at the turnoff and he started to signal, thinking all the time about being home already and of everything being okay. Being okay all the way around. And into the turn he remembered that Sparky had wanted him to help move a heavy table and he had forgotten. "Good place to duck when the Big One hits," Sparky had said.

Daniel hesitated for a split second halfway into the turn, and then he saw the car, strange and silver, upon him, and he heard the colossal clamor of motion and metal and felt the collision that was for him all changing of everything he had known or thought he had known, everything he planned or wanted to plan. And the land-scape of his youth and the life he knew was closing back in on him through the gray dusk now suddenly turning to silent darkness.

Heading west on Highway 46 and coming into Cholame at day's end, the Porsche was passing cars at high speed—ordinary cars, sedans, station wagons. Some of the passes only seemed tight, dangerous, but for this machine it was all in a day's work. The car was ready, preened and tuned to its normal high speeds for tomorrow's race.

To its passengers the Porsche felt eager for greater acceleration. The two friends thought of tomorrow—their route and strategy, the competition, the people from the racing circuit they would see again. It was possible that some of the old Salinas movie crew would be there, along with studio publicists and regular press. It was hard for the driver to escape into anonymity.

"That lunch didn't really do it for me, Dee. Let's stop up ahead for a beer and a snack. I need cigarettes, too."

The wind noise was loud and the driver replied loudly, trying to make himself heard above it. "You and your beer. We'll be in King City by seven or so. Wish we had extra time for a good Mexican dinner. I know a great spot on the main drag—King City Cafe. Best tamales in the state! But we'd better stop ahead. What is it— Cholame? There's some kind of business way up on the right by that big tree. I need to make a couple of calls anyway. You can drive her on in from there."

The mechanic reached into his shirt pocket and pulled out an almost empty pack of cigarettes. He handed one to his friend, who took it and merely placed it, habitually, between his lips with no attempt to light it. Then the mechanic raised his voice to say, "I might have to lean on it some through Paso Robles and on up 101." The young driver nodded and looked at the dash gauges, then pulled down his glasses to look at his wristwatch. It was 5:50 P.M. The car began to slow down for the stop up ahead.

The mechanic looked up over the puff of smoke from his hard-lit cigarette and saw a big, two-toned, two-door Ford sedan turning ponderously in front of them. Reflexively he yelled out something in German, which the driver understood exactly in its tone of panic, for he too saw the car immediately in front of him. Between the time he took his foot off the accelerator and started to brake and say, "He's got to see us this way . . ." the beautiful little foreign machine and its handsome driver were collapsing and crumpling, colliding head-on and then sideswiping the all-American car and its disbelieving driver in unison with death and destruction.

And the mechanic felt himself flying out the door and arcing into the air, still holding the blackened match and smoldering cigarette.

Friday had been picking up for Patrolman Freyling. He had some good hunting since noon, and Pappas would have to pull out five or six citations to beat him now. He had thought about Pappas most of the afternoon—and Ervin, and how nice it was to have a place like the 101 Cafe to call home when you wanted to come in from the road and not go back to the office, or to your real home with all its tensions and troubles and miscommunication. He had the radio. He had Ervin and the cafe gang. And he had Pappas. They all shared a common love for the road and the westering life. A passion for moving, for traveling, for seeing the landscape on the move.

Throughout the day on patrol, as the weekend flow from the Valley to the coast started to pick up, Freyling thought about Erv's conversation during that late-morning meal with Pappas. There was one story about a railroad car running over a buddy and Erv seeing him severed in two, his heart still beating. Freyling knew it had shocked Pappas more than he showed, shocked him back to the traumas of Korea and what he feared seeing again, as a patrolman.

Major accidents were a part of the job. You always had to be ready to handle them, ready to detach yourself from your emotions enough to try and take control of the chaos, because the sequence and progression of accidents—the causes and the effects of events like that—weren't easy to sort out. Freyling usually came in at the end and then had to trace things back to see how first one thing and then something else converged to bring the opposing forces together. Once in a great while he could see something about to happen. There was a prevention aspect to his work that he appreciated. A headlight or a taillight out. A muffler dragging. Bald tires. Jalopies that hindered the flow of traffic. Speeders. Drunk drivers. Teenagers too high on life to know they were courting death—or maybe knowing too well. Obstacles on the highway—anything from sheets of plywood to tree limbs to stalled cars. Deer and coyotes running in front of cars. Hitchhikers. Who was to say when and why bad accidents would happen?

Freyling knew that was what Pappas was wrestling with. Would he be up to it when it happened? When his pie came, Pappas was still a little pale around the gills from Erv's story. That was really why he was lingering over that pie—he was queasy. Freyling could tell. It was just a story, a chapter in the life of old Erv, but Freyling thought about it all day, about what Erv had seen and what he had said about it. The major accidents were horrible. There was always one out there waiting to happen. Always a call just ready to come in. The big one. And it would stay with you, even if you only wondered about it and waited for it and trained for it. It would come, and you were supposed to be ready. But you never were.

Freyling was going over all that in his head around 6:00 P.M. as he headed back to patrol headquarters in Paso. He cruised by the 101 Cafe and thought he might see Pappas there. Then the radio popped and Harriet's voice came in loud and clear.

"Code clearance requested. Code clearance requested. Emergency. Emergency. Code 3! Code 3! Code 3!"

The static crackled, and Harriet's voice wavered a bit, but then she got control of what she was saying. "All units proceed to Highway 46 and 41 at Cholame. Cholame. Code 3. Repeat. Code 3 at Cholame. Emergency. All units proceed to Chomale. Code 3."

It was the big one, the one they had wondered about and tried to prepare for. Pappas would be on 41, but Freyling knew he could get there, too. He had to get there and assist in covering the accident, and assist Pappas, too. He was halfway through his U-turn, hitting the siren and the lights when he picked up the radio mike.

"Freyling rolling red and siren. Rolling red. Will assist! Will assist! Over."

Then he heard the acknowledgment and the radio pop again and Pappas's voice, distant but clear, "Emergency response en route. Rolling red. Be there in ten minutes."

Freyling tromped down hard on the accelerator and the big Buick Super was on its way: 70, 80, 85, the speedometer needle arcing right like a compass needle homing in on due north—and the whine of the siren, loud but strangely muffled against the roar of the big engine. All Freyling could think about was what he would see, what he would find, whether he would be able to see what was essential to see beyond the irreversible carnage. And he wondered whether Pappas would be there before him and whether he was ready for a Code 3, whether they both were ready for how a Code 3 would change everything, the real and the imagined, the living and the dead. Pappas would never be the same after a Code 3. And neither would he. Even the land would be changed where a Code 3 call and an accident such as this converged on some arbitrary spot now marked forever by an Aleanthus tree, a tree of heaven, and in this particular instance, enshrined.

Western Literature Series

Western Trails:
A Collection of Short Stories by Mary Austin
selected and edited by Melody Graulich

Cactus Thorn
Mary Austin

Dan De Quille, the Washoe Giant:
A Biography and Anthology
prepared by Richard A. Dwyer and Richard E. Lingenfelter

Desert Wood: An Anthology of Nevada Poets
edited by Shaun T. Griffin

The City of Trembling Leaves
Walter Van Tilburg Clark

Many Californias:
Literature from the Golden State
edited by Gerald W. Haslam

The Authentic Death of Hendry Jones
Charles Neider

First Horses: Stories of the New West
Robert Franklin Gish

Torn by Light: Selected Poems
Joanne de Longchamps

Swimming Man Burning
Terrence Kilpatrick

The Temptations of St. Ed and Brother S
Frank Bergon

The Other California:
The Great Central Valley in Life and Letters
Gerald W. Haslam

The Track of the Cat
Walter Van Tilburg Clark